Grand Slam

John R. Spencer

To Bill
All best wishes

JWR Spencer

Grand Slam
First Edition
DeerVale Publishing™ November, 2017

This is a work of fiction. Names, characters, places and events are either the product of the author's imagination or are used fictitiously. Any resemblance to actual persons, living or dead, locations, businesses, companies, or events is entirely coincidental.

The author has provided accurate contact and website information at time of publication, but neither the author nor the publisher assumes any responsibility or liability for errors or changes after publication, or for any third-party websites or their contents.

Author contact information at www.solarium-3.com

Cover by Delaney Designs

ISBN: 978-0-9863727-6-6 (paperback)
ISBN: 978-0-9863727-7-3 (ebook)

GRAND
SLAM

I.

Introductory Note

(Skip only at peril to your sanity . . .)

THIS STORY is a tapestry woven from experiences related by some of those involved. There is no single narrator in the traditional sense. Instead, different individuals, named at the head of each chapter, tell that part of the story from their own perspective—often as those events are happening.

So it's important to notice at the beginning of each chapter who is narrating that part.

The "book" The Reporter is working on includes *only* the chapters he himself narrates. It does *not* include the chapters narrated here by other characters.

Some of those involved in the story have never met and, at any point, some know certain key things, but others don't.

Only the reader will get to connect all the dots.

That's part of the fun.

II.
The Plan

One

Kenny Hamilton

"Do you realize how easy it would be to take it?" I ask Brad absently.

"Huhm?" Brad mumbles.

Of course—typical of Brad—he's already half-dozing and not listening to me. Kind of amazing, considering the loud roar of the engines as we climb through a ruffling bank of clouds.

I have to crane my neck hard to see out of the plane's stupid undersized window. Why are airplane windows never at the right height? You can't see anything, unless maybe you're a dwarf.

I watch as the beautiful Caribbean island gradually recedes into the distance several thousand feet below and behind us. Most of the island is already out of sight, a fast memory, fading just as fast as the vacationing and partying Brad and I did there over the last few days.

I can still just make out the outer reef where it wraps around the northeastern edge of Grand Cayman, like a necklace woven of undersea jewels.

Brad is stirring.

"Huh?" he mumbles again, peering toward me through one half-squinting eyelid.

"I said, do you realize how easy it would be to take the place?" I repeat, as the north side of the island slowly disappears from sight through the porthole-like window.

Brad obviously doesn't register what I'm saying. He's a little slow sometimes.

"Take what?" he says, shaking the cobwebs in his head. He rolls his head further right, looking at the back of my head.

"Down there," I point.

He can't see around me. He leans over my shoulder, stretching his neck like a chicken and peers out the window with me.

"Take the ocean? What the heck are you blabbering about, Hamilton?" Brad says, still not fully alert.

I guess I interrupted the beginning of a serious nap. It's also obvious that Brad has a severe headache. Me, too. Too much rum last night. It's only 6:45 in the morning. He'd normally be sound asleep this early. So I guess I can cut him some slack. Planes leave without the courtesy of considering anyone's sleeping schedule. Or hangovers—except maybe the pilot's. The last day of vacation, you just want to rest, but you have to get up before the crack of dawn to get to some stupid airport. Why? Spoils the whole trip.

The woman at the check-in counter this morning really overdid the smile thing as she rattled off, "Good morning, sir!" Her eyes beamed as if she was auditioning for a Broadway musical.

"Not even close," I groaned.

But it's our fault, though. We're the ones who overdid it last night. The drinking thing, I mean.

Brad's other eye finally opens and our eyeballs are about four inches apart. Looks like old Bradley outdid me in the overdoing department. He looks completely addlebrained, and his eyes redder than a late-evening sunset.

The way my stomach feels, I should probably be in a hospital instead of on this stupid, bumpy plane. This is the way most of our mini-vacations end up, with us both in pretty much the same shape as this morning. Trashed. The obnoxiously loud droning of the engines makes the whole inside of my head hurt. I can't imagine how Brad's brain feels.

I jerk his head toward the window. His eyes squint at the brightness and try to focus. He can see just the last fragment of the north shore of Grand Cayman as the plane starts to bank northeast. We watch as the island seems to flip into a different dimension, and disappears from view.

Finally, I think he's caught on.

"Take the—island?" he asks dimly.

He rubs his sunburned forehead, staring at me as if I'm a complete stranger. And in a lot of ways, I am. To him, to everyone. I like it that way.

Never get too close.

Poor Brad tries harder to focus those reddened, drooping eyes. That's what seven days of hard living will do to a guy. Bad headache, burned out, feeling like crap inside and out. I should know.

He lays his head back against his seat. I realize my eyes are grinning at him now, like a kid with a new toy. His tired brain is probably trying to assess my sanity. My brainstorm probably seems like it's from Jupiter, or Saturn, someplace like that. I can see his mental wheels spinning slowly in the mud. *Take the island? Kenny has gone insane.* He frowns at me as if everything smells as bad as my breath, and inside this big, aluminum coffin right now, it does.

"Kenny, what are you talking about?"

"I'm telling you, it would be so easy," I say, my voice wandering in my own mind, already starting to formulate a plan.

I look straight at Brad, my best friend for the last fourteen years. He can see I'm up to no good, as usual.

"How deep did'ya go yesterday?" he asks.

"Deep? What, scuba diving, you mean?"

"Yeah, dummy. How deep?" he presses me.

I can vaguely visualize the depth gauge on my buoyancy compensator yesterday morning, but it's more blurry in my mind than it was in the water.

"I don't know. Eight-five, ninety feet, maybe. Why?"

"Yeah, well, I think you bobbed up too fast, Bucko. Ocean sucked your brain out of your ear or something. Lem'me sleep."

I can't help but laugh. He's a great friend, but I should know by now, don't interrupt his sleep!

I stare out the tiny window again. Grand Cayman is shrinking into the distance but it's still life-size in my imagination as my thoughts shift into the next gear.

"Just thinking out loud," I mumble to myself, but then I realize—I probably shouldn't be talking out loud like this. Too many snooping ears around. I glance at the numbed, bored faces of other passengers around me. Looks like nobody heard me. Everyone else is like Brad, already trying to make up for lost sleep.

Good. Don't want to wreck the whole idea before I even get started.

I look around the cabin further for stewards, stewardesses, plain-clothes sky marshals, secret agents, aliens disguised as half-tanned old ladies in impossibly-and-disgustingly-tight tops and shorts. Nobody is paying attention.

"Just thinking," I whisper again toward Brad.

He moans sarcastically, "Well, that's more than you usually do."

Guess he was listening after all.

He looks at me again, studying me skeptically, through those bleak, puffy eyes.

"Look, Kenny, I'm *really* tired," he mopes. "I've no damned idea what you're talking about. Leave me alone, will ya?" he begs, trying for the twentieth time to find that elusive spot against the head rest where he can get comfortable enough to doze.

I lean toward him again, whispering confidentially.

"I'm just saying, my good Mister Schott, how easy it would be—to take that island. To make it our own. Are you with me?"

I give him my most intense stare but his eyes are already screwing shut, trying hard to play opossum.

"Sure, Kenny," he grouses, "whatever." He cranks his head away.

The sleek, Canadian-built plane shudders a bit as the pilot leans hard into the throttles, finishing our climb, on a heading to the now-legal Cuban airspace, then on toward Miami. There's a sudden bump and a hard jerk left. The plane dips, then lunges upward again like an overly-aged roller coaster starting up the next hill.

My guts do a double dip. They feel like my head—minus the benefit of a skull to hold it all in. Something I swallowed whole from that breakfast bar this morning doesn't want to be down there—and it's about to make a curtain call.

Run for the john, man! Move it!

I scramble over the top of Brad's' knees, jolting him back to half-consciousness and accidentally jabbing him in the ribs. He fakes a quick comeback with his left fist. I arrest his hand just before he makes contact with my ear. Even though he's half-dozing again, catching his arm is like stopping a bat in full swing. The guy is super strong, even if he is kind of soft-headed.

"Your own fault," Brad growls. "Told you not to eat that greasy cake frosting last night," he adds without opening his eyes.

"Well, like you care, but it was breakfast."

I swallow hard as I bolt from the seat, hustling to the back of the cabin. I fling the lavatory door open, wedging sideways into the tiny excuse for a bathroom which, thankfully, is vacant this early in the flight. Man, the stupid aircraft engineers did not build this head for my six foot, four inch frame! I feel like a giant sardine stuffed into an undersized can. I double over, smacking my forehead against the flimsy wall, and throw up.

I twist toward the miniature sink, needing to wash out my mouth, but of course there's no damned cup! I scoop a couple of handfuls of water into my mouth and spit into the toilet.

"Stupid Canadians," leaks out from under my now-even-fouler breath as I stumble out of the lavatory, "who would design a bathroom that cramped!"

I bet I look the same color as that putrid-green galley wall.

"French," says a semi-gorgeous stewardess from her jump seat by the rear coffee station. She sniffs, without looking up from her Spanish-language magazine.

"Huh?" I say, staring at the really stupid-looking bun on her head. The uniform hairdo, no doubt, but even it can't lessen her looks.

"Canadians built it, but the French designed this one."

"Well, those French must not like us much," I say, starting back up the rolling aisle like a drunk.

The stewardess thinks I'm out of earshot and says to her magazine, "Can you blame them?"

I intentionally bump Brad as I crawl back into my seat. "See, bonehead, we should've gone First Class."

He doesn't reply. His mind, such that it is, has drifted into Never-Never Land. I squirm back into my skinny seat and push the button to recline the back. Might as well get a nap. The seat goes back its maximum two and one-eighth inches.

"Damned French."

The pilot banks sharply right this time. I try for a last glimpse of the islands. Grand Cayman is barely visible far in the distance, shrunken to a tiny, flat, brown dot in a very big sea. Even tinier, Little Cayman and Cayman Brac are almost indistinguishable specks parked in the glistening expanse of greenish-blue ocean. The sunlight, reflecting intensely off the water, finally wipes all three islands from sight. My eyes react, blinking.

I stare further into the distance, my vision fixed. Capture Grand Cayman. It sounds crazy, even to myself. But I know I can pull this off. I'll just need a little help from my friends.

"Hey, Schott, you think Traci would want in on this?"

"Huhm?" Brad mumbles from somewhere in the suburbs of La-La-Land. "Want in on what?" He cracks one eye open just enough to let it glare at me. "What are you all lathered about, Hamilton?"

"Traci—my girlfriend, dummy?—do you think she'd go along with this?"

"Kenny, I'm telling you, I'm exhausted. I have no clue what the heck you're talking about. I just really want to sleep. So shut up, would you? Wake me in America."

Poor Brad. No stamina.

I know I can do this. I'll be famous, like my great, great-whatever grandfather, Alexander. It'll be another one for the history books! "The Capture of Grand Cayman," that's what they'll call it.

If anyone can pull this off, it's me.

My blood pumps in a rush. I can feel the adrenaline already! Get a grip, Hamilton. But this would be a kind of world record, I bet. Me, the first person in modern history to capture an entire sovereign nation—little old Kenny Hamilton.

"Big, big world," I mumble to Brad, but mostly to myself. "Little, tiny island . . . ."

Man, this seat is a torture rack. It's killing me! Damned French.

I stretch my neck against the headrest and try to wriggle down into the seat cushion. My eyes close, but my brain is whipping itself.

"Yep. Easy."

Two

The Reporter

"The Grand Slam." That's what all the news and media outlets now call Kenny Hamilton's outrageous plan to capture the Cayman Islands, and there's probably only one or two really primitive tribes somewhere in the deepest jungles of the world who haven't heard about it.

I'm a reporter for a small local newspaper on Grand Cayman. We mostly sell advertising. Yes, it's a real cheapo outfit, I admit, and some of the ads we print are highly questionable. But you've got to live, don't you? I've worked at the paper for about seven years, selling ads and covering mainly local news, what little there is.

Finally, there's some real news.

But my interest in Hamilton's insane plan is more than just professional. That's because I unwittingly became involved in this story myself. My name isn't important, and I was not one of the main players in the whole scheme. Still, after backtracking and researching the threads of how this crazy plan came to be, I almost feel that I was.

How did Kenny Hamilton's great plan work out? As you could expect, it was a catastrophe.

How did I get involved personally? By what you could call a true accident, and only at the very end of the whole mess.

I've spent the last four months researching everything backwards to the beginning. I've spoken for hours and hours—sometimes whole days—with some of the main players. Those who are left, anyway. It's funny how people will talk, and how much they will tell you, if they think it will end up in the newspapers. Everybody wants to be famous, I guess.

Vanity, vanity.

My problem is, I now have so much background information about the Grand Slam that my boss refused to ante up the cost of running the whole story, in serial form, in our dinky, weekly paper.

But I couldn't just let it drop, so I've decided to put it together into a book. I've never tried this before. Maybe that shows. As a writer, I'm still rough around the edges, and my salt and pepper hair is ragged, and I wear fairly foolish looking glasses. Plus, for a guy who's thirty-six, I may be just a little overweight. And sure, I know that probably every reporter in the world dreams of writing a great novel someday.

Novel? Double-*entendre*. I doubt you've ever heard anything as novel as what you're about to read. I know full well that you won't believe some of this. It will sound so far-fetched that you'll think, no, the guy is just making up this part—or he's lost his mind. I have to admit, even to an experienced reporter like me, some of it seemed to be nonsense when I began researching "the back story." It's got to be the craziest thing I've ever run across.

Maybe this will be my break as a reporter, and I'll finally make some kind of name for myself. Then I could find a job as a real journalist. I just hope I can stay here in the islands. It's the most beautiful place on earth, if you ask me.

But I'm wandering from the point.

As I've gone over all my notes and interviews, and looked back at some of the police photos, I've really struggled the last couple of weeks trying to decide how to launch into the story. I feel stumped. I have to wade you through what may seem like a literal swamp of events because I want you to come to know some of the main players the way I've gotten to know them. A story is just a story. It's the people that matter.

"You'll never make sense of this thing," my boss told me when he turned down running all this in serial form.

"I know," I said, "it's been like trying to assemble an oversized jigsaw puzzle with some of the key pieces and the whole outside frame missing."

He didn't respond to my picturesque analogy, but I pressed him.

"Where should I start?" I asked, thinking that with so many years of experience he'd have a great idea.

"You're asking me?" he said with a muddled look.

So much for bosses.

Anyway, I've settled on this. I'll start near the end, since that's where it started for me.

III.
The Plan,
Gone Haywire

Three

The Reporter

Traci Dennison sat as still as she could manage, considering the jitters tremoring throughout her body. She was not one to sweat, even during a major workout at her upscale gym in Philadelphia, but at the moment all her clothes felt damp, down to her underwear.

She was careful not to wipe her forehead under the lazy, low-slung bangs that swept down sideways across the top of her face because she didn't want to give away how panicked she actually was. The walls of the cramped, gray police interrogation room in Grand Cayman's main George Town Police Station seemed to shrink closer in on her as each minute passed. Her muscles were taut, and her whole body felt as if it was turning to stone.

She was absolutely petrified. To make matters worse, the anonymous detective who had refused to give Traci his name also refused to sit down across from her. He hovered closely behind her—much too close for Traci—

increasing the sweat that seeped from every pore of her skin.

What was he doing back there? It made her even more jittery. She could smell a vague aroma of garlic that she assumed was coming from him. Whether from his breath, or his clothes, she couldn't tell. It was just noxious enough to make her stomach feel even worse than it already did.

The man, a detective with the Royal Cayman Islands Police Service, moved a little to her right side, then back, as if he was completely bored and wishing he was out in the bay fishing. But then, she worried, maybe he *wasn't* bored at all. Maybe he was about to run a long, sharp knife into the back of her neck in payment for her crimes today.

Traci knew this fear was just her nightmarish imagination running off somewhere into a mental thicket, but she couldn't help herself. Why couldn't he just be a gentleman, and sit down and look at her, and question her like a normal person?

Maybe because he was a foreigner to Traci, her feelings and fears had ramped up several notches. Her emotional tachometer, like an over-run motor, had redlined hours ago.

Then there was that irritating sound. The detective kept picking at several finger nails with other finger nails, loudly enough to make Traci hear, to make her sweat even more, to rattle her. It was like a mindless woodpecker pecking at a tree branch, but this branch was inside of Traci's skull. It was such a rude, uncouth sound to have to just sit here and put up with. She was sure he was intentionally trying to irritate her. That's what cops do, isn't it?

The detective was not a huge man, but to Traci Dennison he was intimidating and terrifying. Dark hair and dark, thick eyebrows framed his full face. His overly-large, jagged nose gave him a wolfish look, danger cloaked by wile. His smaller but burly figure gave him the look of a half-grown grizzly, ready to take off her head—and maybe an arm or leg, for good measure. The annoyed growl in his voice barely concealed his frustration with Traci, and his dark brown suit only added to the overreaching sense of threat she felt having him so near.

Finally, he came around in front of her.

"All right, Miss Dennison, once more. Where is this Kendall Hamilton now?"

"I've already told you. I don't know." She tried to look confident and sincere, but failed on both counts.

"Yes. You said that. I just don't believe you." He gave her a feigned smile that would have looked natural if he had just bitten into a three week old, moldy sandwich.

"Well, you just have to believe me," Traci protested. "Why would I lie?"

She smiled back, but it was obviously forced. Still, even though it was half-hearted, her smile began to charm the man. It was her famous, one-of-a-kind Traci smile, the smile that had attracted her boyfriend, Kenny Hamilton, to her in the first place. Her smile was unique not so much in its shape or expression but simply because every time it graced her face it seemed to bear up out of her soul some secret happiness and reveling, like a woman who has just climbed her first 14,000 foot Rocky Mountain peak and conquered it.

While the detective would never let himself remotely show it, he did find Traci extremely attractive. She seemed to have not only a winning personality but the looks to match.

Traci had always attracted men, some of whom she liked, but many of whom she didn't. Her light brown hair enclosed a lovely face that was home to two of the sweetest brown eyes ever given to a woman. A little taller than average, at twenty-five she had reached that stage of physical and emotional maturity that had finally taken her beyond girlhood into the realm of true womanhood. Though she had a slightly plumper figure, it was a plump that was perfect, with highly toned muscles under the plumpness, the result of her constant workouts at the gym she not only managed but owned in downtown Philadelphia. In the short time she had run it, after being bankrolled by her very generous grandpa, the gym had become one of the three favorite workout venues for older teens and adults in the whole metropolitan area.

Had it not been for the unusual business of this day— an attempted take-over of the island nation of Grand Cayman—Traci would have been suited out in her typical designer wear, perhaps a silken sweater perfectly showing off the curves of her figure, highlighted by a medium-length skirt of a subtle but striking color. But at the moment, she really didn't need all that to impress this middle-aged detective, whatever his name. The black and gray, quasi-military, one-piece outfit she had on was just fine, because she had only to fall back on that perfect smile, a smile that would normally have been framed by a perfectly made-up face that never lacked the tones and accents that some women seem to naturally absorb into their skin.

This afternoon, her perfectly made-up face was marred by faded rouge and streaks of mascara that had run onto her cheeks and chin after several hours of crying in her jail cell.

The irritating detective moved around behind her again and continued to hover, the garlic smell wafting around him like aftershave on a corpse. He was waiting for a better answer, an answer he liked. Traci turned and forced herself to smile at him again, the same Traci smile that could melt ice cream still in the freezer, the smile that was an electromagnet to men. She worried that it might be her only way out of here. She looked at the detective intensely, and turned up the power.

It didn't work. For the first time in her life, a man snubbed her smile. He got the blatant hint, but he wasn't biting. He had been lured along by such enticements by countless women once they were in custody, but he had never been snagged. It was what the detective and his buddies called the *Try To Buy* look. He wasn't buying.

He shook his head as if addressing an errant six-year-old, ignoring Traci's beautiful face and alluring smile, and returned to her last comment.

"Why would you lie? Let me see, Miss, first, maybe, because you are a criminal and you are under arrest. In my experience, criminals under arrest don't usually come clean so quickly—and not so voluntarily, either— and not without a lot more prying by yours truly. And second, because you are a close personal friend of the man you claim is the brains behind this whole insane scheme."

He mimicked her smile, which irritated Traci and evaporated what was left of her own.

"Let me think really hard," he went on. "Third, everything about you at the moment—your expression, your body language, the perspiration dripping through the hair above your ears—they all shout, 'Hey, Mr. Copper, look at me, I'm lying!'"

His fake smile was instantly gone. He looked really mad now and was becoming more impatient. Traci didn't know it, but because of her antics today, and those of her cohorts, he had missed a lunch date with his wife and young son, a rare date that he had made with them over a week ago, and an opportunity to spend time with his family that would not come around again anytime soon.

Trying to stay professional, he swallowed his anger and came around in front of Traci once more. He sat down ponderously, a look of controlled exasperation masking his face. Her actions today had cost him precious time with his two favorite people, and he was not in a forgiving mood.

"So—where the hell is this Hamilton guy?" he demanded very loudly.

"I can't tell you," Traci whined with a beleaguered frown, cowering. She could smell her own sweat over the garlic.

"*Why* can't you tell me, Miss Dennison?" he nearly shouted.

"Because, I told you, I honestly don't know!" she hollered back. "Don't be such a jerk!"

Instantly, she caught herself, swallowing a breath, realizing she had probably gone too far by yelling at him. She was certain she had made him even madder now.

"*Honestly* . . . ," the detective mimicked, his voice quieter, but almost sneering. "Do you always speak honestly with police detectives, Traci?"

The question smarted, provoking old but very deep feelings. Her troubled past leapt like a specter from the recesses of her memory. Traci had been something of a wild-child in her early teen years, and served two short stints in a juvenile detention center, stints that a judge had hoped would scare her into being smarter about her future.

It very apparently hadn't worked. She was arrested three more times during college. But they were for typical, stupid college-kid pranks, drunk and disorderly behavior, an indecent display of some body parts in a public place, and once for interfering with an officer who was arresting her then-boyfriend for a DUI on the way home from a party out in the woods.

This was different. Today she was under arrest for a crime the magnitude of which she herself did not yet fully understand, let alone appreciate: the invasion and attempted conquest of an entire sovereign nation. A very small, sovereign nation, granted, but a nation, nonetheless.

The detective's patience was nearly gone. His face had turned to dark marble, the veins in his cheeks showing like veins in that stone.

Traci felt even more pressured and worried. Her spirit shriveled inside. She had been questioned by the police before, but had never faced this kind of eyeball-to-eyeball interrogation with an obviously angry police officer. Whatever had happened around the island today besides her part—and she was not yet totally sure—he was taking it very personally.

She put her hands to her forehead and held her head still, but inside of it her mind was shaking itself. She drew back against her chair, the cooling sweat causing her black bodysuit to glue to her back. As she looked at the detective, it was as if he was a mirror, reflecting back the damaged reflection of Traci Dennison.

She was suddenly horrified, baffled at her own foolishness. *How could I have been so stupid, to go along with this?* she silently asked herself. And why? Out of friendship? For Kenny?

Now she shook her head. She stared in and through the detective's prying eyes. Then she relented, if only halfway.

"I'd tell you where Kenny is—if I could. Believe me, sir, I'd love to tell you right now where that rotten jerk is."

This she meant. Her voice trembled.

"So then, just tell me, Traci," the detective said more softly. "Tell me whatever you can about this whole business."

He now opted for the Mr. Personal, Mr. Nice Guy approach, since his rude, loud and aloof mode had so far produced absolutely no helpful results. Besides being very pretty, Traci looked like a decent and reasonable young woman. Maybe—just maybe—a little politeness on his part, he thought, might break through her wall.

"Why in the world would you people have ever even tried this?" he asked with genuine interest.

It was not a standard interrogation question, but, for this Cayman detective it was a very real and pressing question. The whole thing was so outlandish. Who in the world, let alone a bunch of snot-nosed kids barely out of college, would attempt to pull off something this bizarre? To attack and try to take over a whole island nation?

He watched as Traci Dennison shook her head again. If she had any answer, it had never formed fully in her own mind, at least not yet. But she had to admit to herself that it *was* because of her affection for Kenny Hamilton. She wouldn't call it love, but if it wasn't that, it was something very close, some feeling for him that was strong enough to get her to go along with his outrageous plan.

"I don't know, sir," she admitted. She looked up at him cautiously, wanting to cooperate now, to save her own skin. Still, she didn't want to say too much. The sweating had only gotten worse, and now her mouth felt like she had just eaten a T-shirt. "I kept asking him that. He never said. Kenny's just kind of a freak."

"A freak?" the detective asked.

"You know, a freak. A wild man. If something looked like it wouldn't work, he'd always try it, just to prove a point—that he could *make* it work." She saw what seemed to be the detective's confused expression. "Does that make sense?"

"No. I don't follow." This wasn't true. He followed her perfectly. He was just prodding the girl.

A sad, exasperated sigh escaped through Traci's nose.

"I think he just wanted to try it, to see if he could pull it off."

"He said that?"

"Well, no. Not in so many words. But Kenny likes a challenge, taking risks. You know, take over part of the world. A whole island."

"And its people," the officer reminded her gravely.

"Yeah. I know," she said faintly. "But I don't think the people count much to Kenny," Traci added. "Any people."

The words struck her like a thunderclap—and for the first time. These words applied to her, too. He had used her. At bottom, Kenny cared for one person, Kenny. In the end, she didn't count. Her heart recoiled, her mind racing to one word.

Bastard!

She looked up, more frightened than ever, overcome by a sense of utter loneliness.

"Am I allowed to ask your name, sir?"

"Marketta. Detective Dane Marketta."

Traci felt the anger starting to bubble in her chest. Her heart thumped harder. She wanted to cry but didn't let herself give in to it.

"Well, Detective Marketta, let me tell you something. I hope you find that worthless son of a worthless momma dog!" she said bitterly. "And I hope you severely punish the rotten little prick!"

Four

Bradley Schott

I can't believe this. How did they get on to us so quickly? I don't understand it. Did somebody leak the plan? Did cops know before we even got here? How could they have known we were about to hit the island? Unless somebody talked?

Kenny swore we couldn't fail. He kept telling me, "It's a great plan, Brad!" He swore and swore. And here I am, sitting in this hell-hole jail!

Why did I ever listen to him? Ever?

And where the heck *is* Kenny? Do they have him? These cops haven't said. They must know. Don't they? Or are they just playing tricks, trying to get info out of me?

Still, the way they keep asking about him, it sure doesn't sound like they know where he is yet.

I'd sure like to know.

This just can't be happening to me. It was just, what, six or seven weeks since Kenny and I were down here in Cayman for vacation? And then he got this stupid, harebrained idea. I mean, how can a person's life turn to complete dog crap in just seven weeks? Well, in about twenty-four hours, actually. The last twenty-four.

I feel sick.

I can just see part of the one detective through the crack of the door. Wolfish-looking guy. Burly. He acts like a big shot. He came in, gave me the stare, looked at my booking card, and walked out. Didn't say a word. Just the cold stare.

One of their main investigators, I bet. Looks like he's talking to someone else in the hall, now—an assistant maybe.

I bet they left the door cracked open on purpose. They want me to overhear. But even straining my ears, I can't make out anything they're saying. Just sounds.

Maybe they left the door ajar to see if I'll run or something. Then shoot me. "Suspect Shot Trying To Escape." That's what it would say in the newspaper tomorrow. Do they *want* me to run? Is it a trick? Or are they just trying to rattle me more?

Stop, Brad. You're not thinking rationally anymore. Don't go crazy! You're in this mess so deep already, don't make it worse. Come on, why would they want you to run? No, they wouldn't do that. Would they?

Of course not, idiot. Calm down. Take a breath. They need me as a witness. I'm too valuable right now.

Aren't I?

OK, here comes the other guy. He looks friendlier than the wolfish guy. Be cool, Brad, be cool. Act like you're innocent, just play along. You can fool him. He's younger, probably inexperienced. Keep it tight. Don't tell him what he doesn't know. Don't be a fool.

"I'm Detective Carden, Mr. Schott. Are you ready to talk with me?"

He seems nice enough. Sure easier looking than the first guy. Probably in his early thirties. Nice, cropped haircut. Not muscular, but he looks like he could get mean if he had to.

"Don't I get a lawyer or something?"

He laughs, then shakes his head like he's talking to a donkey.

"Lawyer? What, do you think you're back home in the U.S. or something? 'A lawyer,' you make me laugh!" He does it again.

"I'm, ah . . . just asking. I can ask, can't I?"

"Mr. Schott, you can ask for the Queen to fly over here from London and make you cucumber sandwiches for dinner, if you would like. Now, listen to me, carefully. You're in a different country, young man. We operate differently, maybe, from what you expect. You seem to know something about being under arrest. Had some experience that way, have we?" He gives me a snarky smile. "That would not surprise me—not in the least. But don't worry. If the Governor of the Caymans happens to decide at some point that you require legal representation, he will appoint a local attorney for you. Someone who understands our laws."

"But I—"

"And I can damn-sure tell you that there is not a single local attorney in our islands who is going to come over here and represent a poor bastardly excuse for a human being such as yourself, unless he or she is *ordered* to do it by the Governor. All right?"

Oh no, I set this guy on fire.

"All right. Yes sir, officer—I mean, detective. But, well, could I still call one in the States? A lawyer, I mean? I could do that, couldn't I?"

He's laughing again.

"Certainly, Bradley, call your attorney in the States, fly him down here. The only problem will be, I will make sure our Customs folks don't let him past the airport, Smart Alec."

Now he's glaring at me. I am *so* screwed.

"Do you have any other strange requests?" Carden prods me.

"No, look, I'm happy to talk to you. OK? No lawyer. Just tell me what you want me to do." I hope he thinks I'm being cooperative now. I'm not sure I'm putting on a very good act, though.

"All right, then let's go back and start at the beginning. How did you become associated with this . . . ," he looks at his notes, ". . . this Mr. Kendall Hamilton?"

"The Fourth."

"Oh, the Fourth! My goodness, that *is* impressive." The snarky look again, more exaggerated this time. "Yes. 'Kenny,' you called him?"

"Yeah. Well, we're buddies. Ever since junior high school."

"And?"

"Well, that's how. How we became associated, as you put it."

Crap. His face says he doesn't like my answer. Now what? Come on fool, try not to tick him off any more than he is. Stay cool, Brad. Good Lord, it's hot in here!

"I meant, Mr. Schott, how did you and he become associated in this little *event* that occurred here on our island today?"

"Event?"

"Come on, Schott. Let's not drag your feet all afternoon, all right? I'm tired! It's been a very long day, thanks to you, and Kendall, and your other ridiculous friends."

Which friends? I wonder who he has talked to already? Has somebody spilled the beans?

"Well?" he demands.

He's glaring at me. And he's not smiling anymore. If that first face of his could be called a smile. Give him something. Something obvious.

"How did it start, you mean?"

"Sure, Bradley. Tell me that. How did it start?"

He's trying to sound bored. But I know he's not. Far from it. Looks like he's about ready to rip my head from my shoulders.

I'm going to be a wreck. I've gotten too nervous, it's got to be showing. Now I need to use the bathroom.

"I don't want to ask, but can I use the restroom?"

"Can you?" he asks.

"*May* I, please? It's urgent." And it is.

"Surely. I'll walk you."

Hope he doesn't think he has to follow me in!

Alone, finally, in the bathroom. And all I can think about is Kenny, how Kenny always cheated. Cheated on the baseball team. He always wanted the glory, but skipped a quarter of the practices. How did he always get away with that kind of stuff?

High School. Seems like an eternity ago. Who was that beautiful girl back then, the one who liked me? Patty. That was her. Befriended me after she saw me in that school play. Maybe she thought I'd be famous someday.

Great. Now I will be.

Whatever happened to her, I wonder? How come she ever liked me? The head cheerleader, and me, the geek? Life is so strange.

You're in jail, Brad. "Strange" doesn't even begin to

cover it.

OK, why am I regressing to high school? Maybe I'm on overload. Meltdown. They'll be scraping the residue of Brad Schott up off the floor in an hour.

I can't stay in here in this bathroom stall forever. Stalling in the stall. Funny, Brad. Funny. Come on, let's get on with it.

Carden is waiting just outside the door. What a surprise—he doesn't trust me.

"Don't worry," I say, "I'm not gonna run."

"Of course you're not," he says, but with a look that says maybe he wishes I'd try.

We're back in the same little interrogation room and he asks, "All right, start again, how and why did you all come down here? With this Kendall Hamilton?"

"Let me think. Um, it kind of started a couple of months back. Kenny and me, we came down here on a quickie vacation. That's when he had the idea."

"When was that?" Carden wants to know.

"OK, well, it was back in—" When the heck was it? Man, my brain's gone numb. I can't remember! Too much went down today. "I think it was early April, maybe? I don't know. I'd have to check my calendar."

"Go ahead."

"You took it."

"What?"

"My phone."

"Oh, yes, we did. Well, you'll get it back. Maybe." He's glaring at me. He's thinking of calling pest control. "Depending," he says with a question mark in his eyes.

"On what?"

"On how things go here, Bradley. Between you and me, and my boss, Detective Marketta. How the investigation goes. And how hard I have to work. See, I don't like to have to pry things out of people. Especially when they're already under arrest. You're here because you've done some bad things—I'm saying, some *really* bad things. Four people are dead, and more wounded. Do you get that? Do you! And I'm not going to stand here and have to pry every little piece of information out of you. Do you understand, me, Mr. Schott? Are you on board with me?"

Man, I ticked him off again. I don't even get a breath before he rants on.

"Are we going to work together?" he barks. "Or are you going to be a little jerk and just keep trying to make me mad. Do you want me mad at you, Bradley?" he growls. "Is that your plan?"

No good, now he's double-ticked. Stupid move, Brad, stupid move.

"I'm Sorry, Mister—"

"*Detective* Carden," he corrects me.

Well, it's better than that angry growl.

"Detective Carden, sir, I'm not trying to be a pig-head. I just don't know what you want to know. All right, yeah, I'm caught. I didn't plan on that, you know? Obviously," I whisper to myself, then louder, "and I'm hurt, you know?"

Carden watches me gently rub the bandaged flesh wound on the back of my left shoulder.

"Mr. Schott, I cannot express to you how completely I fail to give a damn about your wound," Carden says. "So sorry you have a little ow-wee. It's self-inflicted, if you ask me. That's what happens when you shoot at the police. They like to shoot back."

His scowl just got blacker.

"Yeah, well, you don't know how sorry I am to be sitting here, either." My voice is louder than I want, but I can't help it. "We were the ones who were gonna call the shots. Decisions, I mean. Not 'shots,' like gunshots. Anyway, it wasn't supposed to go down like this. We had a very good plan. And Kenny was certain nobody down here carried guns. The police, I mean. So, see, nobody was going to get hurt." He's not buying this, I can tell. "Well, not seriously hurt, you know?"

"I know? No, Bradley, I don't know! What do you mean, 'not seriously'? What kind of load of horse crap is that?"

"But I—"

"Shut up! You come down here armed to the teeth. You attack our home like a bunch of thug mercenaries! And you say you didn't want anybody hurt? You *are* kidding me, right! Wait," he says, scanning my arrest card, "I thought it says here you went to college?" Now he's talking to a donkey without a head.

"I did—I mean . . . never mind."

"Go on, Schott. Dig your hole deeper. I can't wait. Maybe when you call your smart-ass lawyer, you can ask him to bring you a bigger shovel?"

"Look, the guns, yeah, see, originally, it was just going to be blanks. You know, nothing lethal."

"Stop saying 'you know' all the time, because, no, I don't! You are going to explain it all to me! Got that?"

I wish I could melt down into that rusty floor drain over there.

I better get serious.

"Yeah, I thought—I mean, we thought we had everything handled. Nobody here was supposed to be armed, right? So why would we expect a gun fight?"

"Wait, Bradley, are you an actor or something? Tell me you're pretending. Tell me that you are not really that stupid! You, and your buddy Hamilton."

Actually, the way I feel, I guess I *am* that stupid.

"No, sir, I'm not stupid. We just thought we knew how it would go down, that we could handle—whatever. We planned out every detail. We were really sure the cops down here—the police I mean—you guys— wouldn't be armed. Kenny was sure. Said he checked it all out. So we just had guns for a kind of show of force. To get everyone to go along peacefully with things."

"Go along peacefully! You come down here, you try to commandeer our homeland? Our nation? And you think—no, wait, you're sure—you're sure, 'Oh well, they'll just lie down, roll over, and play dead.' So, in other words, you think we're just as stupid as you?"

That snarl is back.

"Wait, Officer—I mean Detective Carden, please, just give me a second."

"Oh, by all means! Take a second. Take all the time you want, Bradley! You sure as hell aren't going anywhere," he adds with scorn. "And your dinner will taste just the same cold."

Now what? If I say anything more, I'm gonna cook my own goose. I know it. And where the hell is Kenny? The jerk! He should be the one in here talking to this detective. He was the boss of this whole deal, not me. How come I'm holding the bag?

I'm so stupid. Carden is right. I should have told Kenny no, right from the get-go. I should have told him what to do with his big idea.

I look up and Carden is still glaring at me.

"I'm waiting, Mr. Schott."

His face is really red now. He's more ticked than ever. Guess I shouldn't have ditched out on that class on persuasion in public speaking.

"I know, uh—detective, look, I'm sorry. Dragging

my feet, I mean. But I'm scared, OK? We didn't plan on hurting anybody. It just kind of got out of control. And I didn't know Kenny was planning to bring in that live ammo. Never. I just found out about that late yesterday. He told me the team leaders would have live ammo, for safety, he said."

That really did piss me off, too. How come Kenny held out on me like that? Why didn't he tell us all about the live ammo, up front? Now look.

"For safety," Carden repeats, as if his ears are playing tricks.

"Yeah, when I found out yesterday, I asked him why. 'Just in case,' he said. 'In case of what?' I said. He grinned. 'Just in case we have to prove to somebody we're serious.'"

"He said that."

I nod.

"Sounds like Mr. Hamilton was dead serious about your little plan, here."

I can't stop myself from nodding again. Stupid. How come I only see this now?

"Yeah. I guess."

"There sure is a hell of a lot of guessing going on in this room," Carden scowls. "All right. That's a start, Schott. So, are you going to help me out now? 'Cause, just so you know, I have plenty of other folks I can go talk to. Folks who might want our judges to know there was a little cooperation. If you don't feel in that mood, don't waste any more of my time."

Oh man, I am majorly going down in flames! I need to get on his good side before he walks out.

"No, no, wait, I'll help you. Please. I just need to be careful. I've never been in a mess like this. I'm—I'm kind of feeling my way. I don't want to make a mistake."

"Son, you have already made the biggest damn mistake of your life."

I can't even respond, it hurts so deep. When somebody else has to tell you the truth like that, and you're blind. Blind to my own soul.

He's waiting. I have to say something. I have to admit it.

"I guess."

"No guessing about that one," Carden assures me.

Man, I'm dead. I wish I was, anyway. This is gonna hurt a lot more.

"Yeah. All right, sir. I'll help you."

"Let me go find some paper."

He gives a nod and leaves. He leaves the door open a crack. Is it another test? Do they think I'll run?

I just stare through that crack in the door. Twenty-four hours, and my whole life has been flushed down the toilet. And you know where toilets lead.

So where the hell is Kenny?

Five

The Reporter

That afternoon, on the day of the attack, Detective Dane Marketta had been working on Traci Dennison while his assistant, Detective Andrew Carden, twisted Bradley Schott. Both were in custody, from separate arrest sites, and were being held at the Central Police Station in George Town.

Both Marketta and Carden made slow progress.

After an effective chat with Brad, Carden left him in the cramped interrogation room, supposedly to get some paper so that Schott could write a statement. Really, though, Carden just wanted to talk with Marketta to find out if he had learned anything useful from Traci Dennison. Marketta was Chief of Detectives and was leading the investigation into the attempted coup that day on Grand Cayman.

The first time I interviewed Brad, I remember him describing how he had felt that afternoon. After Carden left him in the interrogation room, he just sat there, mentally squirming. He remembered how nervous he had felt as Carden kept pressuring him to confess, and to tell him where the elusive Kenny Hamilton was.

"I told Carden I didn't want to make a mistake," Brad told me, "and make things even worse for myself. Carden looked at me hard, and said, 'Look, son, you've already made the biggest mistake of your life!'"

Brad's day went downhill from there.

He sat alone for another twenty minutes. The intolerable waiting made him even more nervous than he already was, wondering and worrying about his fate. His mind reeled. To make matters worse—if that was possible—the room stank of someone who had been in there before him, someone who had obviously been having bowel troubles. "Probably some drunk," Brad told me.

But Brad was stone-cold sober, and he was in pain. Besides the pain from the gunshot wound in his shoulder, he had suffered some other pretty serious bumps and bruises during his arrest. But none of the physical sources of pain felt as bad as the searing agony he felt deep in his gut—pain, he described it, like a hot fireplace poker wrenching around in there somewhere below his stomach. And it wasn't food. It was fear.

As Brad told me about this, I could actually see the fear creeping back into his eyes, as if he were reliving the events.

He had stared at the grayish-blue cinder block walls that had encased him. It felt like a tomb. The room was far worse than he ever imagined a jail might be. It was worse than the larger holding cell where he and several of the assault team members had been placed after being taken into custody by the Royal Cayman Police. Now he was in a special interrogation room. The little window in the door, he was fairly sure, was a one-way glass. It let the people out in the hall look in at him, but he could not see out.

"It gave me a sick feeling," he told me. "With the sharp pain in my gut—and the constant feeling that I needed to vomit—I felt like living death."

He had never thought he would end up in jail, never even suspected that everything would go so haywire. Being caught, being thrown into jail, had never factored into the wonderful plan that Kenny Hamilton had laid out. Kenny had made the whole plan sound so simple, so plausible, ever since that early morning on the airplane last April when Brad and Kenny flew out of Owen Roberts Airport, headed back home to Philadelphia. It was that morning, Brad told me, when Kenny had first conceived this whole stupid plan. And Brad, trying to be a good friend, and as he typically did, just wanted to go along with Kenny.

So Brad bought into it. But throughout the weeks of planning, even in several nightmares, Brad had never seen *this* coming. Kenny's plan had all seemed so detailed, so perfect.

"Too perfect. That should have been my clue," he told me sullenly.

There he sat in that stinky interrogation room. Carden had not come back. Brad was torn up with worry, apprehensive about what might happen next. And as he now realized—too late—being under arrest in a different country was a different ball of wax from his recent arrest with Traci up in Philadelphia. The police here were different. They were equally as professional as the cops up in the states, but they had a genuine air of superiority that shook Brad. He felt like a little sapling tree standing in a forest of giant oaks.

To make it worse, he sensed that they knew a lot more than they were willing to talk about. "I felt like an overweight bird at the far end of a really thin branch that could break at any instant. And it was like the police were all holding a saw behind their backs," he remembered.

At that point, Brad's biggest concern was about who Carden and the other cops had captured, and who they were talking to. Who did they have? What were the others saying? Was Carden bluffing about Kenny? Did they already know where Kenny was? What about Traci, and the others?

Weeks later, as I interviewed Brad there at the jail, he cursed his best friend. "You were just a spoiled rich kid, weren't you, Kenny?" Brad mumbled, as if he were talking with Kenny instead of me. "Without a real life."

Brad spent a lot of time looking at the floor in those days. But he looked up at me that morning, during our interview, saying, "I've gone back, you know? Tried to figure Kenny out. And all I can come up with is that this whole thing was just because of boredom. Just to see if he could pull it off."

"May be," I replied. "I think Traci said something like that to Marketta."

Brad didn't respond.

I had spoken with Marketta pretty extensively already. He insisted on filling me in on the basics of the attempted coup before he let me actually talk with any of the prisoners.

So, as Brad sat there in front of me cursing Kenny, he was really cursing himself. Brad is a reasonably smart fellow, although, as he admitted to me, he's sometimes slow on the uptake in life.

"Why did I let myself get taken in by Kenny so easily, all those promises of money, and power? Was I still that naive? Or was it really my feelings for Traci that sucked me in?" Brad was asking me, as if I should know the answer. "Maybe I was secretly trying to protect Traci. From Kenny."

I just nodded, not wanting to interrupt his train of thought, which seemed short a locomotive or two.

"I sat there that first afternoon in that stupid interrogation room thinking, *Where is Kenny now, when I need him? Why isn't he here in this stench hole, too?* He promised us he'd be there—to see it all through to the end of the operation," Brad confided to me. "And then the day before we leave Philly—just like that—Kenny tells everyone he's going to stay off-shore, out on that stupid catamaran."

"Why?" I asked.

"Said it was so he could observe, and coordinate everything better. Bull," Brad answered. "The truth is, Kenny weaseled out."

I could see, then, even weeks after Brad's arrest, that he was still confused, still trying to shoulder the responsibility for his own foolishness, and still trying to work out his complete disappointment with his best friend Kenny Hamilton.

Brad's interrogation by Detective Carden that first day apparently didn't help. Brad was still upset with himself, because he let Carden get him rattled. Brad remembered his stomach was doing somersaults as soon as Carden stepped out of the interrogation room, realizing he'd already given in to the cops. To make it worse, the coffee they offered him an hour earlier tasted like it had been brewed a month before.

"Or maybe it got sidetracked back out of the sewer," Brad said. "It felt like that coffee was gonna eat the lining out of my stomach."

His nose screwed up like he could still taste the wretched stuff. He continued his story.

He had stood up, cautiously, even though no one else was in the little interrogation room. He crept toward the small window in the top of the door, hoping to see Traci Dennison, or someone. Anybody he might know. He was pretty sure he had heard Traci's voice, very briefly, out in the hallway.

Pretty sure, he told me, but not certain.

But he had guessed right about the window. It was a one-way viewing glass. They could see in, but he couldn't see out. To him, it was a mirror. And an unwelcome one.

Revulsion suddenly shot through him.

"I wondered, maybe Carden—or someone worse— was right there on the other side of the glass, staring at me eyeball to eyeball, but I couldn't see."

He recalled that he suddenly had a sensation like scorpions crawling up his spine under his battered assault suit, marshaling to strike at the base of his neck. He grabbed at his neck but, of course, there was nothing there.

"I felt like an animal. Caged. But I was too afraid to cry out."

He was still reliving the pain of that day.

"My guts wretched again. I lunged for an old, metal waste can by the wall behind the desk. I puked up what little bit of coffee was left in my stomach. Tasted even worse that time."

He remembered his sweat felt cold and clammy even though the room was sweltering. He tried to clear the poisonous vomit from his nose and sinuses, without success.

"I tried to straighten up on my knees, but I couldn't. It was like some huge hand was forcing me down."

His back ached from the violent upheaval of his stomach. His heart sank as if into the depths of the ocean surrounding the island, his spirits even further. Despair crept in.

And he was struggling, wondering what had happened to Traci. Did they have her? Was she OK? Was she hurt?

Along with the despair, he told me, he felt a deep sense of guilt for what they had done that day. Four people were dead. And it was only then, late that evening after his arrest, that Brad had awakened to the reality—and the enormity—of what he, Kenny, Traci, and the rest had done.

Brad looked at me with a bleak expression, remembering that moment.

"My mind flashed back to the vault, down there in the bank. And all I remember thinking was, *I wish that damned bullet had hit its mark.*"

Six

Traci Dennison

Where the heck are they holding Brad? It's been hours since I was arrested. I overheard Marketta and Carden talking about Brad, out in the hall. So they must have him.

If I could just talk to him first. He'd know what I should say. He's more up on cops. I learned that, that night in Philly. He'd know what we should do now.

I'm afraid.

I'm starving, too. Are they doing this on purpose? Make me so hungry I'll cry, and break down?

Oh, Lord, it's so hot in here. They're probably doing that on purpose, too! What do they say in the movies? "Make 'em sweat!"

No, idiot, it's the Caribbean, it's always hot. Everybody sweats.

Come on, just relax. Relax, breathe. Tell the truth. It's all that's left, isn't it? It's just going to get worse if you keep on lying to these people. You just tried to steal their island! Why shouldn't they be mad? Come on, Traci, don't be a dumbbell.

The door. Marketta's back.

Should I ask him for some food? A snack, maybe?

"All right, Traci. I think we need to talk a little more. I'm afraid you left some things out."

"Oh. I did?" Make it sound innocent. Look straight at him. It'll make it look like you're telling the truth. Anyway, from his eyes, I think he's still in his Good Cop mode. Thank God.

"Afraid so. My assistant, Detective Carden, has been talking to your friend Bradley Schott."

He lets this sink in, then jabs me again.

"Come on, Miss Dennison, of course you left things out. Nobody tells it all, not right off the bat. Not until they realize what really deep trouble they're in. You see?"

"I guess I do. Can I please eat something?"

"Fine. Go ahead."

There's that look again. He's already back to being a smartass with me.

"I don't have anything. But I'm starving."

"Well, you won't talk to me at all if I let you starve to death, now will you?" he says with a muted laugh.

What a jerk.

"What would you like? I could have some prime rib brought in, from one of our best restaurants along Seven Mile Beach. Some great salad bars along there, too. Do you fancy shrimp cocktail? Or maybe some buttered and parslied potatoes. How would that be? We could have our own little love feast here. You, and me."

No laugh this time, just that smirking smile again.

I can't help it. "All right," I burst out, "look, stop treating me like a joke! All right? Yeah, so you're having your little laugh. But this is no joke, not to me!

How would *you* like to be in my place?"

He's quiet, but his eyes seem to sympathize just a little, so I beg some more.

"Look, I'm here, I'm caught. I get it. But I'm still human, huh? I'm not your dog. I'm starved! Please, anything. A snack bar, chips. Anything. I don't care. My stomach really hurts."

"That's not just from hunger, Traci."

"Yeah, I know." My stomach confirms this with an audible, gurgling growl. "But a little food would help. Anything."

"Sure. Of course," Marketta says, relenting.

Wow, his crabby smile is gone. I think he means it. He's going to get me something, before I faint. Or get the dry heaves.

"You like corn chips?"

"I'd eat dog right now."

"We're out," he smiles.

Finally. An actual smile that's not full of contempt. Thank God. He's going to get me some chips. I won't starve. Not today, anyway.

"Thanks. Corn chips would be great. Some soda?"

"Maybe we can find a cup of water."

Water. Oh well, it'll be wet. "A large cup?"

He gives me a weak nod and walks to the door, saying, "Sure, Traci. Anything for my favorite prisoner."

Prisoner. Oh, God, now I am going to dry-heave.

Traci, you fool! See what you've done? Sweet, little, innocent Traci Dennison. Oh, God . . . oh, God.

Some chips and water. But when he comes back, I'm going to have to talk to him. Tell him what he wants. He just bought me.

For chips, and water.

At least I won't be cutting my own throat on an

empty stomach.

Kenny, you rotten bastard.

Seven

Kenny Hamilton

How in hell did everything go so wrong?

It was a perfectly planned attack. It was *not* supposed to go down this way! All those weeks of planning. And two days ago it all turns to crap!

And all that money! What a waste. And what a bunch of worthless friends. They all let me down, Brad, Traci, Broadman—every one of them. I should have known. Don't trust anyone, Kenny. When will you learn?

Well, I'm free, anyway. And they'll never catch me. Morons. Cops are all morons. Especially these island cops! A bunch of baboons. Couldn't find their own butt with both hands and a search warrant.

So they got my crew. They won't get me. I've out-foxed them, I'm certain of it. Even if I say so myself, I'm good. Damned good.

Besides, even if they could catch up to me, they could never pin any of it on me. Not the way I set things up. And those guys won't talk—Traci, Brad, and whoever else got busted. They're loyal to old Kenny. I'm sure of it. They'll take the fall for me.

Anyway, it's their own idiotic fault they got caught. Didn't follow the plan. That's not my fault. If they'd just stuck to the plan, we'd all be living it up at some beautiful tropical resort on Grand Cayman right now, money pouring in, and everybody kissing up to us! Then I wouldn't be here in Jamaica, all alone, and they wouldn't all be in the fix they're in.

Man, I've always known Brad's a little slow, but I thought he was smarter than this. There's no way that he shouldn't have been able to handle things at that bank. And Traci, how could she let herself get caught, just going to nail down the old governor, for Pete's sake? The easiest assignment of the whole operation! And she blows it? What a bimbo.

I thought she was sharper than that. Just goes to show, Hamilton, you really can't count on anybody— ever—but yourself.

All right, think, collect yourself. Don't get ahead of things. There's curve balls everywhere. Watch your back, and play it cool. You don't want to get busted, too.

I'll use the fake passport for the ticket. Just in case my name leaked somehow over on Cayman. Yeah, there's a lot of ocean between there and Jamaica, but why chance it? It's been two days since everything went to hell over there. Plenty of time for my name to get dragged in, if somebody did rat.

But why would they talk? They'd be hanging themselves! They'll protect me. Traci, especially. The girl loves me, I'm sure of it. She won't give me up to the cops. She's tough. A bimbo maybe, but a tough bimbo. She'll keep those sweet little lips shut.

I'm just glad I made it off that catamaran when I did and made it back here. Maybe my backup plan was better than I thought.

OK, so where to now, Hamilton? Not home, obviously. That wouldn't be smart. Where? Somewhere in the Pacific, maybe. Some other tiny island in the South Seas? One without cops!

Is there such a place? There's got to be. I just need to get my butt out of Jamaica and hide out for a while. Let those idiots get through court, and make sure they don't finger me into the crapola pie that they've made for themselves.

Man, I need a vacation. This was hard work. Then to see it all turn to garbage! Weeks of planning—and nearly a million bucks—down the tube!

Oh well, it was somebody else's money. More where that came from. That armored truck heist was truly brilliant. Bundles of money, and I've still got plenty of it stashed. Maybe Traci was right. Maybe there *is* some big guy upstairs. He must really like me!

A vacation? No, that's how this whole plan started. No more vacations. Can't be too visible. I'm just going to have to be on the run for a while, and keep my head down. Make the best of it, Kenny, like you always do.

Maybe I'll just sit here and read, at least until I figure out which way to go. New name, new identity, stay off the grid. Maybe someplace where I could do more scuba diving. That'd be great. I know, I could get a part-time job as a dive instructor.

Who am I kidding? Me, a job? Yeah, now I'm a comedian.

But none of this crap is funny. I feel a little bad about Brad, and Traci. And Arielle. I mean, they were friends, sort of. But how stupid do you have to be to blow a perfect plan like that? They must have gotten sloppy. I told them enough times, "Watch your tails, and stick to the plan!" I kept saying it, day after day for weeks. I guess they thought I was joking.

Well, I'll get over it. They'll just do a little prison time. Probably right there on Grand Cayman. That won't be too tough. Or maybe they'll get shipped off to some jail in England. Now that'd be lousy luck.

Wait, I know—maybe I can figure out a way to spring them. There's an idea! But that'd mean more risks for me, and it might get tricky. It could be fun, though.

No, Hamilton, slow down again. Think that one through. Why stick your neck out for *them?*

Wouldn't that be a hot one for the newspapers, though, if I could somehow spring them all out of jail? I get them busted, then I bust them out! It'd be a riot!

Newspapers. Maybe not. Don't need my picture in the papers right now. But these dang, stupid reporters seem to be everywhere. There's one over there, looking impatient. Wears his cheesy little press badge to the airport. What a dork. Trying to look important. Wait—he just glanced at me. Does he know?

Don't be so paranoid. He can't possibly know who you are—or what you've done.

I need to get moving, if I can decide where I'm going. If I sneak onto a flight with this dummied-up passport, these Jamaican cops will never know. They don't look very smart, anyway.

Suck it up, Kenny. You're smarter than all of them. And obviously smarter than your friends. You didn't get caught! Don't get down on yourself just because the Grand Slam didn't work out. It was a hell of a ride while it lasted!

Wait. That's it, look, right there on the Departures board. Of course. I'll head north to Houston, then back south somewhere. Who would ever figure that out?

All right, where'd I stash that bogus credit card? I wonder if they'll have a full meal on this flight.

IV.
Back To The Beginning

Eight

The Reporter

As you can already guess, Kenny Hamilton's Grand Slam band of mercenaries fell into shambles in a hurry once they landed on Grand Cayman. If you're naturally curious, as most of us are, you're probably wondering what happened, and why.

To answer that, I'll have to go further back. I started from the end of the story because, as I mentioned, that's where I first became involved in it. I'll get to that eventually. But for simplicity, I'll turn back to the very beginning and walk through the events from there.

Believe me, my boss was right. Making sense of those events has been a huge challenge. Reading back over my hundreds of notes and scribbles from talking with some of the people involved, the whole chain of events still seems crazy and disjointed. My challenge, and my real goal, was to try to understand the personalities of these people, the main cast of players. Who were they, and why did they ever get involved in this whole mess?

I've asked so many questions and dug so many details out of them, I almost feel like I was there with them from the beginning of this scheme.

Thank God I wasn't.

It's those details, though, that really tell the story. I've tried to sift the main events down into a running account. You may suspect that here and there I've exercised a bit of artistic license. You'll be right. I've done that so it's more readable and less like a newspaper account. But I'm not going to bore you from here on with who told me exactly what, or when. That's not important. What is important is to draw the big picture and to help you understand who these folks were—who they are—and how they trained their sights on Grand Cayman.

THE PLAN, once cemented in Kenny Hamilton's brain during the flight home from Grand Cayman last April, took shape very quickly.

Kenny and Brad landed back home in Philadelphia late that Sunday afternoon. It had been a brief, hectic vacation in the Caymans, but it had been, as Brad joked getting onto the plane that morning for the flight home, "grand."

It was a typical, second-rate Bradley Schott joke but, sad to say, it planted a seed in Kenny's mind and triggered the plan that he eventually decided to call "The Grand Slam."

Monday morning as faint, early rays began to breach the dark eastern sky over Philadelphia, Brad twisted onto his side in his bed, trying to rouse himself. He had slept like a dead man. He slapped the blaring alarm clock and managed to silence it. But for how long?

His mind rebelled, his heart concurred. But it was

back to work today, back to the daily grind of lining up sales contacts, and working with the sales manager at the auto dealership, a hotshot manager who was newer at the place than Brad himself.

Make the sale. That was the game. Always make the sales manager happy, because that makes the boss even happier. This was Brad's daily reality, and it was a paycheck, nothing more. It was not a job Brad would have sought for himself, but working for Kenny's well-to-do uncle, who owned the dealership, was better than working for somebody of whom Brad had never heard. At least at the dealership he had an "in," his friendship with Kenny Hamilton.

For Brad, selling cars was like being trapped inside the script of a B-horror flick. It was the last thing he would have ever chosen for his career. He had only half-way studied his way through management school in college, hoping that he could get into the big leagues of banking. If not a big bank, maybe he could at least land a spot as the manager of a mid-sized credit union somewhere.

But cars? Selling glitzy new rides that would be scrap metal in ten years? For this, he chided himself almost daily, he had fought for his B-minus grade point average in college?

Oh well, he kept reminding himself, it could be worse. It could be used cars.

He dragged himself slowly out of bed and into the shower. The hot water, with occasional bursts of cold thanks to the apartment dwellers next door, did the trick. He toweled off and pulled on clean shorts and a T-shirt. He hoped that Kenny had beat him into the kitchen and would at least have the coffee started. It was unlikely, but Brad hoped anyway, ever the disappointed optimist.

The kitchen was empty; the coffee pot was, too. He searched against hope for coffee grounds, but the cabinets were just as bare as when they had left for Grand Cayman eight days earlier.

A more persistent search led to the discovery of a bit of orphaned coffee lying forlornly in the bottom of the dark brown glass canister that his best friend Kenny had promised to fill two weeks ago.

Brad sniffed the grounds. Dry as a Phoenix summer, the once-rich aroma had long ago escaped its captivity.

He found a filter and dumped the remaining grounds into the top of the coffeemaker, then put just enough water into the machine to squeeze two cups out of the meager offering of coffee grounds.

A few drops were dripping into the carafe when Kenny wandered through the kitchen door, dark rings under his eyes, and looking only vaguely refreshed.

"Don't bother with coffee. No time. We'll catch some java on the fly. Man, Brad, you're a slacker! Not even dressed yet. Come on, get some clothes on. We've got to get moving."

Kenny was tall, in his late twenties, and as handsome as a son of Philly could get. His dark, curly hair and dark-bluish eyes betrayed a mix of Dutch and German heritage that, along the way and under the covers, had been mixed up with a long-lost Lenape Indian family and—though his Grandfather denied it—included a great-grandfatherly liaison with a reputed descendant of one of Benjamin Franklin's bastard granddaughters.

For Kenny's part, though, he claimed a direct descent from the most famous Hamilton in early America, Alexander. That heritage was, in part, what led to his recent trip to the Caribbean with Brad. Kenny's fascination with the Caribbean started when he accidentally learned—during a college history class he rarely attended—that his forefather Alexander had been born out of wedlock on the Island of Nevis in the West Indies around 1755. That his best-known ancestor had been orphaned at age eleven intrigued Kenny, since he felt much like a social orphan in his own family. How Alexander had grown up to wield such power and prestige as a founding father of the United States was still a mystery to Kenny, but that seemed to intrigue him, also.

As Brad searched for cereal, Kenny stretched and leaned against the kitchen doorjamb, his mind still in the Caribbean. Visions of the great Alexander Hamilton danced at the borders of his consciousness, as another compartment of his brain played with his new plan to capture Grand Cayman.

"Did you know my great-great-whatever Grandpa Alexander was the first Secretary of the Treasury?" he asked Brad out of the blue.

Where is this coming from? Brad asked himself, still trying to fully wake up. The coffee was dripping far too slowly, like sap from a maple tree on a very cold morning.

"Didn't know that," he answered Kenny, his eyes anticipating the last drops of coffee as they trickled down into the woefully bathed carafe. He was hoping Kenny wouldn't see how little coffee was available, so he allowed his body to block the pot from Kenny's view. "What about it?"

"Oh, I don't know," Kenny replied disinterestedly, swallowing a yawn. "Guess I was just born to end up like Alexander, that's all. You know, powerful and rich." He smiled at Brad. "Any coffee, buddy?"

Brad grudgingly poured out three-quarters of a cup

for his friend. Kenny did, after all, pay most of the rent. If he wanted coffee, he got his first.

With the coffee chugged down, Kenny shoved two slices of dry bread into his mouth.

"Want some cereal?" Brad asked.

"Naw, no time," Kenny said bumping Brad's arm and adding, "come on, man, time's a wasting. Get dressed." He quickly swallowed the half-chewed, untoasted bread.

"What's the hurry?" Brad complained, pouring his own half-a-cup, leaving the coffee carafe dry but for a few drops boiling off the bottom of the pot. His brain and muscles were still fighting off the days and nights of fatigue he had built up while on Grand Cayman.

"Hurry?" Kenny asked. "'What's the hurry'? Man, weren't you listening in the cab last night at all?"

"No, actually, like on the plane, Kenny, I was trying to make up for lost sleep. You know, you just ramble a lot. I don't always pay attention."

Eyeing the empty coffeepot, Kenny reached over and smacked the OFF button.

"You don't want to let that run when it's empty, dude. It'll wreck the pot."

Brad began to steam like the last droplets of water percolating up through the coffeemaker.

"You are so rude," he told Kenny with the tone that usually made Kenny instantly mad.

Today, though, Kenny laughed it off. He stopped, gave Brad a look, and then burst into laughter.

"Hey, come on, Brad, smile, buck up. This is gonna be your lucky day! You realize that? Your lucky week, month—life!" Kenny scowled again at Brad's half attire. "Get some decent clothes on, man, we're going down to my office. We've got a lot of things to plan."

"I can't, and you know that. If I'm late to your

uncle's dealership one more time, he'll can me."

"Good. Let him. He's a bozo anyway. Sorry I got you hooked into that job. But I knew you needed the work. But today, I've got *way* better ideas—and I need you to help pull it off. Uncle Terry can go suck eggs."

"So, when my little one-quarter of the rent comes due week after next, and you're stuck paying it all this month, how's that gonna work?" Brad asked sarcastically.

Kenny burst out laughing again.

"Brad, don't sweat the small stuff. Don't you get it? Listen to me. We're done with this place. It's a dump compared to what's coming online for us soon!"

Brad looked around at the classy apartment that Kenny rented for them for the last two years, in a building another one of Kenny's uncles owned. It offered a spectacular view from the twelfth floor of one of the nicest buildings in Philly. Letting Brad off for only a quarter of the rent was purely selfish on Kenny's part, to provide himself some company.

"Dump?" Brad asked, scanning the furnishings that had cost Kenny a fortune, and for which he had paid cash.

"Yes, dump, D. U. M. P. You and I are going for the big time, Brad. I've been working the plan over in my head all night. Barely slept a wink."

That, Brad realized, accounted not only for the dark circles but for the nearly-manic energy Kenny was showing this morning. *If he isn't bipolar, he ought to be*, Brad thought.

"Here," Kenny said, tossing a folded piece of paper to Brad. "This is our list. You call the ones in the 'B' column. OK? You can handle that, can't you?"

Kenny grabbed a third piece of dry bread and

swallowed it nearly whole, then went to the sink and lapped up some tap water from his palm.

"There's ice water in the fridge," Brad told him.

"Yeah," Kenny said between quick swallows.

"Great breakfast," Brad remarked.

"Who needs it?" Kenny laughed. "Clothes, Brad, clothes. Come on, time's a-wastin'."

Good grief. What's he scheming up now? Brad wondered. He wished now he had paid a little more attention the day before on the flight home.

Feeling pressured, Brad hustled back to his own room and hurriedly dressed. He started to tie on a modestly-colored necktie, then paused and looked at it. He was not going to have to sell cars today. He tossed the tie on the bed.

What a relief he felt. No selling today. Kenny was the one selling. He had some kind of plan brewing, though it seemed to be dribbling out of him like the meager coffee servings this morning.

Brad finished dressing and paused in his bathroom to brush through his head of thick, dark brown, curly hair. The shave would have to wait. Kenny was in a hurry. Brad took a final glance in the mirror, content with what he saw. Looking down absently at a toothpaste stain in the sink, he shook his head a little, wondering. Should he just go along with Kenny as usual with whatever plan his friend was scheming up? Why did he value Kenny's friendship so much? Was it just because Kenny was flush with money?

It was a tough question, one he could not answer in the rush of the moment.

He looked back in the mirror and gave himself a nod. Yes, he knew he was sometimes a little slow on figuring things out. Still, for whatever vague reason, he was already wary. Kenny had a way of roping people into things before they even knew he owned a rope.

JUST SIXTEEN blocks away, a pure white cotton comforter lay in loose heaps atop Traci Dennison like a cloak of spring clouds piled up in fluffy layers across a western Pennsylvania mountain ridge. The air in her bedroom was comfortably cool, and only the distant hum of the refrigerator compressor from two rooms away marred the silent stillness.

Traci corralled her long, lush hair into one hand, straightening out several strands that had twisted up into a clump during the night. She took a deep, relaxed breath of air that contained just a hint of the kitty cat that was curled into a small knot between her feet. If this was not the lap of luxurious living, Traci's heart told her, then there was no such thing.

Brilliant early morning rays began to burglarize her apartment, forcing themselves through notches between the slats of the vertical blinds, stealing the darkness from the corners and cracks of her bedroom.

Not quite half-awake, she pulled the comforter higher and tucked her head down deeper, hiding from whatever cold realities the oncoming day might hold. Her kitten Felina adjusted slightly to the movement but was not about to move from her snug little spot at Traci's feet.

Reality began to replace the cobwebs of sleep. Reluctantly, Traci's mind began to focus on what she would have facing her at work today. Business at her gym had been crushing the past few weeks. Popularity had its price. Keeping up with the often frivolous demands of her newest customers sometimes made the job of managing the place very little fun, but the membership was growing like midsummer weeds and the numbers in her income ledger were multiplying like spring bunnies.

Traci was basking in her achievements. These included a local television news spot four days ago about her gym that highlighted the winning personality of Traci Dennison, the young, female entrepreneur who had made the place such an amazing success. What the news reporter didn't know was that Traci's success stemmed largely from the generosity of her grandfather who bankrolled the purchase and setup of the gym, but also from several shots of emergency capital from her well-to-do friend Kenny Hamilton, gifts that had helped the business over several critical growth hurdles and kept it sailing clear of hidden financial reefs that might have sunk it altogether.

As she crawled out of bed, forcing Felina to the refuge of a rumple of comforter that would become her fortress for the next few hours, Traci remembered that Kenny and Brad were supposed to get back sometime yesterday from their vacation on Grand Cayman. Kenny had promised her lunch today to recap the trip. She had desperately wanted to join them for the trip, but it overlapped the day that a local news personality, Kattie McLandrew, had set for Traci's noonday television appearance.

Traci rolled to a sitting position on the edge of the mattress and glanced up at the brilliant sunrays that were jetting across the room just over her head, weaving ocean-like shadow waves across the antique, plastered ceiling. There was no getting around it. Whatever the clock said, morning was here.

Sitting wobbly on the edge of the bed, she caressed her shoulders again with the still-warm comforter. She had never been a morning person. It would be so easy to collapse back into bed and hide from the day.

She resisted. Life was waiting.

It was still early April and the weather outside would not be nearly as friendly as her cuddly bedroom. But she had to face the day. She glanced at the clock. Six-forty-eight. She still had time for a shower.

She didn't quite have her pajamas off when the phone rang. She pulled the top back on and grabbed for the phone by her bed.

"Traci!" came an excited voice.

It was Kenny.

"Well, finally. I thought you'd call me last night."

"Oh, sweetheart, I was too tired yesterday, and the jetlag, you know how that is."

"Sure," Traci admitted.

"Anyway, look, I know I promised you lunch today but—well, something came up, an idea I'm working on, and there's really no time to lose. So can we bump it a day? Have lunch tomorrow? Brad and I are in the car on the way to my office, to get this thing rolling."

"What about dinner after work tonight, instead?"

"No, no, listen, I really need some serious brain time on this. Maybe by tomorrow, OK? Dinner tomorrow? At Delucci's? Will that work?"

"Well, all right. Yeah, if I can get away from the gym by six, I can be there about six-thirty."

"A date, darling! Have a great one! And wait till you hear about this. It's going to amaze you!"

"Love you," she replied.

"I know."

The call clicked off.

If you only *knew,* Traci said to herself.

Nine

The Reporter

Kenny clicked off the call to Traci and, from the way Brad later told it, continued to drive like a madman toward his office, running his mouth at Brad the whole way.

"So, here's the basic idea, we get our own little army together and we just go down and capture the island. Kind of like the old game we played at college, remember? Capture The Flag?"

"Kenny, that was a game. You can't just go waltzing onto an island somewhere and play Capture The Island. Are you nuts?"

"No, Brad, I'm not nuts. Just the opposite. This is genius! It's so simple, it's brilliant. How come somebody hasn't thought of this before?"

"'Genius' might be stretching it a little," Brad said, rolling his eyes to the right so Kenny couldn't see them.

"Come on, play along a little, will you? Sure, no one's ever tried something like this, probably. But I know we can do this. I know it! It's going to take some time to plan, sure, and we'll have to plan it down to the last inch and the last minute, you know? And it's going to take a ton of money, of course, but the money can be gotten. I've got my trust fund, still. I can basically use it for anything I want now, right?"

"I guess."

"No guessing, Brad, it was left to me, and now it's mine. I can do whatever I want with it. And this is what I want to do with it. I'm going to end up owning my own Caribbean island!"

"But what's the point? You don't really think you could hold onto an island forever, do you? I mean, at some point, aren't the actual owners going to object or something?"

"What do you mean, 'owners'? I've already done some research. It's small, yeah, but it's not a private island. It's a whole nation! Grand Cayman, with Little Cayman and Cayman Brac, they make up a sovereign state. A little independent country! They're what's called a British Protectorate, so they kind of rely on Britain, I guess, for military cover, that sort of thing. But the Brits, come on, they're halfway around the world, right? What are they going to do? Are they going to fly an army over to fight us back?"

"Well, yeah, I would think they would!"

"Brad, come on, man, be real. The Brits probably just take a bunch of tax money from them or something. It's not like they're gonna give a hoot who runs the island. What difference would it make to them? They're an ocean away."

"Won't they miss their tax money?"

"Well, duh! So, when we take over, we just keep paying. I mean, look at all the tourist business. I have no idea what the locals do for money, or the economy as such, but crap, look at the tourist dollars pouring in! It's gotta be *jillions!* Just the tourist money from the U.S. alone must be astronomical, don't you think?"

"Well—" Brad tried to say, his mind not able to start calculating that quickly.

"So, we'll just keep paying Britain off. Whatever they used to get, we keep sending it. And that keeps them happy, right? And off our backs."

"I don't think it works like that, Kenny. Between governments, I mean. And countries."

"No? Wait and see. Money talks, right? We take over the island—all three, actually—and we look at the books, we send off our check across the pond every quarter—or whatever—and everybody is happy."

"I think you're making it too simple," Brad said in a strained voice, gripping his door handle tightly as Kenny took a right turn much too fast.

"Woo, that was close!" Kenny laughed, having almost nailed a young woman in the crosswalk. "Trust me, this is going to work. You don't really think the Queen gives a rip about some dinky little island in the middle of nowhere, do you? Come on, think about it, England's up to its neck in its own problems. Believe me, they are *not* going to care!"

"I have no idea what the Queen gives a rip about, Kenny. I just think the whole idea is crazy. I mean, they've got their own police and stuff, don't they, on the islands?"

"Yeah, of course. But they don't carry guns, remember? Guns are illegal on the whole island. So it's kind of like the biggest gun-free zone of all time! We just waltz in, take charge, and the islands are ours. No muss, no fuss."

"So, we won't carry guns either, then." Brad glanced

over at Kenny, whose mind seemed to be racing as fast as the engine under the hood of his B.M.W. "Right?"

"Dummy, of course *we're* going to have guns. We'll have to gin folks up a little. You know, throw them off balance, get the advantage. Of course we'll need guns. We'll just carry blanks. Who's gonna know?"

Brad stared longer at Kenny this time, as if he could see in one ear and out the other.

"Kenny, if we're going to carry guns with blanks, why carry guns at all? And you call me a dummy . . . ."

"It's psychological, Brad! It gives us a huge edge, it'll shake them up enough so they don't resist. It'll make everything a lot easier, believe me. And a lot safer."

"For them."

"For everybody! For us, too. We crank off a few blanks here and there, they get terrified, so they don't try to fight. And they don't get hurt. If they don't fight back, we don't get hurt, either. See?"

"Still sounds too easy, Kenny."

"You just have to believe me, this is going to be a breeze. I told you, I've thought it over all night. I spent three hours last night researching all this stuff on the web. We'll plan this down to the *nth* degree. And nobody's going to get hurt. I promise you."

BY LATE afternoon, Kenny and Brad had finished making dozens of phone calls. Most of the people Kenny talked with were friends of varying degrees, some from his college days, but some as far back as high school. Most of those Brad had to call were complete strangers to him, which gave him a tense, icy feeling every time he started dialing. It reminded him way too much of cold calling prospective car buyers.

After a lot of chitchatting and cajoling, they had

managed to assemble the small starter crew that would be needed to launch Kenny's harebrained scheme to capture the little sovereign realm known as The Cayman Islands.

The plan was now in motion and, at least as it appeared to Brad, there was no turning back. Too many ears were already in on it.

"You don't think anybody we talked with today will snitch about this, do you?" he asked Kenny as they packed up to leave the office.

"What do you mean?" Kenny asked, locking the door behind them.

"I mean will any of them talk to the cops or something. This has got to be illegal."

It appeared to Brad that Kenny had not actually considered this yet.

"Well, let's think about that," Kenny said, waltzing into the elevator. They were alone for the ride down to the lobby of the lavish building that housed Kenny's office. He didn't actually conduct any real business there, he just used it as a place to hang out and look important while he spent his money. "Yeah, I guess it would be illegal—if we were doing it down in Cayman. The planning, I mean."

"Wait, wait, I'm not following this," Brad said with a perplexed look—a look, Brad admitted to me, that was not uncommon on him.

As the elevator dropped slowly down its waterless well, passing the fifth floor, Kenny went on, "See, if we were actually in Cayman right now—and planning to overthrow their government—then yeah, I'm sure that's probably against their laws. But we're not down there, are we? We're here in the good old U. S. of A. If we were planning to overthrow the United States, we could probably get arrested right now. But we're not, are we? We're just talking about overthrowing some other country. So is that illegal in the U.S.?"

"You're asking me? Am I a lawyer now or something?" Brad laughed, beginning to track Kenny's thoughts. "I don't know. Maybe you're right."

"Brad, you should know by now, I'm always right."

Brad looked up at the plastic grating that poorly hid the fluorescent lights in the top of the elevator. He shook his head a little, to himself. He felt the quiet, almost imperceptible hum and vibration of the steel cables as they carried the car downward. That awkward feeling hit him again, the wariness, the feeling that he had already abandoned caution and tied his little raft to Kenny's crazy new plan. Brad had an undeniable feeling that his little raft was about to be cast loose into the swells of a fathomless sea where a dark wall of threatening clouds loomed in the not-far distance.

"Usually, yeah, you're right," Brad admitted. "About most things, I guess," he added half-heartedly.

"What's that supposed to mean?" Kenny asked, wondering if he'd been slighted.

"Nothing. Yeah, you're usually right."

"So like I said, trust me. We're friends. I'll look out for you. This is going to work. The people we got on board today, they'll do a fantastic job. They're all smart, and I think most of them are pretty clever on the fly."

"You think Broadman is the right guy to be one of the team leaders?"

"Of course, he's the classic muscleman, right?"

"Yeah. I guess that could come in handy." The elevator hiccupped to a stop and the doors peeled back. The lobby was all but empty, so Brad kept talking. "Have you really figured up what all this is going to cost, Kenny? I mean, with all the special equipment you're talking about? And the transportation costs for everyone? We're talking about a lot of people." He thought for a moment. "And the guns? Won't they cost a lot?"

"Sure. This time, *you're* probably right. We're going to need some extra cash, I think," Kenny answered pensively.

When they first started talking things through earlier that morning, according to Brad, Kenny expected that his personal trust fund would be more than sufficient to fund the whole enterprise. That was before he started adding up hard numbers during the afternoon. Brad was right.

"So where's the extra money gonna come from?" Brad asked.

"I could beg some more from my rich relatives. But I don't really want to." They paused by the high, front entrance of the building. "I'll figure something out."

"Hey, listen, I'm not heading home yet," Brad told him as they walked out onto the sidewalk under a fading evening sky. "I think I'll run some errands. I'll catch a cab home."

"Yeah, fine buddy. I just want to go home and lie down. Too much brain work today, and too much last night. I'm beat."

Brad wanted to say that might be because Kenny generally did so little of it, but he held his tongue.

"My head's exhausted. See you later," Kenny said as he walked off toward the parking ramp.

BRAD LOOKED across the cafe table at Traci Dennison. He studied her nearly electric brown eyes. She gave him only half a smile, but it was enough to start the melting process. Any smile from Traci, however vague or half-hearted looking, was like medicine to Brad.

When Kenny had broken his lunch date with Traci on the way into the office this morning, and then passed on dinner, too, Brad saw the opportunity. By midafternoon it was obvious that Kenny was getting frazzled and tired and would want to head straight home after their day working on his Grand Cayman scheme. So when Brad found a private moment, he called Traci and asked her to dinner. To his delight, she said yes.

The dinner, however, came with a price tag. Traci told Brad that because of the press of work at the gym every day, she was having trouble getting time for her own workouts. She promised she would have dinner with Brad only if he would come to the gym first and workout with her.

For Brad, this was like being offered an extra serving of his favorite ice cream, along with a hundred dollar bill. Having the opportunity to spend time watching Traci working out was like inviting a seven year old into a toy store, hardly what Brad would call punishment. In fact, it was a delight. Dressed in her workout tights, Traci's figure and personality both seemed to shimmer with a kind of man-attracting, invisible force field. If his schedule allowed it, they worked out together a couple of times a week. For Brad, this wasn't easy. He always had to work hard to keep up with Traci's incredible energy level. Still, he loved every minute being with her.

During their workout earlier that evening, Brad watched her as if she were a film star up on the big screen. Beads of sweat oozed from her forehead and cheeks, bathing her face and neck. Brad could almost feel the warmth emanating from her whole body. He wished he could just take her in his arms and kiss her lovely lips. But he knew he'd likely get slapped.

Then the dream vaporized when she said, huffing between breaths, "You're not working very hard, Brad!"

"What?" he said absently. He was busy admiring her smile, her figure, and the energy of life that bubbled within her, and around her. He had never felt so close to someone with whom he was really not close at all. Not that he didn't want to be, but Traci had strong feelings for Kenny, and she always kept Brad at an emotional arm's length.

By the end of the challenging, hour-long workout—after the stress of putting up with Kenny's wild scheming all day—Brad was done in. He didn't care that she kept him at a distance emotionally. Just being near Traci was enough. He was excited because he was about to have a quiet supper with her—though he knew it would lead nowhere. He was ever-patient, even though he knew that his patience would purchase nothing.

As he gazed at her now across the restaurant table, her sparkling eyes drifted between his smile and the plate of appetizers that rested between them. Each time she looked up, he smiled back at her. Tiny beads of sweat still glistened from each of their foreheads, as they cooled down from the workout.

The waitress brought the drinks they had ordered, and they took a few moments to sip before ordering a light supper.

"Are you sure about this?" Traci asked when the waitress had left, picking up their conversation. "Are you even supposed to be telling me this?"

"About the great Kenny plan, you mean?"

"Well, yes. Don't you think Kenny is going to be a little ticked off that you didn't let him tell me himself?"

"Look," Brad said, a bit awkwardly, "I know how tight you two are. Yeah, maybe I should have waited, and let him tell you. But it's been kind of bugging me all day. I mean, we've talked to so many people about Kenny's wild plan already, and you were still in the dark. It just didn't feel right. I guess I felt you should know sooner, rather than later. Because I know he wants you in on it."

"What?" Traci said too loudly. She looked around and made an embarrassed grimace toward a couple seated nearby. Then, in a nearly whispered voice she said, "What do you mean, he wants me in on it?"

"He wants you to be part of the whole thing. You two are so close, why wouldn't he?"

"U-hum," she nodded. "I suppose," she added, her face still marred by a look of shock, but also something else.

It was a puzzling look. Brad couldn't read it.

"Well, to be safe, maybe you should play dumb when he does tell you. Cover for me, OK? I don't want to upset him."

"Oh, but why not, Mr. Schott?" she teased.

"Come on, Traci, you know perfectly well. You know what his temper can be like."

"Yes, I do." She gave him an even odder look. "So, when do you think Kenny plans to tell me?"

"Well, soon. Maybe tomorrow. We have a kind of preliminary meeting set up for tomorrow afternoon."

"What does he think I'm going to do?" She was more than a little irritated, but she toned her voice down. "Brad, I've got a business to run. I can't just go dancing off into the wild-blue anytime I want, like Kenny."

"Don't think there will be any dancing involved," Brad replied with mild sarcasm, trying to make a joke.

Like most, this one failed, too.

"Well, forget it. If you little boys want to go play cops and robbers with somebody's island, then go! But don't try to suck me into the whirlpool."

"Look, Traci, maybe you're right, maybe I shouldn't have even brought this whole thing up. It would've been better to let Kenny fill you in. About your part, I mean." A look of childlike shame crossed his face. "I don't want to make any trouble between the two of you." He paused. "Or the two of us," he said, examining a water spot on his spoon.

"Brad," Traci smiled, as if addressing an eight year old, "You already made trouble—just asking me out to dinner."

The waitress appeared out of nowhere with their meals, and whisked away into the shadows just as magically. Brad looked at Traci, nodded, blushed, and sipped his drink again, pretending to concentrate on which utensil to pick up first. He felt sweat on his forehead again. This time, it was from the emotional workout.

Traci waited silently, patiently, her food untouched. Finally, he looked back up at her again.

"Look, I know this whole scheme Kenny has cooked up seems crazy. Probably is."

"But you're helping him, aren't you?"

"Yes. Well, so far I have. But, to be honest, I'm a little nervous about it. We could get in big trouble."

Traci smiled again, this time a smile of sympathy. Brad smiled back. An urge leapt up in him to just lean over, smash through all the food, grab her, and kiss her. But he managed to contain it. She was Kenny's.

Finally, she speared a piece of chicken with her fork.

"Well, if he thinks he needs me, I guess I can play

along. For a while," she added. Her mind and emotions were doing a juggling routine.

"It's gonna be pretty risky, Traci."

"Come on, you know me, Brad. I don't mind risks. And it wouldn't be my first rodeo, you know?" She laughed lightly, remembering some of her escapades during college. Then her face turned serious. "He's got a backup plan, I assume. In case something were to go wrong?"

"I don't know yet." Brad looked at her, trying to read another enigmatic expression that had crept over her face. "Why? What are you thinking?"

She sipped her cocktail again, a not-very-potent combination of rum, 7-Up and a pinch of peach schnapps. It bit back, and she felt as if a little spider had run up her spine.

Watching her intently, Brad finally read through her expression.

"You want to prove to Kenny that you're tough enough for this, don't you? Just as tough and smart as he is."

"Kenny? Tough? He's a marshmallow. No guts." She laughed, again too loudly. "Brad, you're sweet, but I think you're the one who is always trying to compete with him. Trust me, Kenny is not tough. He's a spoiled rich kid from uptown who just plays at looking tough. Down in my neighborhood, they'd eat him for fruit on their cereal."

"So why would you go along with this thing?" Brad asked, genuinely confused.

"I could ask you the same," she bantered, taking a bite of pasta.

He made a funny look, scrunching his lips. He wasn't sure yet why he had agreed to be part of his friend

Kenny's wild plan at all, let alone be the number two man. Except, perhaps, that Kenny was also his landlord and he really didn't want to be out on the curb.

"Well," he replied, "it *would* be something to remember. You know, some real excitement for a change, not just sitting in a stupid movie theater, imagining that you're up there on the screen, doing something brave, and daring. This would be the real thing."

"Adventure . . . ooh . . . ," Traci cooed with an eerie drone in her voice.

"Look, I'm due for something real, OK? Selling cars doesn't do it for me. What a crap life! Life has got to be more than that. Get up, work, go to bed, sleep. How boring is that?" Brad made an exaggerated moan. He grabbed a dinner roll and started pulling it to shreds.

"Yeah," Traci agreed, "you're right. I feel like that at times. Back in college, at least there was variety, and lots of fun. Wild times." Her eyes pictured some of that fun. "Now, it's the doldrums. Don't misunderstand, I love running the gym. Grandpa sold his whole plumbing business so he could set me up in it. How easy was that for me? Still, a lot of days it gets me down. All the bookwork, that kind of stuff. If I could just run it, play around, and pay somebody else to do all the business stuff—I'd love that! But I'm not making enough money yet to hire somebody for that."

"Traci, I'd take that job in a heartbeat," Brad told her sincerely.

"Would you?" She looked at him with a new kind of interest. Maybe Brad was more than he seemed. "Anyway," she gave a nod, "if there's money in this thing you and Kenny are cooking up about the Caymans, that interests me. Think of all those banks down there. I hear it's quite the place to hide secret accounts. Big ones. If we could run the country, wouldn't we kind of run the banks, too?"

Brad chuckled, "I'm not sure, but it's probably the other way around."

"Who really runs the island? I mean, now?" Traci asked.

"A governor, I think."

"Well, with Governor Kendall Hamilton the Fourth of Grand Cayman, I mean, come on, there's got to be money in that somewhere, huh?"

Her mind began to drift. Personal check registers with large balances seemed to appear like flocks of imaginary swans on the horizon. She took a larger gulp of her drink and started digging into her meal with more vigor. She knew almost nothing of Kenny's plan yet, but her natural curiosity was starting to percolate.

"You don't really think it'll be that dangerous, do you?" she asked Brad, her eyes seeming to lose focus just a little. She gave him a bigger smile. She did like Brad. Next to Kenny, in fact, he was the only guy she really liked to be around these days.

Brad somehow sensed what she was thinking. Maybe it was just the drink, but she seemed to be warming up to him. He felt he had to put on a good show. Moxie, and bravery. Even if it was fake.

"Naw, Kenny's pretty sharp. If he plans something out, he'll account for the road hazards. And, yeah, I'm sure he'll have some kind of backup plan. We'll be fine. 'Money and manpower,' that's what he's been saying all day. Kenny's already got a lot of the first. And this Broadman guy he reached today, sounds like he can produce the second."

Traci's head felt like it had grown three hat sizes.

"Let me eat," she said with sudden attention to her plate. "I think this booze's too much after that workout. I'm getting kind of lightheaded."

I wish I was causing that, Brad mused. *She is sure something.*

Ten

Kenny

My head hurts. I need some sleep tonight! I can't keep hours like I did last night, doing research half the night. We'll never get anywhere with this plan if I wear out before we start! Thank goodness Traci's not hanging around tonight.

I don't even want to eat. Too tired. Maybe a drink.

Brad's right. This thing is going to take serious money. More than I can turn up in cash, anyway. My trust fund could get used up in a hurry.

So, who could I tap this time? Uncle Martin? Just tell him it's an investment opportunity. It is, kind of. Only half a lie. Just keep the details back from him, until later. Hell, I'll be able to pay him back twenty times over— once we pull this thing off!

No, Kenny, forget him. He's too sharp to buy into a scheme like this, even if I lie about what we're really doing. He's a damned banker, he'd ask too many questions. They always do. And he'd want some kind of collateral. And I sure don't have much left.

Come on, think, man, there must be some way. Where does a guy go for some quick cash?

Maybe a brandy will help, I'll—

No, it won't. It'll put me to sleep before I get this money thing figured out. I better make a sandwich.

Cash. From somewhere that can't be tied back to me. A source. Where?

Wait a second. Broadman. Of course, I almost forgot. He mentioned it today—he worked for that armored car company a while back.

An armored car. It's perfect.

No, wait. Come on, Hamilton, way too much security. And the guards on the truck would be armed. You'd never get them out of the damned truck, let alone any cash.

That brandy sounds good after all.

Where else? Who keeps a lot of cash lying around? Rob a bank? No, if we got caught then the whole Cayman plan goes up in flames.

Maybe I should call Broadman tomorrow. Tap his brain. He's pretty shady, maybe he'll have an idea. He drove those cash trucks around for a while. We can't hit a truck, but . . . .

Wait a second. Why not? That's it, *hit* a truck.

Hamilton, you could have made genius, if you'd just studied a little harder.

Where the heck did Brad park that stupid bottle of brandy?

Eleven

The Reporter

At some point, Kenny Hamilton realized he was going to need a lot more money for his Grand Slam plan. Characteristically, he wasted no time going after it.

According to his partners in crime, Kenny had grown weary of begging money from rich relatives and well-set friends, though he had quite a few of both. He had started down that road as a teenager and, at first, he had not felt the least guilt or remorse grabbing onto money whenever he could put the touch on someone. But now, at age twenty-seven, he was getting tired of it. He still had a trust fund left by his parents, which held six million dollars at the time of their deaths. But after only nine years, Kenny had blown through most of it. About eight-hundred-thousand remained, and at the rate Kenny burned cash, the account would have a short life expectancy.

That fact, as Brad later told me, may have been part of what drove Kenny into pursuing the Grand Slam idea to begin with. Kenny wanted money, as much as he could lay hold of. But he also wanted the power and prestige that money brought. Maybe, as Brad said, Kenny saw a new life as governor of The Cayman Islands as the perfect blend of power, money, and prestige.

SITTING ACROSS from Kenny Hamilton in the back of one of his favorite hangouts, a pub in downtown Philadelphia, was Jason Broadman. Brad and Traci had joined them. Although the pub was seedy, smelly, and in pressing need of fresh paint and flooring, Kenny had picked the place because at mid-afternoon like this, the pub was nearly empty and they could talk without a lot of strange ears close by.

True to his name, Jason Broadman was just short of six feet tall but was abnormally broad across the chest and shoulders, as if he had been fashioned after one of the old, staved beer barrels that used to grace this little pub eighty years earlier. His partly-balding head held shiny brown hair that swept back into a ragged wad at the base of his skull, where today, missing its usual red rubber band, it hung loosely like a lopped-off squirrel's tail. He had made an attempt at shaving earlier in the day but the attempt had largely failed. The fact that he was still hungover from his previous night's escapades did little to improve his rough appearance.

If Broadman wanted to be here right now, it didn't show. Sitting next to Brad Schott's five-foot-nine, slender frame, Broadman overshadowed him like the Jolly Green Giant.

There was even greater contrast between them, though. Brad always looked just a little uncertain about himself—about life, in fact. Broadman, on the other hand, had a casually mean look that seemed perpetually stuck in his eyes. His whole expression displayed his assumption that he was superior in brain power and muscle to those around him, and to most of those in the world, in his modest opinion.

"Piece of cake," Broadman bragged to Kenny, smiling as he did so at Traci Dennison who was sitting between him and Hamilton.

"You sure?" Kenny asked.

"Of course. I worked for Glad-Hand Armored for three years. I know all their key routes, *and* I know roughly how much will be in each truck on a given day."

Glad-Hand Security Armored Services was a locally-owned armored car service in the Philly metro area. As one of their drivers, Jason Broadman had been trained in the use of weapons, and was used to risky, hair-raising situations. So he was not afraid of taking the company on. In fact, he was ready for a little payback. He had gotten the axe a year and a half earlier when a bag of small bills came up missing from his route. Broadman, who was not the actual culprit, stomped out of the Glad-Hand garage that afternoon leaving the image of his thick, middle finger burned forever into the mind of the company's cowering route manager.

Broadman's recent months had been spent collecting state unemployment benefits because he had not been offered any job that he thought was worthy of his time or abilities. He was the kind of person who thought all of life's opportunities should be served up to him on a silver platter. So, the opportunity Kenny Hamilton was now offering him sounded not only exciting but actually challenging, for a change.

"So, how exactly do we pull this off?" Brad asked, still unclear on the details of this opening salvo of Kenny's planned Grand Slam operation.

Brad had purposely sat across the table from Broadman. The man smelled too much of some oriental spice from whatever he had eaten for lunch. The smell of strange food in the middle of the afternoon was not appealing. To make it worse, Brad wasn't sure which part of Broadman's anatomy this smell was coming from.

"Well, first, 'we' don't," Kenny replied. "You and I are going to stay completely clear of this part, Brad. We need to keep our noses clean. I don't want to chance us messing up the plan before we even get it going."

"Kenny, don't you think that somewhere along the line, the authorities—somebody—is going to catch on to what we're up to?" Brad responded, with a worried expression.

"Eventually, maybe," Kenny admitted. "But not until we're already on the island, and in charge. That's why we have to be so careful now. Then, it won't matter. By the time any authorities figure out how we pulled this whole thing off, we'll be running our own little, newly-created nation in the middle of the Caribbean." He grinned at Brad with a typical, smug smile, a smile that drove Brad nuts because it always seemed so self-satisfied.

"I guess," Brad mumbled. He worked on his beer. There was no persuading or redirecting Kenny at this point. His mind was obviously set.

"But aren't those armored cars, like, really tightly sealed? What if the thing just floats?" Traci Dennison asked.

"Yeah, they're tight. But not that tight," Broadman responded with exaggerated confidence.

Kenny had pulled Traci away from the gym late this morning and spent two hours with her over lunch explaining this first step, and her part in it, before he dared introduce her to Broadman.

Brad knew why. Broadman was such an intimidating presence, Kenny probably wanted to be sure Traci was on board before she had to deal with Broadman in person. Brad suspected something else. Kenny didn't want to look foolish in front of Broadman by having Traci cave, lose her nerve, and refuse to take part in the operation. Brad glanced at the look on Kenny's face, knowing Hamilton was probably worried that this was exactly what was about to happen.

And it's not just that, Brad was thinking, *Kenny's nervous because he's asking his girlfriend to jump into the middle of something from which he himself wants to steer completely clear. It just doesn't feel right.*

What Brad was feeling was no doubt true. Kenny wanted Traci to be part of his great scheme, but he was probably worried that Traci might bail out at some point. Anybody jumping ship along the way could fry the whole plan, and Kenny knew it.

Kenny leaned closer to Traci, his voice soothing and reassuring.

"Traci, this is not going to be that tough. Just takes a little nerve. I know you can do it. Look at you—you're tough as nails."

"Fingernails, maybe," she said doubtfully.

"Look," Broadman said, "I will make absolutely certain we account in advance for anything unexpected that might happen. It'll go off without a hitch. I promise. You just need to trust me, Traci." He gave Kenny a sideways wink of reassurance but at the same time gave Traci a gentle squeeze on her knee.

She frowned at him and carefully placed his heavy hand back on the booth seat.

"What if the guards won't open the doors?" Brad pressed.

He read the reaction on Kenny's face. *Now Brad's going to weasel?*

"Kenny, I'm in, OK?" Brad assured him. "I just have some questions, things I wanna get clear. Like, what if the guards are really dedicated and think they have to protect the money?"

"Look, folks," Broadman interrupted, "the second that truck starts sinking—I guarantee—their desire for fresh air is going to outweigh any concern they'll have for the cash—which isn't theirs, remember. They'll bail. As soon as they do, the cash is ours."

"You're certain?" Kenny prodded him, trying to reassure Brad and Traci.

"Trust me on this, Hamilton," Broadman said, "this little piece is the simplest part of what you're trying to pull off. We're just talking here about ripping off a little armored truck. You're talking about ripping off a whole island!"

"Three islands," Kenny smiled.

"Yeah, well then, leave this part to me and my help. We're good. We'll get the job done." Broadman kept his hands to himself, but this time the wink went toward Traci. "You'll do great, tough girl."

Kenny smiled at Traci and Broadman with the same smug grin, nodding, "That's exactly what I'm counting on."

Twelve

The Reporter

Jason Broadman had assembled a small, two-man team for the day's work and the three of them were in position and ready.

Ronnie Vaughn was a civilian-trained, expert scuba diver, qualified in both inland water and open ocean work. He would not only be handy today, but even more so once they headed for the ultimate target, Grand Cayman. Vaughn was only twenty-six, of a medium build, with reddish hair and slightly-too-round of a face, and had lived a hard life growing up in New Jersey. A father who was far too rough in his discipline had trained Ronnie to always be ready to strike back, whatever the world threw at him. So far, he had found nothing in life he was unwilling to do to make money, or get ahead of someone else.

The second man, Rick Kell was another large, strapping man like Broadman, though his head seemed a little too small for his body, and his light green eyes seemed always ready to cross at any second. Kell was as tough as an old army boot, and had the looks to match. He was steeped in arms training, the result of twelve years in the Ohio National Guard. He had wanted to get into the regular Army Special Forces, but had never shown the natural intelligence needed. He finally got disgusted with never being able to move past corporal in the Guard, so he quit and returned to civilian life. Kell was three years older than Vaughn and not as sharp mentally. But in a fist fight, there would be no doubt that Kell would come out the winner. His piercing dark blue eyes seemed full of some hidden anger that was just waiting to get sprung on an unsuspecting world.

The late-morning Pennsylvania sun shone down around them as they sat in their prearranged position. Broadman checked his watch and winked at his buddies. They waited.

TRACI DENNISON gunned the engine of the rickety Honda and merged into the center of three lanes as she approached the upper deck of the I-95 Girard Point Bridge which spanned the Schuylkill River. The Delaware Expressway was packed this morning, crazed drivers hustling everywhere to get somewhere faster than they really wanted.

It was a cool spring day but her hands felt hot on the steering wheel, as hot as the car's troubled, battered engine. Broadman had stolen the Honda from a parking garage downtown just two hours earlier and slapped a temporary license sticker on it, one Brad Schott had obtained—by a five-finger discount—from his old boss. Kenny's uncle had indeed fired him two weeks earlier, as Brad feared, but had failed to make sure that Brad turned in his keys to the office at the dealership.

Traci swerved left, trying to get around an erratic car

that changed lanes just ahead of her. Traffic picked up even more behind her but slowed when she bolted back into the center lane, along with dozens of other vehicles funneling onto the bridge deck like sand through an hourglass.

Traci's hands shook with the jitters and she felt a sudden wave of nausea. She knew she would have to push the Honda to catch the Glad-Hand armored truck that was moving more slowly but was already nearing the mid-point of the bridge. Its driver, obviously a professional, was driving cautiously, staying in the far right lane.

No wonder the driver is being cautious, it occurred to Traci. Jason Broadman knew about this truck, knew its daily route, and had promised Kenny and his friends that there would be at least two and a half million dollars in cash riding in the back on its way to the NewSense Bank in Swarthmore.

Traci passed a slower car ahead of her and wove back into the center lane, then gunned the tired, little engine harder. She caught up to the armored truck and veered into the far right lane behind it, nearly clipping a semi-tractor as she did so.

The armored truck finally passed the mid-point of the bridge and emerged from under the massive overhead superstructure that supported the center span. Then, for only a few moments, the driver ignored the traffic around him, distracted by a call through the security panel from his guard in the back.

"Beautiful view today, huh?" the guard called.

The driver glanced out through the thick, bulletproof passenger window, enjoying the stunning view of the sun glinting off the rippling waters of the river far below.

Traci, by sheer chance, picked this same moment to

make her move. She pressed the gas pedal deeper, jerked the car to the center lane of the downward slope of the bridge and then—holding her breath as if it were her last—rammed the little Honda hard into the driver's door of the armored truck.

Looking right and distracted, and never seeing her car veer toward him, the armored truck driver jerked his eyes back to the road but panicked, and overreacted to the impact. He yanked the wheel hard to the left and, stupidly, hit the brakes hard at the same instant.

The stench of burned rubber assaulted Traci's nose for several seconds as the armored truck slid hard sideways, the six tires shrieking in their futile attempt to maintain traction against the concrete pavement. The truck leaned over hard to the right, then whiplashed and tumbled, as an edge of the front bumper caught in an iron drain grate. The momentum of the truck flipped it twice, flinging the grate cover into the air like a bottle rocket. The truck bounced off its nose, then catapulted up and over the low, concrete excuse-for-a-railing at the edge of the bridge deck.

NOT TWO hundred feet upriver from the bridge, Jason Broadman and his two men were ready. Broadman and Rick Kell, dressed as fisherman, sat casually in their Bass-Tracker boat, fishing lines in the water. Kell had an open beer balanced on one knee and his red and blue Phillies ball-cap cocked sideways on his head, the perfect image of the contented fisherman watching with disinterest as the busy world passed by.

The third man, Ronnie Vaughn, was already in the water in his wet suit and dive gear, his goggles hanging around his neck, waiting.

Up above on the bridge, Traci Dennison was

desperately trying to take a breath and keep from wetting her pants, while trying to regain control of her car. In what seemed to Traci like slow-motion, the Glad-Hand truck made two more erratic loops through midair, like an Olympic diver finishing a two-and-a-half twist, then struck the water upside-down with an incredibly loud *whack.* It circled on its roof for five or six seconds, then whale-rolled over onto its right side.

As Broadman had predicted, the locked cash bags inside the armored truck now meant nothing to the two well-underpaid security guards. Less than five seconds after hitting the water, the back door of the truck was forced open by its electric motor control just before it shorted out from the water gushing in, and the rear guard escaped as the truck floundered and began to quickly sink.

Just a few seconds later, the driver managed to kick out the right front window by the passenger seat. Although it was inch-thick, bulletproof glass, it was very weakly mounted in a thin steel frame. Three forceful kicks dislodged the glass and sent it to the bottom of the river, the truck anxious to follow. The driver gulped air, wedged his overweight body out through the window, and fought toward the surface as the window frame tried to pull him down. The air in his lungs gave him just enough buoyancy to spring him loose, and he escaped upward, losing only one shoe that got caught by its lace in the damaged window frame.

The two soaked men, panicked, tried to swim away from the heavy truck but the suction it created as it sank into the river pulled them back toward the vehicle and dragged them, against all their efforts, into the whirlpool it formed as it went down.

Broadman had the Bass Tracker, aided by the current

of the river, racing swiftly toward the wreck, but with absolutely no thought about whether the driver and guard might drown. His only goal was to drag Ronnie Vaughn, his man in the water alongside the boat, to the sinking wreck and quickly as possible. Once over the sunken truck full of cash, Vaughn would start retrieving the heavy bags of money. Controlled by its now-fried electric control, the rear door would remain fully open as the vehicle went down. For Vaughn, it would be like waltzing into an unguarded, underwater bank vault.

Dragged through the water like a half-drowned water skier, Vaughn used one hand to pull his facemask into place as they reached the spot where the short-lived whirlpool had closed over the wreck. He let go of the side of the boat and dove quickly toward the truck, a high-intensity spotlight strapped to his head, lighting the way.

Rick Kell jumped into the water in his fishing getup to make a show of pretending to help the driver and guard. The driver had already gone under for the third time and was nowhere in sight. The guard who had been in the rear of the truck had somehow managed to escape the suction and had swum a few yards away, but he was panicked, flailing his arms and letting out shrieks as he tried to breathe. His clothing was fully soaked and his heavy leather combat boots were acting as lead anchors.

Kell, supported by a light-weight, neoprene wet suit hidden under his fisherman's clothing, had no trouble staying afloat, but he intentionally made slow progress swimming toward the terrified guard. Kell's goal, and that of Broadman when he laid out the operation, was to focus anybody else's attention on the attempted save of the drowning men and keep curious eyes off the Bass Tracker and what was about to be loaded on board into a large, white beer cooler.

Ronnie Vaughn's strength and expertise as a diver was showing. He worked quickly and efficiently, up and down, covering the short eighteen-foot distance between the sunken truck and the side of their boat multiple times in under ten minutes. With each trip, he brought up one or two water-soaked, locked bags full of cash. The heavy coin bags he left below. The loot added up quickly, even as the first patrol cars were arriving on the bridge and near the east shore of the river.

Rick Kell watched the exhausted guard take a last gasp and sink, while Kell held back, just ten feet away, pretending shock at the sight of the man drowning before his eyes.

Once the guard had disappeared, Kell himself began to feign drowning, acting as if his soggy fishing clothes were starting to pull him down. He flailed wildly and splattered as much water as he could, yelling for help, still trying to draw everyone's eyes away from the robbery in progress. He slowly carved an unnecessarily wide arc through the water back toward the Bass Tracker, and caught the hint when Broadman gave him a thumbs-up, meaning that they had finished loading all the loot worth taking.

When Kell finally reached the boat, Broadman quickly pulled his soaked friend aboard. Ronnie Vaughn remained low in the water alongside the boat to conceal his presence from any cops or onlookers.

Broadman hit the electric start switch on the one-hundred-fifty-horse outboard motor and gunned the boat toward the west shore, opposite from where several police cars had begun to arrive. Hitting the shore hard, they loaded the beer cooler into a white rented van. They and the van were gone from the area five minutes before anyone told authorities there had been a fishing boat in the river near the wreck, or that when witnesses looked again, the boat was gone.

TRACI WAS still trying to recover her normal breathing, each hard breath pumping in and out erratically. It was not so much breathing as trying to swallow pails of air. She felt as if her heart would blow through her chest at any second. She could still sense the smell of the burnt tires. She feared it would stay in her nostrils for hours, maybe days.

After torpedoing the armored truck, she had hit the brakes just enough to avoid crashing into it a second time. She steered the bashed up Honda into the passing lane and rushed onward toward the west end of the bridge, dodging two more semis and whipping recklessly between a pickup and a meat delivery truck.

As planned, she ditched off the expressway at Enterprise Avenue and wound her way into the parking lot of a small air charter company not far from Philadelphia International. She let the battered Honda coast to a stop until it bumped into a guardrail at one side of the lot. She gulped down more air and got ready to ditch the car, silently praying that there were no cop cars that had seen her or followed her off the bridge.

She jumped from the driver's door and hopped the guardrail, walking west through two other small parking lots. Her legs were shaking like willow branches in a storm, still feeling the effects of the impact with the truck. In the third lot, she found another member of Broadman's crew, Bryan Cantor, sitting low in a purple '67 Mustang in the shadow of a large building, waiting for her.

He pulled the earbuds from his ears and gave her a

wide, warm smile. His geeky, frizzy brown hair, wire-rims, and not very sturdy looking frame told Traci this guy must be the computer whiz Broadman had bragged about.

Traci wobbled down through the car door and into the passenger seat of the Mustang. Cantor, looking both ways, cautiously pulled out of the lot. He drove slowly and carefully back toward Kenny's new digs at the High Point Hotel downtown, not wanting to frazzle Traci's nerves any more than they already, obviously, were.

Cantor kept quiet the whole drive, but several times he heard Traci mutter under her breath, "Oh, God . . . oh, God . . . ."

Thirteen

Brad

"How much?" Kenny asks excitedly.

Broadman has almost finished counting the loot from the armored truck. He and his crew who pulled off the heist are gathered around a coffee table in our plush new hotel suite here at the High Point.

"Enough," Broadman smiles. "We missed a few bags. Cops were getting too close to launching their rescue boat. But I count just under one-point-seven-five million."

"Million, as in *million?*" Traci asks in disbelief. Her eyes are glued to the stacks of damp, wrinkled bills on the table.

"Not a bad day's work," I laugh. I'm finally getting into the mood that Kenny has been trying to sway me into for two weeks!

"It's good. It'll buy us a lot of help," Broadman says. "And with this little scheme of yours, Hamilton, we're definitely going to need lots of help."

"You think you can get the twenty guys you talked

about?" I ask Broadman.

Before he can answer, Kenny says, "I don't think twenty will be enough. We need a small army. Not a softball team."

Broadman gives him a look that implies Kenny has challenged not only his brain, but his integrity. Something like a muted growl emanates from the back of Broadman's throat.

"Look, Hamilton, you're already asking a hell of a lot. I can get the twenty names I gave you last week. And maybe another thirty, if I work at it—other people the first twenty guys will know. My people are good. They'll have their own connections."

"Can they all keep their mouths shut?" Kenny wants to know.

"No question."

"And they're trained, right?"

"My people? You kidding? Most of them are part of a little-known right-wing militia. They're trained, they're hardened, they're good. And they're not chickens," he adds, swallowing more beer. "The bulk of them are ex-military. And I can tell you, they're anxious for a little *real* action. This tramping around in the woods playing army on weekends is a bunch of crap."

"Real action. Like capturing an entire Caribbean nation?" I grin.

Broadman gives me his usual tough-guy stare, the one he seems to save for me in particular, the one that means I must be the stupidest person in the room—and probably on the planet.

"All right. That's perfect," Kenny finally says, taking a sip of beer. "But get me another fifty after that."

Broadman's expression tells me Kenny just barfed in the stew.

"Are you nuts, Hamilton?" Broadman says with a head-wagging scowl. "Look, you got a lot of cash here, but just how far do you think you're going to stretch it?"

"One-point-seven-five should buy me plenty of help, Jason, if you don't get too generous with your offers. These people need to work reasonably. After all, every one of them is going to end up owning a little chunk of one of the most beautiful Caribbean islands on earth—for free."

Broadman gives Kenny another razor-sharp look. The guy should have been an actor, with facial expressions like these. This new stare from Broadman suggests Kenny is the biggest cheat on earth. Kenny smiles back at Jason with his typical cocky look. He doesn't care what Broadman thinks.

"Look, I'm—" Broadman begins to say, but Kenny cuts him off.

"No, *you* look!" Kenny says, his beer bottle smacking down hard on the coffee table, sending a small eruption of foam out the neck. "I'm not in the begging or bargaining business! You can remind every one of these guys—or gals—that the best of them may end up helping me govern the islands. If they do their jobs." He smiles a half-sober grin at me. "Right, Brad?"

I nod, "Sure. We'll need help governing. Of course." I'm trying to reassure Broadman.

Bryan Cantor finally looks up from the cash on the table. He has a happy, silly look. I can't tell if it's because he's picturing a big chunk of Grand Cayman on his personal asset sheet, or picturing some of the exquisite women that are likely to come with the deal. The silly look behind his dorky glasses makes me wonder if any woman would give him a second glance. Looks like the classic computer and techie nerd. Gotta wonder how he ever got hooked up with Broadman.

Broadman is fuming, but hiding it. He takes a slow breath.

"All right, Hamilton, fifty more. But don't expect me to get these guys on the cheap, OK? Men and women like this don't work like that. They know the chances they're going to be taking—and they'll expect fair payment for those risks."

"Sure, of course. I know that," Kenny says, wiping the mouth of his beer bottle on his sleeve, and taking a swig.

Kenny is smooth. I'll give him that. He's a big shyster at heart, but he always manages to sweet talk people around to his point of view. I guess I'm a classic example. Traci's no better.

I still can't believe they pulled off the armored car thing this morning. I thought Kenny was insane to even suggest it. But look how easy it was! Except for the guard, of course. And the driver. I think Traci is still kind of in shock about them. She just sits over there by herself, curled up in that cushy chair.

She looks like she'd rather be anywhere but here right now. Maybe Saturn, somewhere like that.

I don't blame her, I guess. She's the one who actually launched those guys off the bridge. That's got to be hard to live with.

She smiles back at me. Maybe she feels a little sympathy from me. She deserves it.

Anyway, the master plan is actually coming together. We've got the money, now. Maybe Kenny's idea will actually work. I mean, Broadman and Traci and the others have been back here for nearly two hours, and so far no cops have come knocking at our hotel door. They must have found that stolen Honda by now. Of course,

Traci wore latex gloves, so the cops won't find any fingerprints.

I hope they don't find anything else, either.

Broadman said he left the Bass Tracker tied up on the shore, but he and Kell wore gloves, too. And I'm sure Vaughn had on diver's gloves, so the boat should be clean. Nothing, at least, to tie it back to the armored truck accidentally going off the bridge.

Broadman figures it'll be several days before they can salvage the truck and realize how much money is missing. Anyway, by the time the cops start piecing all this together—if they ever figure out it wasn't just a traffic accident—Kenny, and Traci, and me, and the rest of us, we'll be reclining in the sun somewhere on one of the beautiful beaches of the Caymans Islands.

I think we are actually in the clear. Amazing!

I look at Broadman. At least he's simmered down. He's eyeing the money on the coffee table again. I can see how the guy's mind works. Those piles of cash signal that there's a lot more coming, down the road.

"All right, Kenny," he finally says, "I'll get you those fifty more. You're the boss." Broadman laughs, but it's a faked laugh. "And they'll be good, too. Not as good as me, but good enough for this little operation. A cake walk, if you ask me."

He picks up several large but still damp bills and curls them through his fingers. I can see he loves the feel of cash in his hands—money to feed his habits, of which I'm guessing there are plenty.

"I've no doubt you'll come through," Kenny replies.

He looks at me, then past me, to where Traci is still curled up in an almost fetal position in her easy chair.

Fourteen

Traci

I feel rotten. My stomach has hardly settled down since Bryan got me back here to the hotel. The sick feeling keeps coming and going. When I don't feel sick, I feel numb.

It was sort of disgusting watching Kenny, Broadman and the rest. They sat around gloating, bragging, laughing, counting all that money, like they were kings or something. And I was the only woman. I really felt out of place.

I couldn't handle it. Too depressing. I spent the day just sitting here in this overstuffed chair, feeling like an overstuffed person. My head feels like a balloon filled with acid. It's like I'm hardly even here to the rest of them. Nobody gave me a second look. Except maybe Brad once or twice. But he was caught up in the money thing, too.

It's always about money.

I can't shake this horrid feeling. The news on TV said the two guys in the armored truck drowned.

I did that. Me. Something vile that I did was on the news. They're gloating over money, and I just want to sit here and die. I feel gutted.

How could I have been stupid enough to believe Kenny, that this would be OK? Yesterday, he promised, "Nobody will get hurt!" Bull. He *must* have known it was a lie! He knew that truck was supposed to fly off the bridge. That was the whole idea! Why the hell else were Jason and his guys down there in the damned boat?

Why do I *ever* listen to Kenny? Why do I trust him so much? I don't understand myself. Isn't that something? When you can't even trust your own feelings?

My heart isn't in this anymore. Not after this morning on the bridge. I just don't know if I can go through with it. I promised Kenny, I know. And Brad. I hate this. But I'm stuck. It's too late to get out.

I'm a big-time criminal now. Big-time.

It took hours before the rest left, and left me with Kenny. Broadman hung around forever. That guy creeps me out, the way he stares sometimes. It's like he can see right through my clothes. Maybe it's my imagination. Still, he scares me.

Now Kenny's trying to act like nothing happened today. Couldn't he see how upset I was all afternoon? He pulls me closer on the couch. What does he want? I can read Broadman's eyes, but I can never read Kenny's. The street lights outside shine a hesitant glimmer into the hotel suite. They look like I feel.

The place is swank, of course, all luxurious like this couch Kenny coaxed me on to. Nothing is ever too good for Kenny. And nothing's ever enough. I'm not sure I'm enough.

The room finally cleared out an hour ago, after a raucous afternoon poker and pizza party. I think Brad's gotten delirious, too, with this new sense of power. I could see it grow on him all afternoon—fueled by liquor. He went off somewhere to celebrate with Ronnie Vaughn and Rick Kell. I hope they don't go crazy drinking and end up in jail. That's all we need! They were already pretty-well lit up when they took off.

Once they left, Kenny did something that completely surprised me. It was so out-of-character. He made us a dessert, deep-fried ice cream, a treat he discovered in Mexico several years back.

"So how do you deep-fry ice cream, and it doesn't melt?" I asked, watching him make it.

"Simple, watch."

It was truly delicious. The outer crust was almost as sweet as the ice cream it hid. And the ice cream didn't melt! Don't ask me how.

Another side of Kenny I didn't know. A very different personality from me. He's far from the domesticated-type male but he's impressed me with his cooking skills tonight. He claims he learned from an Aunt Elinor he lived with one summer when he was fourteen. His folks booted him out for three months.

He may have learned cooking from Elinor, but I don't think he caught much else from his sweet old auntie. He sure didn't catch any of her moral values. The way Kenny describes her, I doubt that summer was very pleasant. She sounds like a warm, delightful lady, one with very deep Christian values. Kenny must have run afoul of her rules every day. Seems he was wild even back then.

He pulls me closer on the couch, stroking my hair. It's like we're sinking into a well full of cushions. Yeah, I know what he wants. He's not getting it. Not after today.

"I was just wondering," he grins, "what traces of fried ice cream might taste like on those beautiful lips." He outlines my lips with his finger.

The warmth of our bodies feels wonderful. I need that comfort right now. I don't need anything else, though. Except for him to look at me—and really see *me*, for a change.

"You liked it, didn't you?" he asks.

"What?" I say. I'm lost in my feelings. The image of that truck plummeting off the bridge is haunting me.

I can't think about it. It grinds into my heart like a dull knife.

"What do you mean, 'What'?" he asks. "The ice cream. Did you like it?"

"Yeah, it was wonderful. You're pretty clever. Except when it comes to being able to tell how I'm feeling." I push him back a little and make him look at me. "Like now."

He gives me a blank look and says, "I know how you're feeling. You felt left out. Because we partied all afternoon."

"See, you don't get it. That's not it at all," I say, disappointed.

He makes a frown at me, like he's waiting for a brick wall to talk.

"Well, give me a little help. A clue." He waits. "You *weren't* feeling left out?"

Where did he get such a thick head?

"Kenny, I've been scared to death, and depressed— all day! I *killed* those two guys! Are you really that callous?" I almost yell.

"Sorry, Traci. I mean, I knew you were—" He pauses. "Look, I could tell you were a little upset, when Bryan brought you back. But—I didn't realize it affected you this deeply."

He finally looks at me. The real Traci. He's trying to hold a wounded animal.

"I'm sorry," he says.

His expression says he means it, but he still doesn't understand.

"Kenny, I'm not a little upset, I'm *really* upset! You promised yesterday, remember? Nobody would get hurt. What the hell did you think was going to happen when a truck crashes sixty feet off a bridge?"

But I can't just blame him. *I'm* the one who rammed that truck. What did *I think* was going to happen?

"I'm sorry," he says again.

"You made it sound like it would be so easy, Kenny. But on that bridge this morning—I knew what I had to do—but I flinched. I almost didn't ram them. And I *never* thought they'd drown. Broadman was supposed to save them!" I give him a hard look. "Isn't that what you promised?"

He's quiet.

"Well, that's what we hoped," he says, but it sounds false.

I'm crying. I can't help thinking about it. I feel like something really horrid is stuck deep in my stomach, some kind of creature that isn't me, and doesn't belong there. But now it's part of me.

I want to puke it up—and I can't.

Kenny's getting irritated.

"Look, Broadman said those trucks are airtight, enough to float for a few minutes. Time for the guards to get out."

"They did—if you believe Jason. So why didn't he help them? How could he just let those guys drown?"

Kenny's eyes roam, looking for an excuse.

"I guess Jason got frazzled. And he didn't want to get caught with all that money."

"So they just left them, drowning?"

"He figured the cops could save them in time."

"And you believe that?" I demand, although Kenny obviously wants to believe whatever Broadman told him.

"Traci, I can't be everywhere. I can't do this whole thing on my own! I've got to rely on other people for some of this stuff. Broadman said the guys in the truck would be fine. I believed him, yes."

I don't know whether to believe Kenny or not. But what else can I do? I'm in it, now. Deep. What would I tell the cops, even if I had the courage to turn myself in? Which I don't.

I'm in the quicksand. If I struggle, it's just going to make it worse.

Kenny pulls me toward him. I don't resist. One thing I've learned about myself—long ago—I have a hard time resisting the attention of a handsome guy. Kenny's so alive and attractive. But he has a sort of built-in mischievous expression. I think he has an abnormal sense of fun. I guess I like that. And he's so excited about this Grand Slam thing of his. Maybe it's that untamed energy that draws me to him.

Well, after today, he's got me on the hook—and he knows it.

He brushes my hair back from my face, which I'm sure is a complete mess. Tear-smeared mascara, battered rouge, the wreckage of Traci Dennison after she kills two men.

Kenny's got the "guy look" in his eyes. No surprise. In the year and a half we've known each other, he's been putting the moves on me any chance he gets. That first day he came into the gym as a potential customer, he started sweet-talking me on the spot. That was a compliment, I guess.

When he showed up for his first workout and begged me to "show him the ropes," I guess I started to fall for him, too. Head over heels. Or heart over head, maybe. What a schmoozer. "I'd've paid ten thousand a week to be a member of your gym," he told me, "just to spend time with you."

What's strange, though, he says he's had no lasting attachments with all the girls he's dated. That's probably a flag, right? I've never been much good at reading red flags.

Even more strange, after us dating for a year and a half, I don't feel we're really very close. He's tried to get me into bed the whole time. Typical guy. And the whole time, I've resisted. I want more than that. Sex like that is easy, and cheap. You get what you pay for—which is pretty much nothing. Life has taught me the hard way. I know how easily someone can hurt me, and abuse my feelings. It's not going to happen again.

I want more, but I can't tell if Kenny does. He's always willing to break rules to get what he wants. What would he do to keep me?

"What'ya thinking about?" he suddenly asks.

I guess my vacant stare at the street lights outside was telling.

"I don't know," I tell him. "Lots." This time, I pull him closer. "Are we going to last?"

"What do you mean?"

He stares, trying to figure out what's going on in my head. Good luck, Kenny, even *I'm* not sure.

He kisses me softly.

"Come on, lighten up. We've lasted this long, haven't we? Right now, I just want my girl Traci. And she's looking lost."

"After today, I am."

"Stick with me, Traci. We'll make this happen. We're going to have our very own Caribbean islands! And I'll be more careful from now on. For you, I mean. No more big, risky stuff for you. OK?"

"I guess."

"Come on, you trust me, don't you?"

It's a question I've asked myself over and over.

"I guess." Sounds like a refrain to some song I don't know.

"I'll protect you."

"Will you?"

"Of course. Come on, I love you."

Sounds like he means it. He holds me tighter. But there's that nervousness creeping around inside me again. Can I handle his attention, but keep setting limits? Or is his personality going to overpower me? I don't know. I pull back.

"What's wrong, Traci?"

I shake my head. Is something wrong with me? I take risks all the time. I've had a lot of wild times, even as a teenager. Always trying to impress my old boyfriends. Still, even then, it was like the word "caution" was written in invisible ink somewhere between my heart and my brain.

I kiss him, but not too long.

"I know you want more of me, Kenny. I'm just not ready."

I feel his grip relax. I just popped the romance balloon. He looks at me with a patient nod.

"Sure. I get it," he assures me.

But does he? Really? Does any man ever know what any woman really feels?

"I feel a lot of things for you Kenny. I'm just feeling mixed up, now. My life is beginning to blossom finally, the gym is going great guns and . . . well, I don't want the blooms crushed."

It's a nice metaphor but, no, he doesn't get it. He's Kenny, after all.

I'm not going to settle for cheap anymore. I want real, genuine love. Deep, not just some flighty moments of lust and desire. I don't want to end up like that again, disappointed, feeling like castoff furniture.

Kenny leans in, barely two inches between us and asks, "Hey, are you OK?"

"Wow, you sound like a paramedic or something."

"Maybe you need one," he laughs.

Maybe I do. Or maybe a shrink.

"Yeah, I'm OK," I lie, and change the subject. "Something bothers me, though."

"What?"

"This thing you've dreamed up, taking over the Caymans, it's—I mean, do you realize how really dangerous it is?"

"Of course I do. I'm gutsy, not stupid!" His arm snakes around me again, tighter. "That's the point. All the risk is what makes it fun!"

"But," I offer weakly, "I'm worried."

Kenny frowns. "About what?"

"Well, don't you think God might, like, get back at us someday?"

He looks like he's been hit by a flying wrench thrown by a ghost.

"What are you talking about?" He gives me an intensely strained look. "God?" he asks. *Really?*"

I'm completely embarrassed. I don't even know where that came from. It's just this lingering feeling that keeps creeping around in my mind.

"What in the world does God have to do with anything?" he says, trying to muffle his anger.

"I'm—I can't tell you. It's just this feeling. I mean, my idea of God is, well, it's pretty much non-existent. Some big distant being somewhere. I'm not one of those crazy people who hang their whole life on the idea. It's just"—I really don't know how to explain it—"I can't get the thought out of my head. It's like, this whole plan of ours is going to make him mad."

"Traci—"

"Like today. You said nobody would get hurt—and look what happened. But it doesn't matter what we *meant* to happen. It's what *did* happen."

"OK, look—" Kenny says, still trying to derail this, but I cut him off again.

"I didn't think I'd react this way. I've been—I've been feeling closed in all afternoon, like in a steel box. A prison. And I'm afraid God's already mad at me!" I gulp a breath. "And that's not even counting what we're still planning to do on the island," I blabber on.

Kenny looks dumbfounded. He takes the drink he's been balancing on his knee and sets it down on the floor. His expression is strained.

"Traci, stop it. I'm not worried. First of all, I don't think there's really a God. Anyway, not like people think. And besides, even if there were, why would he care diddly-squat about you or me? With all the big, ugly things going on in the world—why would he give a damn about us?"

"That's rude, Kenny."

"Fine, it's rude! If you ask me, God is the one who's rude. If he *does* exist, as far as I'm concerned, he's nothing but some kind of cosmic clown. Spends his time making life crazy, trying to distract us from having any fun."

He's really upset that I brought this up. I didn't know this was so sensitive. Must have to do with Aunt Elinor.

"I'm sorry, Kenny. I worry, I can't help it. It's just—there—in my head, and I can't shake it. This has bugged me all afternoon!"

"Yeah, well you worry too much, Traci. You need to get over it, because *that* bugs the hell out of me! Sure, what happened today was bad. But it couldn't be helped. All right? We did what we had to, and those two guys got hurt in the process."

"Killed, Kenny. Not hurt."

His lips and whole expression get tight. He's regressed into a pouty teenager. Now he's the one who looks like a wall of stone.

I pull away from him and get up, wandering the room. I still feel lost. Lost from myself, lost from Kenny. I sigh loudly.

"Come on Traci, sit down. What's important is that you're here with me, right now. Quit fretting about the future." He eyes me. "Come on, why don't we sleep on it?" He gives me that schmoozing smile again. "Just one night," he proposes.

I brush a big, sweaty lock of hair behind my ear and stare down at him. Yeah, he's a guy. And he could talk a cat out of its only remaining life. My heart whispers, *Stay, Traci.* But deeper yet it yells, *Stay back.*

I come to the wall, and I kick the baseboard.

"I can't. Not tonight." I turn, embarrassed.

Kenny just sits there. His eyes have lost focus. Maybe

it's the all-day boozing.

"Tell me honestly, Traci," he says. His voice sounds distant. "Do you want to just back out of this whole thing?" He waits. "You want out?"

Oh God, I wish he wouldn't always put me on the spot like this! How can I answer that? If I back out, he'll think I don't care for him at all!

Why is life always like this?

He tosses the lure again.

"Think of it, Traci. I'll be Governor Kendall Hamilton of The Cayman Islands. My own country. *Your* own country. Think of the wealth. A life of happiness, prestige, on a tropical island—with me."

This always happens, too. He keeps hooking me back into things.

I've just got to act grown up. My gosh, I'm twenty-five, I'm a woman, for crying out loud! I can handle this! My folks always stifled me. Maybe that's why I got so wild in college. The little girl in me still wants to get out and play!

Look at him. He's like an overgrown kid himself. Dying for some real excitement, not something in books. How can I let him down?

I can't.

"I'm still in, Kenny. You know I'm in."

A dreamy look appears in his eyes. He beckons me with, "Life is going to be so good, Traci. Come on, stay."

This is going to take every ounce of strength in me.

"No, Kenny. I can't. I've done enough for you today."

Fifteen

The Reporter

From what Brad and Traci eventually told me, the plan gained momentum rapidly after the armored car rip-off. Kenny was in a kind of manic euphoria, sleeping only two or three hours a night, and driving everyone nuts with an invisible whip during the day.

During one of those sleepless nights, according to Traci, Kenny must have realized that part of the reason for her anxiety was that she was the only woman in the operation. It not only made her feel awkward, it made her even more unsure of herself. After that, Kenny started paying a lot more attention to Traci and coddling her some.

"He didn't want to lose me," Traci confided in me. "For selfish reasons, of course. So he moved pretty quickly to fix the problem."

"WHO CAN you think of, guys?" Kenny asked them.

The "guys" at that moment were Brad and Traci. It was just five days after the armored truck heist and they were in the plush hotel suite where Kenny and Brad were now living. The three of them were killing time, trying to tie up some ragged ends of Kenny's blossoming plan to capture Grand Cayman, while Broadman and his buddies were out recruiting the extra help Kenny wanted.

"We need another woman on one of the teams," Kenny said with a mouth half-full of cheesecake.

"Why?" Traci asked, suspicious for more than one reason.

"Well, I need her to help infiltrate this bank that I want to get into. We're gonna use it as a kind of diversion, during the assault landing," Kenny explained, trying to veil his real reason from Traci. "And, anyway, we're gonna need our own bank, right, once we're there? To hold all our money and things?" he smiled. "Who can you think of?"

Traci didn't respond to his look, so he glanced at Brad. Brad considered the women he was friends with for several moments, but came up blank. It was a short list.

"Don't know," Brad said, his eyes still squinting in thought. "To be honest, I can't really think of anyone. My mind always comes back to Traci."

It probably wasn't the smartest thing to say in front of Kenny, but Traci couldn't help smiling at Brad's overly obvious display of his feelings for her. Brad floundered on.

"I meant, I don't know any other women as sharp—or capable—as you, Traci."

"Mentally sharp, right?" Traci laughed, goading him.

"Well, no. Sharp in the looks department, too," Brad added hastily, his face reddening a little. He cleared his throat.

"Oh. I see," Traci said in a forced, overly-serious tone. She couldn't prevent another smile showing.

Brad glanced toward Kenny and realized he wasn't helping himself.

"Sharp, in every respect. I mean—what can I say? You're a really sharp woman, Traci. You've got brains, and—you know." He looked away. "I don't have to tell you, Kenny."

Brad had tried and failed to extricate himself from the awkward hole he was digging. He smiled warmly at Traci again, as if compelled.

Kenny's eyebrows rose ever-so-slightly, implying that Brad could be such an idiot at times, then gave them both a subtle, knowing look. Traci belonged to him, and Brad knew it. But Kenny wasn't stupid, and he must have realized that something had begun to develop between Traci and Brad, too. If Kenny sensed this, he let it go. It would only muddy the waters right now, and both Brad and Traci knew that Kenny wanted nothing to muddy any water or interfere in his Grand Slam plans.

"Come on, Traci?" Kenny pressed her. "Doesn't anybody come to mind?"

Traci mentally scanned the contacts list in her computer in the gym office. *Ah, of course,* Traci thought. *She would be perfect.*

"How about Arielle?"

"Who?" Kenny asked blankly.

"Come on, Kenny, don't play dumb. Arielle Kemper. You've seen her, my friend from my waitressing days. She comes to the gym. Usually Thursday afternoons."

"Oh, man," Brad butted in, "you mean that really gorgeous brunette? The one with the really big—"

"Yes," Traci cut him off, "the girl with the large, striking breast line. What did you call it that time?"

"Glorious . . . ," Brad admitted with a sheepish but dreamy expression. "And the thin waist, and really nice—"

"Yes," Traci cut him off again, "and those, too."

"Sorry," Brad mumbled, turning bright red this time.

With Brad's graphic prompting, Kenny obviously recognized who Traci meant but he downplayed it, trying to hide the fact that he, too, had given Arielle a second look more than once. It might upset Traci just when he was trying to help her.

But Traci wasn't stupid, either. She had noticed Kenny watching Arielle at the gym.

"Not sure who you mean," Kenny quibbled.

"Oh, come on Kenny, you do too. She's stunning!" Traci declared. "And, she can cook like crazy."

With what sounded like a pretended critique in his voice, Kenny said, "I'll take your word for it. But is there anything in her head besides recipes?"

"Don't be a smartass, Kenny," Traci snipped. "It so happens Arielle maintained a three-point-eight-five grade average for two years through Hillside Tech, and waitressing that whole time—*and* helping out in the kitchen at the restaurant, too. She's smart. And trust me, we've arm wrestled. She's very strong."

"I can imagine . . . ," Brad said, as he did.

"Let it go, Brad," Traci chided as Kenny turned away smirking.

"So, what does she do these days? Can you break her loose?" Kenny asked.

"She finished a four year degree in biology. Works at a medical lab downtown. Does all kinds of really technical tests and things."

Exactly what Arielle did at the lab, Traci didn't really understand. She was just reinforcing how smart her friend was. Brad was trying *not* to imagine Arielle as an expert in biology.

"Call her up," Kenny said. "Let's have dinner tonight or something."

"I really need to get back to the gym, Kenny. I'm way behind on the books."

"Well, call her anyway. I'll have supper with her."

Kenny alone at supper with Arielle? Traci knew better. She had not been kidding when she said Arielle Kemper was stunning.

"I guess the account books can wait," Traci said. "What time do we eat? And where?"

Kenny started to answer when his cell phone interrupted him. The conversation was short and terse. He nodded several times.

"OK. Good. Yeah? OK. Tomorrow morning, about ten. Here at the hotel." He scratched at the day-old stubble on his face. "Bring whoever you've got so far. I'm going to background check them all. What? No, I'm not worried about criminal background. The more the merrier. I just want to know if they've ever been snitches or anything, you know, too friendly with the cops." He nodded again. "OK, eleven, then. See you."

Traci and Brad waited to hear.

"Broadman checking in. He's got fourteen new guys so far, and he says there's at least thirty somewhere in the pipeline. I'm impressed. In just five days." He looked at Traci. "Times-a-wastin', sweetheart," he said, trying to sound like Humphrey Bogart. "Get this Kemper woman on the line. Supper's at six. You pick the restaurant."

Sixteen

The Reporter

For Kenny Hamilton, Arielle Kemper was a real a find—like a lost gold mine. Not only was she fantastically beautiful, she had a captivating personality and an over-the-top confidence that was exactly what Kenny needed to move his Grand Slam plan forward. He wasted no time in sending her off on her first assignment. She proved to be the right choice.

As Brad Schott once put it for me, "Arielle Kemper could talk a snake out of its brand new skin."

KENNY SLOWLY poured himself another half-glass of Southern Comfort, smiled, and asked, "How'd it go, guys?"

One of the guys who was not a guy—very far from it—smiled back.

"It was simplicity itself," Arielle Kemper said with a poorly-concealed wink.

Arielle was not only stunning to look at, she had an invisible aura that drew everyone's attention wherever she went. With an infectious smile that made people either helplessly smile back or else laugh for no apparent reason, Arielle had proven to be the perfect pick to wheedle their way into the good graces of the Comptrell Trust and Savings Bank in George Town, Grand Cayman.

Brad tried not to stare at her. He suspected Arielle could probably worm her way into Fort Knox with nothing but the flutter of a single eyelash. With Arielle, the Grand Slam team had struck it rich in the conniving department. Looks aren't everything, Brad understood, but he knew there were probably few men around who would want to say "no" to anything Arielle asked of them. Brad also realized, unfortunately, he was in that bunch.

Just four days after meeting Kenny and Traci for supper, Arielle had flown down to George Town with Bryan Cantor, Jason Broadman's computer wizard. The sole purpose of the trip was to introduce Arielle to the staff at Comptrell and allow her and Cantor to scout the place out. The male staff at Comptrell would be talking about, and daydreaming about, Arielle Kemper for the next few weeks, until her promised return visit to the bank.

She and Cantor had returned to Philadelphia the evening before, just two days after they left the States.

Poor Bryan Cantor, geeky as he was, could not help himself. Though he would never tell Kenny, he had tried to hit on Arielle at least five times during their brief trip, especially late at night after several drinks in the lounge at their luxurious hotel. But as he described it later to Jason Broadman, hitting on Arielle was like bouncing a racket ball off a concrete wall. She seemed impervious to compliments, and apparently—unlike Cantor—had a will made of iron. What Cantor found infuriating was that despite her aloof attitude, she always seemed to be luring him along toward some intimate pleasures—pleasures that never materialized.

"I think it's just how she's wired," Cantor told Broadman.

"No, Bryan, I don't think it's her wiring that bugged you," Broadman laughed.

Cantor was now sitting with Broadman and several others in Kenny and Brad's hotel suite at the High Point, and was still in a pout. He kept his eyes down and let Arielle do most of the briefing.

"We met with Dave Sloan," Arielle continued, "he showed us around, and we made the appointment for the big day." She smiled approvingly with a conceited pleasure at her own success. "Except, of course, he doesn't know it's going to *be* a big day," she said with a lyrical laugh.

"Who's Sloan?" Brad asked.

"He's the local manager at Comptrell-Cayman," Arielle explained.

"That's the bank, right?" Brad asked, having been out of the loop when this scouting trip was planned a few days earlier.

Arielle answered with a flavored smile that said, *Of course, dear Brad.* Brad tried not to melt.

"Got it," Brad said, glancing out a window. Anything to take his eyes off Arielle.

Jason Broadman brought a half-eaten piece of cold sausage over from the kitchen counter and plopped down into a spot on the couch that was too narrow for him, between Brad and Arielle. The other two adjusted. Broadman leaned toward Arielle, pretending to confide a non-secret.

"So, Miss Kemper, you twisted Mr. Sloan around your pretty little finger, right?" Broadman wound an imaginary piece of string around his own finger.

"Like you can't imagine, Mr. Broadman," she smiled. "Putty. Worse—jello." She beamed another self-confident smile. "This is going to be some kind of fun!" She stretched the last few words with a feigned southern accent.

Kenny stretched his legs out from his easy chair, slouching back into the rear cushion. He said with an obviously pleased tone, "So, you and Cantor show up out of the blue with the blueprints Bryan found online, and they waltzed you right downstairs into the main vault. Just like that? Hard to believe."

"It was simple, Kenny" Arielle said.

"They're dumber than I expected," Kenny chuckled.

"Well, not *that* simple," Cantor chimed in from across the room. He was, at least, paying attention. "Finding those blueprints took some real effort."

"Come the 'big day' as you call it," Kenny went on, "you show back up at the bank, with more of this cock-and-bull story about fixing the seepage in their basement, and they'll waltz you right back down to the vault again. Right?"

"I don't see why not," Arielle said, as if this may have been the stupidest question she had heard in her life. "We promised them we'd have technical drawings for the repair work when we come back."

"And then," Kenny added, ignoring her flippant tone, "we pull the plug on the whole government of Grand Cayman."

"So, what are the blueprints of?" Rick Kell asked. Being essentially a fifth wheel in the operation so far, Kell was also consistently several curves back along the road.

"They're prints of the basement and vault area of Comptrell Trust and Savings," Bryan Cantor said.

"So, what, are we really after stuff in the vault then? Cash? Jewelry? What?" Kell pressed greedily.

"Not a damned dime," Kenny said, although Brad wondered if he was shading the truth a little. "It's a diversion," Kenny insisted, "plain and simple. We have to have a diversion, see, to get everybody off-guard—the authorities, I mean. Just before we execute the main assault landing. As we hit our primary targets, the fuss at the bank will throw the cops for one more loop—and we breeze on in and take everything over."

"And you got these blueprints—how?" Kell asked Cantor.

"We slipped in a back door and confiscated them," Bryan laughed.

"Wait, the bank leaves their back door open for burglars?" Kell said with a raised eyebrow.

"Not a door in a building, thick-head. A back door in a computer program. I took the blueprints off their web server. The morons have the entire plans of the whole bank—upstairs and down—right there in a 'Blueprints' folder tucked alongside their accounting software. I hacked through a back door in their system and swiped the blueprints." He shook his head. "Fools."

"Sneaky, huh?" Arielle grinned. She nestled up against Jason Broadman, provoking a smile from him. A leer, actually.

"And, just lucky for us," Kenny informed them, "the vault actually does leak."

Kell's eyebrows went up again, his mind still stuck on what they might pilfer from that vault.

"It leaks, like, you mean, they lose money out of it?"

"No, Rick. I mean it leaks, literally. The basement floor, around the vault area. Not surprising. They dug so deep so close to the coast, the ground water keeps seeping up around the floor sill. So, when Arielle and Bryan showed up day before yesterday, pretending to be reps from the architectural firm in Little Rock that designed the place, they persuaded the bank folks that they were there to finalize some redesign work to fix said leaks." Kenny smiled at his own cleverness.

"Nixon should have called that firm," Brad laughed, but no one got it.

"Wait," Rick Kell said, "how did you figure out who designed the bank?" He looked truly buffaloed.

"Well, Rick, see, their names are written in big, block letters on every page of the blueprints," Cantor told him as if poor Kell had been born the night before.

"Oh." Kell frowned again. "And nobody at this bank is smart enough to call Little Rock and ask questions?" Kell asked in disbelief. "To check Arielle and Bryan out, I mean?"

"Apparently not," Broadman said, pawing a little at Arielle's very warm arm that was nuzzled against his ribs. The smell of her shampoo was enticing him. Actually, just being in the same room with her was enticing him.

"So, see, on the big day," Arielle went on, "me and my *other* handsome 'co-worker' here, Brad, we'll show up at the bank again, you know, to do a final, on-site assessment of their leakage problem. Before the remodeling begins. And while we're there, we pull off this little robbery thing," she said with a coy smile. "Which—like Kenny says—won't be an actual robbery."

"Just a ruse," Kenny added. "All the island cops will go ballistic," he assured everyone, "because it just so happens that Comptrell is the biggest veiled bank on the whole damned island."

"Veiled?" Traci asked.

"Veiled, as in, they're harboring all kinds of not-quite-legal money laundering accounts. Bryan here also got inside their accounting software . . . ,"

"Piece of cake," Cantor smiled.

". . . and the people at Comptrell are holding hidden off-shore assets for two of the biggest corporations in the States. And three of the biggest shell corporations in Russia—accounts that are actually owned by former members of the old Soviet Communist Party. Oh, and there's at least one account from a huge criminal enterprise group that's centered in Qatar, but that money is so hot, nobody in their right mind would claim it—if it gets snatched. So, once we're in control of the island, we probably *are* going to snatch that one. You know, help prevent crime," Kenny grinned.

Kell let it all drop because his head began to spin as the dollar signs multiplied. Then the dollar signs were quickly replaced by the image of a dark-red Maserati Quattroporte that he had been fantasizing about since Broadman first drafted him for the Grand Slam project.

Kenny smirked at his ingenuity like a drunken cheerleader, adding, "Wait, did I mention that Comptrell also holds some hidden accounts for a former President of Russia, and several U.S. senators—and at least three state governors? Accounts none of these people ever want found? Oh, almost forgot, there's three accounts that belong to an Ayatollah in Iran, who is supposedly holding all this loot in trust for the good of the Iranian people. In case they ever get attacked."

"Oh, my gosh," Traci moaned, "we are going to get so busted . . . ."

Traci's reaction caught Kenny by surprise. But it was Traci, after all, who had dragged her friend Arielle into this before Kenny had offered Traci any hint of what he was going to ask Arielle to do.

Traci looked positively desperate but then, realizing everyone in the room was staring at her after her remark, she tried to collect herself, saying, "Sorry, didn't mean to get us off-track. It's just—this whole thing gets me a little overwhelmed at times."

Kenny moved over and sat on the arm of her easy chair and put his own arm around her.

"That's because you are such a loving, sweet woman, Traci, so you can't comprehend how many bad people there are in this awful world," Kenny teased.

"No, it's exactly because I *can* comprehend all those bad people. It's just that—I'm beginning to feel maybe I'm one of them."

"Everything is going to be fine. This plan is brilliant, it'll work perfectly. That's why I did this little dry run with Arielle and Bryan. Line up all our little duckies in a nice, neat row."

"I guess," Traci conceded with what was becoming her favorite expression.

She was still not convinced. She looked over at Arielle, who seemed to be enjoying herself far too much sitting between Jason Broadman and Brad. Traci looked back up at Kenny. The wink Kenny gave her, and the warm, reassuring grin that spread across his face, made her think of a clean-shaven Cheshire Cat smiling at a very perplexed Alice.

"That easy, huh?" she asked.

Kenny leaned down and kissed the top of her head, the softness of her hair caressing his lips.

"Like Arielle said, simplicity itself," he said with a

soothing tone.

"But you said the bank heist was phony," Traci said. "Now you're saying we might take some of the money."

Kenny's grin only widened.

"Yeah, we might have to swipe a few illegal accounts. Darn it. But nobody's going to claim them. Just say, we're cleaning up the Cayman economy a bit. But what I said is true, Comptrell is a diversion, mainly. The banks down there are very careful about the privacy—and secrecy—of their clients. We start messing with a bank and *boom,* I guarantee, every cop on the island will be headed in one direction."

"They'll never know the rest of us have come ashore, till it's too late," Jason Broadman smiled.

"So our real objective is still taking the island, right?" Brad asked. Like Traci, he was becoming a little skeptical of Kenny's motives and wanted reassurance.

"Of course, buddy. You know that's been our goal since the beginning! But first, we'll bring the police to a fast boil with this supposed bank heist, to get them off-guard. They'll look like the Keystone Cops of the Caribbean."

Traci thought back. She did remember Kenny talking about needing a major diversion to distract from their teams landing. *The bank would do it*, she admitted to herself.

Brad glanced at Traci, who smiled at him. That was all the reassurance he needed.

Kenny was still bragging up the greatness of his plan, adding, "By the end of that first day, the cops and authorities will have been sweating it out for six or eight hours at the bank—then they suddenly find out they're no longer in charge of their own island."

This appeased Brad further. He swilled a gulp of beer

too fast and almost sneezed it out. Arielle leaned away from him and let out a hushed laugh.

"So let's get on with it," Kenny nodded. He turned to Jason Broadman, Rick Kell, and Bryan Cantor. "You guys need to take off. You've got gear to scout out and get bought. And we still need those extra people, Jason. Just keep me informed how you're doing. And let me know if you think up anything else you're going to need."

"You know I will, Mr. Money Bags," Broadman said with half a snarl, trying to impress Arielle, who he was leaving on the couch with Brad.

"I can't wait!" Arielle smiled at Broadman. "I'm excited!"

Broadman wasn't sure what she meant by this, but he took it as flirting. He left the hotel suite with Kell and Cantor in tow, trying to interpret Arielle's words and the smile that had accompanied them.

"But Arielle was just being Arielle," Traci would later tell me. "The moment Broadman was out of sight, I noticed her focusing on Kenny and Brad. I think she felt a little jealous, because she could see they both liked me."

Her friend was a flirt, Traci knew, but Arielle also had a keen sense of relationships and sometimes saw what few others would notice. Traci searched her memory, redrawing the scene in her mind and trying to explain it to me.

"In a way, it was funny. I think Arielle must have seen the question mark in my expression as I watched Kenny go to the mini-bar for another beer. But Arielle was also scrutinizing Brad who was right next to her— but whose eyes were fixed on me."

Seventeen

Traci

Kenny has the whole crew gathered this afternoon in what he calls our temporary operations center. It's a large pair of rooms in the ratty basement of an old hotel out in a Philly suburb, near the interstate. He rented this place because there was way too much traffic always coming and going from the hotel suite at the High Point downtown. Kenny was worried somebody would get curious, or suspicious, and call the cops. You know, wondering if he's selling dope or something.

I still can't believe the cops haven't caught up to us over the armored truck robbery. I think we've gotten away scot-free. It's been a little over two weeks, and not a peep from the cops. If they knew anything about us, you would think they would have busted us by now. But Kenny is sure we're in the clear.

"There's no way they'd let us slide this long—if they knew," he whispered to me at the restaurant last night. "Told you we'd be fine," he said with his usual causal, confident look.

Then he called me late this morning and told me to get out here to our operations center for a last minute meeting. He wants to go over the plan with the whole crew and make sure we all know our parts.

Typical Kenny. Why didn't he tell me about this meeting at supper last night? He forgets I'm still trying to run the gym! It's hard enough without getting called away every couple of days at the last minute like this. I've worked as fast as I can training the woman he found to cover for me while we're away. But I had to just walk out this afternoon and wish her good luck, because we're flying to Florida tonight!

That's Kenny, though. He's kind of a last minute guy. It says something about our relationship, I guess. And me.

In fairness, though, he's been working pretty hard, too, with Brad and Jason Broadman. This whole last week they've been getting the rest of the people lined up and working to make sure Broadman has bought all the gear we're going to need to capture Grand Cayman.

As I look around the operations center, the stuff is piled everywhere, in shipping boxes, and small crates, and heavy, aluminum travel cases.

Kenny is trying to corral everybody into chairs at the front of the room. He looks impatient. That's not unusual, either.

Even now, as the "big day" is closing in, I get queasy when we talk about the plan. It seems so big, so overwhelming. I can see Brad is feeling that, too. But Kenny keeps telling us every day that we can pull it off. Well, I'm on the hook, aren't I? I can't back out.

Anyway, it's too late. We'll fly out tonight to some staging place in south Florida, then from there it's on to Jamaica. What can I do? Like I told Kenny, I'm in.

Broadman came through, pretty much. Besides his original help, Rick Kell, Ronnie Vaughn and Bryan Cantor, he's managed to round up another seventy-two people. Sixty-eight men and four more women—although, honestly, looking around the room, I have trouble telling which of the bunch are the four women.

One of the new guys is *really* strange. Kenny has decided this guy is going to lead Team Four. His name is Anson Dahlgren, and he looks like a runaway from the set of some overblown beer commercial. His dark brown hair is shaved off both sides of his head, from the ears about three inches up, leaving a big shock of straight, shaggy hair crowning his head like a really bad toupee. To make it worse, his skin has some kind of disease. I don't know what you call it, but it's really ugly. Looks like some orangey-reddish blotches of alien skin have attached themselves to him and won't let go. He's had on long sleeves the couple of times I've seen him, I guess to help cover it up.

Anyway, I try to avoid looking at Dahlgren. He's just plain scary. Looks like he's always mad about something, and ready to pay the world back for it. I have no idea where Broadman found him—or the rest of them. But then I don't really want to know. Right-wing militia groups, street gangs, who knows?

"OK," Kenny hollers, more impatiently as people finally sit, "pay attention. I don't want to have to repeat all this."

He sounds like a real commander all of a sudden. Must have practiced again after I left the hotel last night. Brad's been coaching him, trying to make Kenny get more authority in his voice. It's working. He sounds like he knows what he's doing.

Heads lean forward, eyes and minds sharpen up. I'm

near the front by Brad on a brand new loveseat that looks really out of place with all the ragged, castoff furniture the hotel has stored down here. Jason Broadman is standing, imposingly, just behind us. Arielle is next to him, half-leaning on a stool, and half on him. She seems to have taken a liking to Broadman. I can't believe it. He is not remotely her type. Well, better than Dahlgren, I guess. At least Broadman has most of his hair.

There's no accounting for taste, I guess. Or lack of it. It's not that late in the day and already Broadman smells. The guy needs to shower about three times a day. I'm never around him when he doesn't stink. Don't know how Arielle can stand it. Maybe working in that lab with all those body specimens has killed her sense of smell. And her sense of being grossed out.

"So, here it is," Kenny half barks, "what I'm calling the Grand Slam. Listen up."

"Grand Slam," one of the new guys in the back chuckles, "that's when you steal all the cards in Hearts, right?"

I think it's a guy.

"No, if you're talking cards, you're thinking of Bridge, not Hearts," Brad tells the guy.

Huh. I never knew Brad knew anything about cards.

"Actually, it's a baseball term," Kenny says. "It's when all three bases are loaded and the batter hits a home run, driving in four runs. That's a grand slam."

"Oh," the guy at the back nods.

"Let's get back to the point," Kenny says. "We'll have four marine-borne teams for the assault, and two main drop zones. We've got two fast yachts rented that will be stationed at a private marina in Jamaica on the fourteenth. We're flying down to Jupiter, Florida late tonight to our staging area. Then we fly to Jamaica on the thirteenth, and rest up for a couple of days."

"So we get to party that night, right?" someone asks.

"No, you *don't* get to party. I need everyone cold sober—and not hungover—on the sixteenth. Trust me, you'll have lots of time to party when we're done," Kenny says with a patronizing smile. "We'll tie up any loose ends while we're in Jamaica, then board the yachts the evening of the fourteenth. They'll carry two teams each over to Grand Cayman. It's about a day and a half sail on these rigs we rented, so you'll have plenty of time to tune-up plans with your team leaders."

"We'll arrive near Grand Cayman during the night—well, the early morning hours, actually, on May sixteenth," Broadman says. "That's the day."

"So why the long stop in Florida? What's the plan there?" another anonymous voice asks.

"Work, and start earning your keep," Brad chimes in, provoking a smile from Kenny.

"Like Brad says, starting tomorrow you're on duty—and from then on," Kenny tells the crew. "Do what you're told, when you're told. Listen to your team leader. Check the binders you each got. Everything you need is there, names of your teammates, basic assignments. Tomorrow in Florida we'll break out into teams. You'll have five days to practice your landing and attack plans. Brad rented an indoor-outdoor soccer field in Florida, so there'll be plenty of layout to simulate your landing zones on Grand Cayman. Your team leaders were briefed in detail last week and they'll run you through your paces."

"And after Florida?" Ronnie Vaughn asks.

Kenny looks impatient. Vaughn is one of the team leaders and he should already have memorized these details.

"Already been explained, Ronnie."

"I know. I thought the others might be curious."

"Sure," Kenny nods. "A private charter flies us from Florida to Jamaica, we rest up, then you yacht over to Grand Cayman. We'll anchor about five miles offshore, just before daylight on the sixteenth."

"And once eight o'clock ticks up, we'll hit the water in twelve-man inflatables for the final approach to our landing spots," Broadman adds.

Kenny looks at him, getting ticked off at all the interruptions. "You want to finish?" he asks Broadman pointedly.

Broadman half returns Kenny's stare with a kind of apologetic expression. Never seen that look on him before. I guess he knows who's paying the bills.

"No, Hamilton. Your show. Sorry."

Kenny nods, saying, "Teams One and Two disembark into their boats, like Jason said, and come ashore here," he says."

He points his laser pointer at the huge aerial map of Grand Cayman projected on a ten-by-twelve-foot screen on the front wall, zeroing in on a spot along the south coast about three miles west of Bodden Town, as the crow flies. He clicks his computer remote and an area of the map blows up larger. He zooms in on a set of buildings.

"You land right here," he tells them, highlighting a spot of rocky looking shoreline, "just below Pedro Saint James Castle."

"Which is—what exactly?" Rick Kell asks.

"Well, besides being probably the oldest building on Grand Cayman, it was the original seat of government, back in the 1700s. Before George Town became the capital. It's just a museum now, but I'm going to make it *my* seat of government."

"Kenny and I did the tourist thing there one afternoon, when we were on Cayman in April," Brad says. "It's awesome, has a really old, colonial feel. It'll be perfect."

"So anyway," Kenny says, tolerating Brad's interruption, "Team One will secure the house, grounds and shoreline, Team Two will blockade and guard this one entrance road that leads into the property," he says, pointing. "Then four or five of them will head downtown, to the cruise ship docks."

"Then?" Ronnie Vaughn asks, his expression suggesting he's asking for the others again.

"Then you sit tight, and wait for my orders. You should make the beach about eight-thirty, if the waves aren't too bad. Brad and Arielle will be arriving at Comptrell Bank, just as they open, at the same time you're landing. They'll have come ashore on the west end by a separate small boat before sunup. They hang out at a little cafe near this marina—here—until it's time to head to the bank."

"Eight-thirty in the morning? I'm surprised any banker can get out of bed that early," Anson Dahlgren jeers, spawning laughs.

"The bank, see, is going to be our big diversion," Brad chimes in importantly, "to keep any cops from paying attention when the rest of you come ashore."

Kenny doesn't seem to mind Brad exerting some leadership, but he quickly steals back the floor.

"Their job," Kenny says, "Arielle and Brad, is to cause havoc at the bank—a supposed robbery. That will screw up the police so bad that any response to our arrival at Pedro Saint James—or on the north side—will be just an afterthought. They'll be so twisted up and preoccupied at the bank, they won't realize what hit them."

"I *really* like that part," Arielle smiles, almost a purr in her voice. "Hope we don't disappoint you, boss," she adds, giving Kenny an alluring wink.

I'm beginning to wonder if I should have gotten Arielle involved in this after all. Seems like she's got an eye on just about every guy in the room. I don't get it. She didn't used to be like this. Maybe there's just too many overcharged male hormones percolating around here. It's like she's caught a disease.

"Come on, everybody, don't keep interrupting," Kenny orders, "or we'll never get through this. Teams Three and Four will have dropped off the other yacht along the north coast. They motor in and come ashore here," he shows us with the pointer again, "by Old Man Bay, landing at the same time as One and Two. There's a soccer field, right here," he says, zooming in further, "where Old Robin Road meets North Side Road. I'll have six large passenger vans pre-stationed at the field. It'll make a perfect staging area. And it's strategic. It'll give Kell's and Dahlgren's teams quick access to move toward East End, or west toward Rum Point. It also connects to Frank Sound Road—here—which is the only main road across the island from north to south. If the cops *do* respond to our arrival—very unlikely—but if they do, I'll be able to quickly move you in any direction we need."

"Clever," Broadman comments, emitting a slurred belch, a result of the rum and Coke in his hand.

Must be practicing his part.

"Yes, it is clever," Kenny smiles. "Again, this will all happen simultaneously with Arielle and Brad showing up at the bank."

"Communications?" Bryan Cantor asks.

Kenny smiles. Finally, an intelligent question.

"See the smaller metal cases over there? Every one of you will have a small handheld radio. They're specially set up. Not only can you set them to one channel for your team, but they also—at the same time—keep scanning the other team channels. So if you need to listen in on the action of a different team, you can do that."

"Groceries?" Larry Pinter asks. Pinter is almost the strangest looking of the bunch. He's small and looks part shark and part terrier, with short, fin-like arms, and legs that are too short, too. His whitish-blond hair is cropped short in military style but his broad, pronounced nose overshadows his other features, except maybe his slanted, almost fish-like eyes that don't ever seem to be looking in the same direction. I think he's supposed to be on Team Three under Rick Kell.

Kenny taps some keys on his laptop and zooms in on an area near The Reef Resort at the far east end of the island.

"See this little strip mall, here? There's a small grocery store right here. All the groceries you'll need for day one."

"What if the store's closed?" Pinter asks.

"Then we open it," Kenny says with a hard tone of voice.

"Oh." Pinter smiles. He likes the idea.

"I was just about to get to this. I've arranged for two more rented vans to be stationed in the lot of the strip mall, for backup," Kenny explains. "Sometimes the rentals down there aren't real reliable, if you know what I mean."

A new glint appears in his eyes, like he's savoring his

own cleverness.

"Here's the good part. We're going to create a whole second diversion on the opposite end of the island. While Brad and Arielle are screwing around at the bank in George Town, some of Team Three will be bashing up cars at this strip mall, then they'll hit the grocery store. You'll run the staff into a back room, or a cooler. Lots of yelling and screaming, waving guns, that sort of thing. All in fun, of course. A little, low-tech kidnapping way out there on the east end of the island will spread the coppers even thinner—way beyond their capacity to respond to anything else."

For the first time all afternoon, Kenny smiles at me. He really has thought a lot about this. Even I'm getting impressed.

"Team Three, make as much mess as you can," he adds. "That'll draw whatever police are out at the Bodden Town station. And that clears the area for us at Pedro Saint James, because then all we have to worry about is a possible police response coming out from George Town. With the robbery alarm at Comptrell, though, I doubt there'll be any officers left."

"OK, some of my crew heads to the strip mall. How big a mess do you want?" Rick Kell, the leader of Team Three, asks.

"Throw together whatever you can, Rick. Roust the grocery store, scare folks with your weapons. I mean, don't hit anybody, or anything. Just shake 'em up. Oh, there's an ATM in front of the store, too. Probably some sort of alarm on it. Hammer it—hit it with a van or something. That ought to generate some more emergency calls." Kenny laughs. "Only wish I could be at the George Town police station to see it all. It'll be just like the old Keystone Cops movies, I promise.

You're all going to have a lot of laughs!"

"Why get so carried away on the east end of the island? Won't we be pretty far from the main action?" Kell asks.

"That's the whole idea, Rick," Kenny says. "We want the cops running in as many different directions as possible—right after the alarm goes down at Comptrell."

Kell answers with a confirming nod. There's suddenly a predatory look on his face. He can hardly wait.

"And the rest of Team Three, and my Team Four, what are we doing?" Anson Dahlgren asks. He picks at something deep inside his nose, not seeming to realize that everybody is looking at him.

He probably doesn't care.

Kenny has it under control, though. He and Brad have obviously thought this through.

"I've already sent a small advance team. They flew to Grand Cayman yesterday. They'll rent six speedboats, to be in place by the fifteenth, the day before the assault. Six boats, from six different companies, so nobody gets suspicious. Three of the boats will be pre-stationed at Rum Point dock, and the other three at Water Cay."

"Why do we need them?" another new face asks.

"So I can respond with more manpower wherever I need to. I'll call the plays as we go. Most of Three and Four will standby at the soccer field until I know where I need you most. Say, if I need reinforcements in George Town, some people from Four will van to Rum Point or Water Cay, take the speed boats, and shoot across to Governor's Creek—this little bay here—then work your way downtown. Check your folders, so you know which boat you might be in."

"Why land up there?" someone asks. "Why not shoot

straight down toward George Town?"

"Because you'd be landing right near the police headquarters. Too visible. I'll have some rental cars stationed up here"—he points to an area just north of George Town—"to take you down into the city. Less noticeable that way—until you're right on top of them. The car locations are in your folders, too."

"Where would we dock?" another voice asks.

Kenny's red laser pointer draws a circle again around the small bay labelled Governor's Creek, which connects to several residential canals and marinas.

"Here," he says, circling the marinas. "Plenty of places to tie up."

"Then?" Kell asks.

"You pick up the cars I'll have stationed nearby, and advance downtown through these back streets," Kenny says, pointing.

"We just—what—drive around?" Kell asks, looking confused.

"Don't play stupid, Rick, you know this part from your first briefing. You'll head to either Comptrell or the Central Police Station. Or Government House. Wherever we need help."

"And the rest of us?" Anson Dahlgren asks. "My team, I mean?"

"Well, depending on where I need you, anyone left from your Team Four, Anson, and Rick's Team Three, will shoot down Frank Sound Road and pick up Bodden Town road here, and head west toward Pedro Saint James. To backup Teams One and Two. Got it?"

Dahlgren looks mildly confused. Apparently that first briefing didn't help him either, but hopefully it's sinking in now.

"All right, is everybody with me so far?" Kenny asks,

one eye on Dahlgren, who finally looks up from the floor.

Dahlgren gives a half-confident nod. Kenny goes on.

"OK, here's where it starts to get a little tricky," he says slowing down so that everyone will pay closer attention. "Brad and Arielle are at the bank. They'll have managed to get into the basement vault and will be ransacking it while folks upstairs call for help. There'll be a couple of security guards on duty. But, of course, they have no guns, and Brad and Arielle will—to keep the bank staff at bay."

"I can already see the look on Frank Bennington's face!" Arielle laughs with a smug glint in her eyes.

"Who?" Larry Pinter asks.

"The bank manager," Kenny explains. "It's all arranged. Brad and Arielle are supposedly there to finalize a plan to stop water leaking into the vault. They'll make sure that Bennington has master keys for some of the safe deposit boxes—so our folks can 'inspect' the walls at the back of the boxes."

"And as soon as he opens them, we'll trash the contents," Arielle smiles.

She's really enjoying this, apparently. But she can do it. I remember what her dorm room looked like in college.

"While that's going on at the bank, Traci and Bryan Cantor will have headed over to Government House," Kenny goes on.

"That's, what, like their senate or something?" another newcomers asks.

"No, as a matter of fact, it's the official residence of Governor Theodore Edwards, governor of the islands," Kenny replies.

"Oh! Extreme!" the guy smiles. "We're gonna steal

the governor?" He laughs with a wicked, dog-like snarl.

"Government House is right up over here," Kenny points. "A hop, skip and a jump. Traci and Bryan and five others from Team One will take it. They'll be totally unexpected, of course. More fun for the cops—who'll still be swarming and fumbling all over themselves down at the bank." He stifles a laugh. "Anyway, if Traci and Bryan need help, some of Team Four will come across in the speedboats and head their direction. But, truthfully, I think seven people at Government House is going to be way more than enough. From what I've read online, they have no real security around the governor—day, or night."

"The rest of us?" Jason Broadman finally asks.

"Like I said, I'll have to call most of the plays the day of the game. We've got to be flexible, you know? There's no way we can calculate in advance all their exact moves. The cops, I mean. The good thing is, we'll have the whole Grand Cayman police force far outnumbered. Almost eighty of us, and, as best I can figure, there's only about forty-five street officers on the whole island."

"Which didn't exactly answer my question," Broadman points out, trying to sound respectful.

"No," Kenny says, "I'm getting there. The rest of Teams One and Two will do several things. Most important, you'll hold onto Pedro Saint James. That's going to be my base of operations, home of my new government. Once it's completely secure, I'll spring some of you to help capture the Central Police Station—if we haven't done that already. It won't be hard. It'll essentially be empty by that time. But this is important. That's where their police communications system is based. So as soon as we breach the place, we'll knock out their whole radio system. You have somebody tapped to do that, right Jason?"

"Yup."

Kenny nods, "Right. So from then on, the rest of us spend the day rounding up any stray cops who haven't gone into hiding and lock them in their own jail. To keep them off the streets, you know, until we get our new government up and running. Then we'll recruit them back, to be on *our* police force."

There's Kenny's self-satisfied smile again. Ever since I've known him, he's had that kind of cocky look. Inherited it from his dad, I think. I've seen a couple of pictures.

"Cute," Arielle comments. "Pretty savvy, huh?" she smiles at Broadman.

Broadman returns her beguiling look with an unusual sparkle in his eye. I'm surprised he's not panting. It's getting thick in here. What a creep.

I can see what Arielle's thinking. She's picturing those Cayman police officers, their cool, summer-like uniforms over well-built, muscular frames. She's been spending too much time at my gym, gawking. And she obviously doesn't realize that a bunch of their cops are women.

"What about Comptrell, afterwards?" Broadman presses Kenny—barely able to peel his attention off Arielle.

"We'll wait and see how it plays out," Kenny tells him. "We'll have Brad and Arielle inside. They disrupt the place, then hunker down in the vault with Bennington, the Chief Operating Officer, while chaos erupts around the rest of the island. Once we're sure we've got all our key locations secured—and the coppers locked up—I'll send some of you to escort Brad and Arielle out of the bank. They join up with us, and we all have a crazy and highly over-priced supper somewhere!"

"We're, ah, missing a big piece here still. You haven't talked about the airport," Broadman prods him.

"Oh, right. I was getting to it. That's the easiest part, really, though the timing will be a little tricky. The advance team I told you about? They'll still be on the island, just to make sure everything's tidy and in place. They'll be at three different hotels, of course, the five of them. After we've hit Government House and have the governor, assuming he's home—which he usually is, swimming and doing his usual Mr. Governorship thing—the advance team will buzz over to the airport to see if there's any coppers left there. Most will have already shot downtown to the bank. The advance team will report to me, and I'll fire some of Rick's or Jason's teams over to the airport to secure it."

"Aren't there customs officers at the airport, too?" someone asks.

"Yeah, a few. But they're pretty useless. Passport stampers, that's really all they are. They—and anyone else who tries to cause trouble—get locked away in this small private hanger, right over here. One of my advance team, John, worked as an air traffic controller for about a year. He'll take command of the traffic control and the tower, and shut everything down."

"But there could be a bunch of planes *en route* to the island, Kenny," Bryan Cantor says.

"Yeah. Your point?"

"They'll have to land."

"No, they *won't*. They'll get a warning, with enough time to divert. Our new tower operations guy—John—will tell them there's been an explosion inside the terminal and the airport is closed. We'll send the planes up to Cuba, or over to Jamaica. No sweat, no harm. They all carry plenty of fuel for this kind of unexpected thing."

Kenny smiles at his own ingenuity.

"Go on, Traci," Brad whispers, nudging me and noticing that I've gotten very preoccupied with my phone.

I'm checking how many airlines fly early routes into Grand Cayman on an average morning, I whisper back, "Go on, what?"

"Looked like you had a question a second ago. Ask him."

I frown at Brad because I'm not sure I want to ask right now in front of everyone. And I'm not as worried about airplanes as I am about something else.

Brad nudges me again.

"Are you sure about the number of police?" I ask Kenny.

"Look, before the few that are on duty know what hit them, we'll have most of the island locked down, and the duty cops locked up. At least a half to a third of the cops will be off duty, remember? At home or in bed, resting for the night shift. Really, there's not going to be much resistance."

I listen, but I still worry. Are we getting too over-confident? Oh well, that's Kenny's nature. He's always had it made in life. Look at how his parents spoiled him, before they died. Then all that money, when they did. He was born into wealth, nursed in the lap of luxury. Why would he not expect everything to go easily?

Rick Kell breaks in again.

"Won't there be some tourist boats off on day trips and things? What if they wander back ashore in the middle of all this?"

"Well sure, there may be a few," Kenny admits. "So what? What are they going to have on board? Swords? Cannons? No, fishing poles, rotting fish bait, and some drunk, sunburned tourists." He gives Kell a snide laugh.

"What about cruise ships?" someone asks.

From the voice, I think it's one of the four women. But, honestly, I'm not sure.

"Me and a friend was down there on a cruise once," she says, her voice as thick and ragged as her hair. "There were, like, three or four huge cruise ships that all came into the harbor at once—early in the morning."

Kenny is unflustered.

"Possible. But remember, I said we'd send some people down to the main docks as soon as we get Pedro Saint James nailed down. So by the time the cruise ships have anchored and started ferrying passengers ashore, our people at the docks will just turn the shuttle boats around, tell them a plague hit the island, or some crap like that."

It's obvious Kenny really has covered all the angles. This is what happens when he can't sleep.

"The cops have cars, right?" I ask, pushing back to my last point.

"Sure. A couple may be patrolling around. But their cops mostly hang around the stations, unless somebody calls. It's bad for tourism for the coppers to be too visible. I've researched this and it looks like during the morning hours there's only going to be maybe eight or nine actually on duty in the George Town area. Maybe five or six more—*maybe*—out toward Bodden Town Station, and East End Station. Small potatoes. They won't be a problem."

"Firefights?" Anson Dahlgren asks with a lurid

anticipation in his voice.

"Won't happen," Kenny assures him. "Remember, you're all carrying blanks, and the Cayman cops don't have guns. They're illegal on the whole island, remember? Yeah, sure, you know some of the foreign property owners probably have a few firearms squirreled away here or there, in their houses. But nothing we can't handle. We'll be a lot scarier than anything they're used to, in our black assault outfits and all. And our assault weapons. Most of you will be carrying a SIG MPX machine pistol. Short, light, easy to wield. A few of you will have an MCX patrol rifle. For longer shots."

"Longer shots? With blanks?" Vaughn asks, confused.

Still unflustered, Kenny says, "Come on, you know, Ronnie. It's all for looks. To scare the hell out of people. Psych them out!" he adds, giving Vaughn a buddy nod.

"OK. I get it." He nods to himself. "Yeah."

"You're sure about the gun situation?" Rick Kell presses him. "As far as the cops. They have nothing, right?"

"Absolutely positive. Look, I've been down there, some of you have been there. The cops carry mace and a few of the better trained ones get to carry Tasers. But you'll have them totally outgunned. At least, that's what they'll think, even though we're carrying blanks. Trust me. Crank off a few blank rounds and they'll scatter like bats when a light turns on."

Kenny laughs at his little joke.

"Why are we carrying blanks? Sounds kind of stupid to me," one of the tougher looking men near the front asks. He's obviously disappointed. He's about forty, I'd say, with prematurely-graying hair and eyes chiseled from granite. It looks like he's been around the block more than once.

"Well, come on," Kenny answers, "we're not going down there to hurt anybody. Just to capture the island. And we hold it as long as we want. If I'm right about most of the lovely citizens there, they're not going to give a rat's ass who's actually running the government. Most of them probably can't tell you who's running it now, for crying out loud! I mean, how many of you—right here in the room—can tell me who your congress-men and senators are?"

Kenny's getting a little heated again at all the questions. I know him. He doesn't like it when people challenge him. He told me once that even in high school, he'd get mad any time a teacher would challenge an answer he gave in class. Kenny has a hard time not being right, I guess. Anyway, all these questions are not what he wanted today. He just wants to lay out the plan, make sure everybody is committed, and go get a supper at a nice restaurant somewhere.

I nudge Brad. He nods, and tries to break the tension.

"Look, everybody, they'll probably end up thanking us when it's all over," Brad laughs. "You watch, even the cops will probably thank us for showing them how vulnerable they've been all these years."

"Exactly," Kenny adds. "Brilliant point, Brad. Not only will you all end up with a really nice, big house somewhere on the island, every one of us will probably get our names on a big brass plaque somewhere, to boot. Maybe the Queen will fly over and congratulate us on our initiative."

Muffled cackles circulate through the room.

"OK, so some of us stay out at Pedro Saint James, right?" asks Ronnie Vaughn, who will lead Team One. "Why there?"

"Aren't you listening, man? I already explained this. It's going to be my headquarters. So you capture it, and sit on it. How tough is that? Keep everybody away, and wait for me to land."

"What?" I ask, looking up from my phone. Obviously, I've *really* missed something. "What do you mean, when you land?"

"When I come ashore," Kenny says.

My face must look like I was just pricked by a big thorn.

"Wait, what—?" I stammer. I'm sure everybody hears the surprise in my voice. "You mean, you're not landing with one of the teams?"

"Nope, I'm going to be floating," he tells me. "Literally. I'll be on a large catamaran off the north coast. Observing, coordinating everybody."

"Well, maybe I should stay out there with you, then?"

Wow, this is awkward.

"No, Traci, I've already explained this, too. You and Bryan are leading the group that will take Government House, to capture the governor. I did that for a reason. Think! With your savvy—and that hugely-sweet personality—you'll bowl the rickety old governor right over. Huh?" He coaxes me along with his smile. "Come on, Traci, he'll love you! He'll do whatever you ask him to. Don't you think?"

Kenny comes over, leans down, and gives me one of those sideways shoulder hugs like a brother would do. Of course, we are in front of a whole room of near-strangers.

"You get to hang out in the governor's mansion, Traci! How can you beat that assignment?" He gives me one of his lovable, almost-fiancé smiles, coupled with a little nod that says, *It'll be easy!* "Just wrap him around your little finger, like Arielle does!"

I'm not sure I wrap exactly like Arielle.

"I guess," I say, on the edge of an embarrassment cliff, about to fall.

I feel everyone's eyes on me. My God. I wish Kenny had clued me in on this before. Why would he spring it on me now, here, in front of everybody?

Well, it's not like I can argue, with all of them staring at us. So I just shrug. Put on your big-girl pants, Traci. Anyway, maybe it'll be better on land than bouncing around on the waves all day with Kenny. I get seasick pretty easy. I force a smile.

"Sure, I can handle it. How tough can it be to capture and schmooze some old fart politician, right?" I laugh for everyone's benefit, but mostly to persuade myself.

Brad gives me a subtle squeeze on the arm. I lean my head toward him just a little as Kenny turns away.

"Wish it was you going with me instead of Cantor," I whisper to Brad.

"Yeah? Me, too," he whispers back.

"Anyway," Kenny says, walking back up front, "whoever gets to the George Town Police Station first, you secure it and hang tight. Just in case any patrol cars are out—or in case they call in off-duty folks for backup. Keep them out of the station. Once we control the main station, we'll control the jail. And we're likely to have a few customers for that."

Broadman decides to show off again.

"I found out they have one quasi-tactical police truck they keep out back of the main station," Broadman says. "That can be our mobile command post—once we're in charge. That is, if we can get the dang thing started." He laughs too loud. "*Hell yes,* this is going to be fun!"

One of the men hanging back by the small kitchen at

the back of the room gets a nod from Kenny. The guy proceeds to pass out cold beers or ice waters to everyone.

Kenny rambles on for a few more minutes, but everyone's attention has faded. Beer looks more interesting. He tries anyway.

"Remember, everybody, read through your individual assignment folders in detail. Memorize them. No screw ups! You screw up, you don't get paid! Oh, that reminds me, see Broadman by the door as you leave. He's got an envelope for each of you. Cash, and some team ID cards for each of you. And make sure your passport is with you tonight! Remember—no screw-ups!"

Some wiseacre near the back chimes in, "Uh, hey Hamilton, I don't think we're gonna need passports to attack Cayman!" and he gives a belly laugh.

Kenny waits for him to shut up, which takes a few seconds.

"No, but you *will* need one when we land in Jamaica. Anybody else want to throw a rock at me?"

For the first time this afternoon, he scowls at the whole bunch. I can see what's going on in Kenny's head. *Do I really want to trust this bunch of losers?* He seems exhausted, and all he's done so far is talk.

Brad takes a huge swig of his newly delivered beer and leans toward me.

"So, you OK with everything?"

"The plan? Sure. Why not?"

"Come on. I saw your face a few minutes ago."

I make a little pout with my lips. "It's all right, Brad. I just kind of hoped we'd be on the same team."

"Yeah, me, too. Would have been nice." Brad looks toward Kenny. "I'm not sure why he picked me to go to the bank with Arielle."

We both look at Arielle, who has moved away to the side of the room, a small swarm of worker bees beginning to hover around her.

"Just hope she keeps her hands to herself. While you're stuck down there in that bank vault," I tell Brad.

He glances at Arielle. I can read it in Brad's eyes. He's not sure he'd mind if she didn't.

Men.

Well, what can I expect? The girl has something, I'll give her that. Something I obviously don't have. Stupid me, I'm the one who talked her into being part of this gig.

"Anyway," Brad smiles, "hey, you'll be with the *real* governor of the island. And I'll be stuck at Pedro-Saint-Whatcha-ma-call-it with Mister-Make-Believe there," he says, nodding toward our ringleader.

I can't help cracking a smile. Sweet-talking some old governor out of his own government?

Maybe this will be a little fun, after all.

Eighteen

Brad

It's really hard to not get bored in a long meeting when you already know everything that's gonna go on.

Well, almost everything. I'm like Traci. I had no idea Kenny isn't coming ashore with the rest of us. Not until he sprung it on us in the meeting. Staying out on a catamaran? What catamaran? He never said a word about it before. At least, not to me.

Kenny always has something up his sleeve, I guess.

Anyway, after his really long-winded explanation of the assault plan, he finally wrapped up the briefing. Only thing that made it tolerable was getting to sit next to Traci the whole time.

I drank a couple too many beers after the meeting, after Kenny headed off somewhere with Broadman and Rick Kell to work on something. I have no idea.

Anyway, he didn't give Traci another look before he left. I could see she was in the dumps. I think she didn't understand all the operation details until today. And I was getting a headache. Her being so down, I asked her to supper. We went to this really small little grill down the street from our temporary "Ops Center." The restaurant looked like a hole in the wall, but Traci knew the place, and turns out it has really fantastic food!

The headache wasn't going away, so I drank a couple of Southern Comfort Old Fashioneds with dinner. That didn't help much. So I had a three-shot Drambuie after. I think. Maybe two. Not too smart, Brad. But I don't feel the headache anymore.

Traci hit the liquor hard after supper, too. She's more pie-eyed than me right now, so guess who's driving her home?

That stupid curb back there was *way* too close to the street. Damnit! At least it's her tires, not mine. Hope I didn't bang up the rim.

Wish we were home already. Roads are tricky tonight. Wish we were already at her place. Who knows? She seemed a lot more friendly toward me at dinner. More than usual. I think Kenny kind of ticked her off this afternoon. Maybe that could be a good thing, you know? My little chance?

She is so sweet. No. She's perfect. Arielle's hot. But Traci is perfect.

Tracy is twisting her neck like a sick goose and suddenly breaks my train of thought with, "What the heck's flashing back there?"

Oh man! Oh crap! Never a cop around when you need one—*always* around when you don't want to see one!

She cranes her neck some more, peering with squinty eyes out the back window.

"Brad!" she shouts, scaring me half to death. She jacks my elbow up and down. "Don't pull over—*don't* pull over. Hide!"

"Hide!— What? Traci, it's a cop! I *gotta* pull over!"

"You're shit-faced! They'll nail you. We'll both get arrested. I've done this before," she whines, ready to cry, something busting out of her memory.

"Calm down, Traci! I've got them. I mean, I've got this. I'm OK. I can pass their little tests." My head feels like it won't stay centered. I bump the curb as I stop.

Traci reacts, "Bull—you're double-shit-faced."

I make my eyes open as wide and clear as possible as the officer walks up from his patrol car.

"You got any gum?" I beg Traci.

"Doesn't work."

"Anything will work, Traci!" I argue. OK, I know I'm drunk.

"Brad-ley,"—it sounds like she just ran the hundred yard dash—"listen to me, it won't help," she says in a forced, calming-down voice. "You'll just smell like booze and Juicy Fruit."

Cop's at the window.

"Put down the window, Brad," Traci orders me, like I'm a moron.

I hit the power switch. Nothing.

"Push it forr-wward a little, then back," Traci instructs, her index finger flicking at the air.

I do. The window hums down. I can just imagine the booze smell floating up out of the car—right into the guy's big nose.

We're cooked.

"Good evening, sir. May I see your driver's license and registration, please?"

Sounds more polite than my mother's pastor.

Driver's license. What the heck does that look like? Now what's she doing? Oh man, Traci's digging in my back pocket!

"Good grief, Traci, quit! I can get it!" That was too loud. Calm down, Brad.

I dig out my wallet and thumb at it like my fingers are dead. There. I hand over my license.

Traci turns front, pouting, then whips open the glove compartment and digs for the registration. I think she's trying to hold her breath. And she tells me gum won't help.

"Any weapons in there?" the officer asks abruptly.

His hand just went to his right hip. I don't want to look.

"What? Weapons?" I ask with a forced laugh. I stare hard at Traci. "There aren't. Are there?" I plead in a strained whisper.

She looks at me through her upper eyelashes. The mascara is starting to run from unfocused tears.

"No, stupid. I don't carry weapons. You know that."

"Not yet," I moan quietly, my teeth almost locked. "Just give me the stupid registration."

It's cool out this evening, but, man, am I sweating! My socks are getting damp. I hand the registration to the officer.

Are we both idiots? Tonight, of all nights? Spoil our whole evening? Worse, maybe spoil the whole Grand Cayman plan! This is not gonna end well. Kenny will murder me. Then her.

"Excuse me, Mister Schott. Did you know this expired last month?"

"My license?" I ask, eyes even bigger.

Traci's head whips sideways, a icy stare boring a hole through my right ear.

"Are you kidding me?" she says in a hoarse murmur. "Your license expired in the middle of all this?"

I turn and give her a look. It's a helpless, pathetic

look that pleads, *I've been kind of busy!*

"Not your license, sir," the officer says, "this vehicle registration. Expired two months ago."

Without thinking, I point at Traci.

"Her car."

If this were a cartoon, smoke would be rising out of Traci's ears.

"Officer, I'm sorry," she says, leaning toward me, her hand landing nearly in my crotch.

"Traci!" I yelp.

She blusters on.

"See sir, um—well, I have been kind of busy with some friends lately. We've been planning—"

She wrenches to a stop. I almost choke as she swallows the next words. I may be drunk but she's lost her mind.

"She was going to get it renewed tomorrow," I butt in.

I can see the cop has heard this one at least six thousand times. Traci's holding her breath again.

"Tomorrow's Saturday, sir. DMV is closed." He makes a curious nod, as if Traci and I just landed from Pluto.

"Oh. Yeah. I remember that. I meant Monday."

Traci offers him her sweetest smile, but it barely hides her panic.

"I'm sorry, sir, it's my car, but . . . ," she says with her winning smile.

"Is that a fact?" he says pleasantly.

"Yes. Brad—uhm, Mr. Schott was driving me home."

"Why? Have you been drinking, ma'am?"

He must be a comedian on the side. The car smells like the cooking kettle of a brewery.

"They're going to know," she whispers toward me in

a voice I don't think the cop can understand.

"Know what?" I whisper back, leaning toward her.

"The armored truck!" she whispers hotly, her mouth almost inside my ear.

The guy didn't hear it.

"Just give me a few moments," he says as he departs for his cruiser.

His flashing lights are lighting up three city blocks. Every Lookie-Lou up five stories is probably watching us.

"We're dead," Traci says with a long exhaling moan.

"Whadderrr you talking about?" I say, the words slurring beyond my control.

"We're dead, Brad! They're gonna connect me somehow." A drunken dread forms in her eyes.

"Connect—? What are you talking about?"

"The armored truck, stupid! Somehow they'll connect my name. We're *both* going to jail! Oh crap. Oh crap, crap, crap!" she blathers, her whine turning almost to a growl.

"Are not! Traci, how could they connect you? With what? If they knew anything, they'd've come and hauled you off a long time ago! Don't be foolish."

"Me foolish! Am I the one driving drunk on my butt?"

"I am not on my butt." My nose runs and I wipe it on my jacket sleeve. "Maybe half," I admit. "I was doing it for you, Traci! You're a lot worse than me—drunk-wise."

Suddenly, for no reason, she bursts out laughing, and sobbing a little. "You're right. I love you. You're always so funny. Even if I'm in a big pickrul—pickle!"

She pulls the rearview mirror over toward her so she can see out the back without turning around.

"We're screwed," she whispers as if I might hear. Dread haunts her voice. "Why hasn't he come back?" The laugh has stopped. Now it's fear.

"Traci, lighten up. We'll be—we're OK. I'm probably going downtown. If he makes me get out and try to walk the line thing. You'll be OK. They'll give you a ride home. Some handsome young police officer."

"I'm not that lucky," she whimpers, watching the mirror.

She sees her runny eyes, and wipes them carefully with two fingertips. It just smears the mascara worse.

"Never wear makeup when you're drunk, Brad," she says confidentially.

"Don't worry," I laugh, the tension broken for just a second.

But the cop is coming back.

Nineteen

Traci

It feels like we've been here for hours. It was so stupid of me—to let Brad drive drunk like that. Of course, I was too plowed to do it.

They took us both to some police substation, first. I have no idea where it was. Bad neighborhood, though. There were a lot of questions. Most didn't make sense to me. But I was still pretty polluted.

Anyway, they've brought us downtown, now, to the cop headquarters. Walking in, it was like going to a funeral.

Their questions earlier didn't make sense to Brad, either, I don't think. He was pretty badly drunk, too. I don't know where he's at now. They're keeping us separated. I'm not sure why, but I have a suspicion.

Brad was great, out at that substation. He tried to laugh everything off, convince them he wasn't really that drunk.

That was funny. He could hardly stand up straight.

But I'm not laughing now. I'm worried that somehow

or other they'll connect me to the armored truck robbery. Have they already? Why else would they be so secretive? And why would they be keeping me so long? I mean, I wasn't driving. No law against having a few, then riding in a car, right? But they're keeping me in the dark.

But then, it was my registration that was overdue. Maybe that's all it is. They want to write me a ticket for an expired registration. That would be some great luck.

Or maybe I'm in "protective custody," they call it. Because I'm so drunk. Till they find Mommy and Daddy. Good luck. Look in the cemetery.

They have to know about the armored truck. They must. Brad didn't think so, the last time we got to whisper, before they took him away.

They've got to know. They're going to hang me.

The door of this little room opens again. It's three cops this time. Two uniforms, a third in jeans and a polo shirt—with a stupid little badge stitched onto the right breast. How cheesy.

What I don't see at first—the third guy has the looped end of a leash in his hand.

A humongous German Shepherd plows after him into the room. The horrid creature strains at his leash the instant he sees me, and is sniffing me long-distance.

This can't be happening. Oh God. I'm terrified of dogs!

"He's hitting on her," the plainclothes dog-handler says very seriously.

"Probably not the first," laughs one of the uniforms. "Bet every guy in town has hit on her."

Jerk.

"Yeah," Uniform Two says, "I understand she runs that real popular gym down here."

"What are you doing?" I cry, trying to wedge myself and my chair further into the corner. But the chair is bolted to the floor. I hate dogs, but I'm petrified of big dogs! I'm yelling, "Take him out! What's he doing?"

The Shepherd is still straining on his leash. The handler gives him just enough slack so he can get right up close to my legs. I pull them both up so I'm now wriggled into a fetal position in the chair. I may pass out! Feels like a million creepy things are wriggling all over me.

"Relax, lady," the handler tells me, "he won't bite. Unless I give him the command."

Suddenly, though still drunk, I feel stone-cold sober.

"I don't care! Get him away!" I shout, trying to shrink into a smaller ball in the chair. The dang dog's breath is so foul it could rot three-week old garbage.

"What do you think?" the first uniform asks the dog handler.

"Well, he's hitting. So he's picking up something from that car."

My heart sinks. My car? No, that's not it. *That* car," he said. They have to mean that Honda, the one I drove in the robbery.

The other uniformed guy is sniffing now. Maybe he's a dog, too.

"Is that Red Door?" he asks, looking me hard in the eyes.

"The what door—what are you talking about?" I'm about to break down completely. *Please, God, just kill me. Something! Get me out of this!*

"Red Door," he says again. "Is that what you have on? Your perfume?"

It clicks. Of course.

"Yes. It's my favorite. I put some on this morning,

like always. That a crime now?" I don't want to give anything away. But I've got to know if they know. About the armored truck thing. "Why is your dog after me?"

"Who said he is 'after' you, ma'am?" the dog guy says.

It's always "ma'am this" and "ma'am that" with these guys. Shouldn't they have a women officer in here? A matron or something? Isn't that standard—with a woman prisoner?

"I meant, what do you mean he's 'hitting' on me?"

"He loves you," the Uniform Two says, smirking.

"You're an ass," I say with as much credibility as I can muster, being this drunk. And he really is.

"Sorry, ma'am. Just a little joke. 'Hitting' means he's picking up a scent."

"Of what?"

"A scent we're looking for. You wouldn't know anything about this, I'm sure. But we're working on a murder case. Robbery, actually, and two murders. The murder of two armored car guards. Several weeks back."

I'm trying to hide the distress on my face.

"No, I don't know," I plead, sounding as ignorant as possible—which is not easy. My heart rate just exploded.

"What, you don't read the papers?" the dog handler asks?

"Actually, not very often. They're so depressing."

"Well, we have a sketchy description of a woman who was driving a car on the bridge that morning. Your face and hair color—they kind of match up."

"I don't have any idea what you're talking about," I lie. I make a puzzled frown. But I don't know if it's believable.

"Well, I'm sure that's probably true," the dog guy says, "but we took Scout here," he says nodding at his mongrel, "down to the vehicle impound lot a half hour ago, and let him sniff around the car again."

He waits. He's wants me to make some kind of mistake. I'm saying nothing.

But I can't bear the silence.

"My car?" I ask innocently.

"No. The car that was used to ram the armored truck—and send it over the bridge rail."

I nod a simple nod that I understand, then shake my head again so he knows I know nothing about this. My chest is working harder than normal, trying to keep up with my heart. I can't help it. And I can't stop it. Unless I can manage to just die. I think every pore in my body is starting to leak sweat.

All three of them stare. Four, with Fido. He's begging for a closer sniff.

"My puppy, here, he's really well trained in this sort of stuff. When he smelled you here in the room, he connected you to that car we just left. The one that collided with the armored truck."

"What?" I play dumb. "You mean, my perfume?"

"Or something else," he says with a smartass look.

"It's a really popular perfume," I tell him, which I know he already knows.

"Yes, I know."

He waits again.

"Can't help you, I guess," I tell the all three of them. Four, if you count the stupid dog.

"Let me talk to you in the hall," Uniform One says to the other two.

Scout's ears perk up, like he's imagining fat doggy biscuits, but he doesn't want to leave me. I'm his new best friend. He has a spooky look in his eyes. It's not hunger, exactly. It's like, he's know something I don't, and isn't about to tell me.

His handler jerks the leash and he bounds out through the door like a two-month old puppy.

I can't tell if I'm still breathing. Maybe I did die.

THIS SEEMS endless. They've been out there in the hall talking for at least half an hour.

What the heck have they done with Brad? In the drunk tank, maybe? Poor guy. Just because he wanted to be nice to me. He's such a killer-good friend.

The door opens. Just the two uniforms this time. Thank you, God. No dog.

"Miss Dennison, is there anything else you think you should tell us about?" the first asks. "While you have the chance," he says, trying to sound ominous.

"I have no idea why you're keeping me here," I say with some more protested innocence and a little faked indignation. "No law against drunk riding is there?"

"Well, be that as it may, I have just this tiny suspicion that you *do* know something about that armored car incident, Miss Dennison. And all the money that went missing." He looks at me real seriously. "Is there something you're not telling us?" He looks at me harder. He waits. "See, how it usually goes with this kind of thing, the longer it goes, the worse it gets. For you. So, if there is something you'd like to tell us, this would be the best time."

I bet I look like a piñata to him. Full of cop candy and investigative goodies—just waiting to be smacked by the right bat.

I shrug, getting more sober by the second.

"No. Really, I don't. Know anything, I mean. I think,

yeah, maybe I did see something in the paper—or was it on TV? About some armored truck wrecking. It went off the interstate bridge, didn't it?"

"Uh-huh."

Nothing. He's giving me no clues. He's still waiting for me to stub my toe. I'm doing my best innocent act. I've practiced that before, too.

"Well, you know I would always want to help the police, any way I could. Kind of our civic duty, right? But I don't know anything—except what I've read, I mean." I shrug bigger this time. I smile, innocently, lavishly.

Uniform Two's eyes perk up. He wants doggy biscuits, too.

"Yeah. Well, I guess we're going to leave it there for tonight, then," Number One says. "I talked with the Prosecutor's office, their guy on call. He says we don't have enough to hold you."

"Not yet, anyway," Number Two adds, with great disappointment. He was looking forward to standing real close to me, fingerprinting me—getting a bigger dose of Red Door. "The prosecutor said what you said. It's a pretty common perfume. Not enough to lock somebody up. Just on suspicion."

"Suspicion of wearing perfume?" I say, a joke to lighten things up. It falls to the floor like a lead balloon.

The first guy looks pretty disappointed, too. Thought he was going to get credit tonight for breaking a big robbery and double-murder case. Probably would have meant a promotion. Maybe a small raise.

Tough luck, Bucko. It's not your night. And it sure as heck is not my night.

Suddenly, he sits on the edge of the table across from me. He returns my smile. Don't know what that's supposed to do. I stay deadpan.

He gives me that penetrating cop look, the *I know you know* look. I play dumb—one thing I'm actually pretty good at. I've been in this rodeo before.

"So, you're going home tonight. Of course, we're not going to let you drive. You're still over the limit, I'm sure. So we'll even give you a ride home."

I break half a smile and exhale too obviously.

"You two?"

"No, Traci," Uniform Two says, "actually the canine unit who was just here, Officer Bragdon and Scout. Seems they're headed uptown, toward your neighborhood. So he offered."

I feel the anxiety start to eat a bigger hole in my stomach. Not the dog, please! But can I say no? Do I want to take a chance on pissing them off—even more? They're already mad because they couldn't get through this perfect little facade of mine.

"Can't I just walk?"

"Uh, not a good idea," he tells me. "You're in kind of a—a vulnerable condition, so to speak. Downtown gets kind of rough this late at night."

No, I am *not* going to press my luck. I'm going home in a canine car. Oh, fun. Maybe Scout will take one of my legs home to his doghouse. For supper.

Steady, Traci.

"OK. The dog car. I get it. But can you tell me what happened to Brad?"

"Mr. Schott? He's been booked in on DUI. Blew a point-one-six on the breathalyzer. He'll be spending the weekend, and see the judge on Monday. Unless somebody bails him out."

Oh, God. Kenny is going to explode. We're supposed to fly down to Florida tonight! Think, Traci. Think.

"Well, I could, right? I can bail him out, can't I? I mean—well, he was doing me a favor, driving me home. So I wouldn't drive drunk."

"Your home, or his?" Mr. Nosy-Parker Uniform Two has to ask.

"No, it's not— No, see, we're just good friends."

Nosy-Parker nods, knowingly. Thinks he knows everything. Jerk.

The first guy, at least, is trying to be polite.

"Yes, you could post the bail for Schott if you want. Nineteen hundred and seventy-six dollars. But you can't drive him home."

No way can I afford that. My brain won't handle all this. And the more I blab, the closer I'm going to come to making a really huge mistake.

"OK, wait. Did you give him a phone call?"

"Yes."

"Who'd he call?"

"I can't tell you that."

Figures.

Then it hits me. My brain just thawed! Brad gave me his envelope just before we got to the restaurant—the envelope of cash Broadman handed out to everyone. I shoved it in my purse—with mine. They just bring me my purse, and I've got plenty to bail Brad out.

"Where's my purse?"

"The sergeant has it locked up. For safe keeping."

"Would you bring it here, please?"

"Why, of course, Miss Dennison. Anything at all, for you," he smiles. And I almost think he means it. Is *he* hitting on me, now?

Lots of canines around here.

They both leave. I'll bail out Brad and—wait—

Oh no! Oh my God, have I totally lost it? My brain

thawed another layer. Traci, you idiot! Don't you remember where all that cash came from? Soggy, wet, wrinkled up cash—from the armored truck?

Oh, this can't be happening! What if the desk sergeant got snoopy and found those two envelopes in my purse? What if they have the serial numbers of the cash stolen from that truck?

Oh, we are so, *so* screwed . . . .

Uniform Two comes back, alone, with my purse. He drops it on the table.

"There you are, Miss. Will there be anything else, Miss?" he asks with a barely-masked snide tone.

"Thank you, officer. You're such a gentleman," I say sweetly, thinking he's a complete moron.

I wait. I'm watching him, now. He doesn't say a word about all the cash.

They didn't check it? Or they didn't connect it? Or, am I just sitting here stupidly waiting for the other shoe to drop?

Do I dare even open my purse?

Well, I'm sure not sitting in this stink-hole the rest of the night.

"Did, ah, did your sergeant go through this?" I ask as innocently as I can manage.

"No. No, see, you're detained, but you're not actually under arrest. So we don't inventory personal stuff. Unless you're under arrest. It's against regs."

I nod, saying, "Sure, I see."

"Should we look through your purse, Traci?"

I try not to look too startled.

"Why?"

"You tell me. We don't have a warrant, but we could go through it OK—with your consent, I mean."

I pretend I'm thinking about this, but actually I'm not

thinking even a little bit. I've gone numb upstairs.

"Well, I don't know," I tell him. I hum and haw just a second. "I have some personal stuff in here. You know. Girl stuff? And some things about one of my patrons at the gym," I say, making this up on the spot," that's pretty—ah—well—sensitive. Private, you know?" I smile.

"You don't want me to go through your purse then?" he asks with an insinuating tone.

"No. Not really."

The dog handler cop suddenly pops his head back in the door, minus the dog. Thank goodness.

"Hey Jack, the friend Mr. Schott called just showed up and posted his bail. A Mr. Hamilton. Says he's a friend of Mizz Dennison here, too. He'll drive them both home."

There is a God. Thank you, thank you.

I zip the purse more tightly shut—so tight I almost rip the little tabby thing off the zipper. I wait, smiling at them. The two cops take a sideways stare at each other. They're probably wondering, *What did we miss?*

The uniformed guy turns back to me with a fake smile and says, "Well, thanks for allowing us to show you our evening hospitality room tonight, Miss Dennison."

The dog guy offers me his arm, adding, "You're free to go. I'll escort you down to reception." He jerks his arm into a perfect "V."

Smart ass.

I brush past him and march blindly down the hall as quickly as my wobbly, trembling legs will take me.

Twenty

The Reporter

Brad Schott nearly went berserk that night, locked in the drunk tank at the Philadelphia PD. Traci went nearly as crazy worrying about him. I can still remember the emotion in Brad's voice, and the look in Traci's eyes, when they each recounted, separately, this part of the story. It was as if they had both walked barefoot across a bed of razor wire that night, and it only got worse once Kenny showed up to post Brad's bail.

"WHAT THE hell were you thinking!" Kenny shouted angrily at Brad and Traci as he pulled away from the police headquarters. "What? What!"

"Guess we weren't thinking," Brad said quietly, trying to calm Kenny's fury.

"No. Really? *Really!* And the whole time—idiots!—the whole time, you both had all that cash on you?"

"Well, see, I gave mine to Traci—" Brad started to explain but was cut off.

"From the armored truck!" Kenny almost screamed.

"And that didn't register? A little bell didn't go off in your heads, saying, *Stupid alert, stupid alert!*"

He was yelling, but trying to control it. If his face got any redder, Brad thought, blood vessels would start popping under the skin.

"No, Kenny," Traci said, nearly sober now, "it didn't register. OK? Because we didn't exactly plan to get pulled over for drunk driving."

"Oh, no? This wasn't some kind of clever little trick you two cooked up—to just blow up the whole damned plan at the last minute? A plan I've spent weeks—and almost a million bucks on? You were just being a little careless, right?" he said angrily with three levels of insinuation in his tone.

"We went out to supper, Kenny. I just had a couple too many!" Brad said, getting irate at Kenny's overblown reaction. He was one of Kenny's best friends but Kenny was treating him like an imbecile.

"So you were driving drunk because she was too drunk to drive?" Kenny said, exasperated. "Ok, now I get it!" He took a breath. "You realize, we are this close?" Kenny railed on. "*This close* to pulling the whole thing off. And you two go and almost ruin the whole plan! I thought you were both a whole lot smarter than this!" He stopped only long enough for a deep breath. "How on earth did they *not* piece together Traci and the armored truck heist? How stupid can cops be? Still, they could have. That's the point. They *could* have!" He was almost slobbering with anger and slapped the wheel so hard the car jerked over the center line. He was probably more dangerous behind the wheel right then than Brad had been earlier, driving drunk.

It all broke down into silence. None of the three could say anything rational for another five minutes.

"Look, Kenny, I'm sorry," Traci finally said. *"We're* sorry. We'll be more careful."

"You damn-sure better!" He drove another entire block seeing purple. Then he glanced over at Traci beside him. "You still have the cash?"

"Of course. I have both our envelopes in my purse. Thank God they didn't search it."

"You and your silly God," Kenny sneered.

This shut Traci up again. When Kenny was mad, he was always this rude. It seemed to come out of nowhere.

Traci still couldn't believe her luck. The cops had been so close to solving the armored truck robbery—closer than they could have possibly imagined. A simple, routine "officer safety" check of a woman's purse during the initial traffic stop, and the whole Grand Slam scheme would have gone up like a mushroom cloud.

Yet Traci had walked out of the police department without a hitch. Miraculous, she thought. Regardless, Kenny was still fuming.

"Thank goodness the stupid cops are dumber than you two!" he said, starting to get hoarse. "Oh—and you might want to know—when Broadman heard about this, he almost pulled the plug on his whole crew! Said he wasn't going to risk working with this kind of stupidity."

"Well, he—" Brad caught himself, breaking off before he said what he really thought of Jason Broadman. "But you calmed him down, right?"

"Yeah. Eventually. After I managed to calm myself down!"

Kenny took a corner hard and almost clipped a parked Mazda that was too far out from the curb. He recovered, and took several deep breaths. Apparently he was still trying to calm himself down. The only good thing, as far as Brad and Traci could tell, was that he had sobered up since late afternoon.

Imagine if he had shown up at the police station plowed, Traci was thinking. Kenny must have laid off the booze after the briefing ended, so the odds were good that they would still make it to the airport in time to meet the others, assuming Kenny kept at least one eye on the road.

Kenny turned toward the back seat and scowled at Brad, then looked at Traci again. As angry as he was, Brad hoped that Kenny still cared about them both. They were his friends. As far as Brad knew, he and Traci were probably the only really genuine friends Kenny had ever had. Because of how rich Kenny's family was, Brad knew it had been difficult for Kenny to find friends who didn't just want to leach off his money and his free-wheeling spending habits. At times, Brad himself felt like one of the leaches. For whatever reason, Kenny didn't seem to mind. Besides, Brad and Traci had hung in with Kenny all these weeks on the Cayman plan. Even Traci, after the trauma of killing the two guards in the armored truck, hadn't quit.

Kenny couldn't ask for two better friends, Brad told himself. So Kenny was mad. He'd get over it.

It was about then that Kenny, with a forced calm, said, "Anyway, change of plans. You two are getting on a different plane. You're flying on to Jamaica tonight."

"What?" Traci said, startled. She stared at him in disbelief for the second time today. "Kenny, what are you talking about?"

"We're going to your place so you can get clothes, then we're stopping at the hotel so Brad can pack what he needs. Broadman is booking you last-minute tickets right now. We're sending you ahead to Jamaica. You're going to hide out there—and I mean that, you're going to *hide!*—until the rest of us fly in on the thirteenth."

"But—" Brad stammered.

"Look, you two, I'm not going to take any more chances on the cops tying Traci into the armored truck robbery! After your little escapade tonight, you both need to be out of here. Gone!"

"Well, but what about finishing up all the logistics while we're in Florida?" Brad asked. "I was supposed to help you with that."

"Yeah, buddy, but now you're not. You two are getting an all-expense paid mini-vacation, got it? Jamaica. All by your lonesome. Broadman will help me finish up in Florida." He eyed Traci. "And you *both* better behave. Hide—and behave."

He smacked the turn signal lever like he was whipping a mule, then looked back at Brad again. Brad knew the look.

"I'm sorry, Brad. I just can't afford any more screw-ups. Not this far into the game. OK, so you were careless tonight, but it was really, *really* stupid. I just can't afford that. Broadman agrees. The only way he—and all his people—stay in, is if you two fly the coop. Tonight!"

"But Kenny—" Traci tried to say.

"End of discussion! It'll keep you out of reach—just in case the cops decide after all that they have more interest in either of you."

Traci swallowed hard at this. She was not about to tell Kenny about the dog, and the perfume—which he had bought for her last Christmas. Better that she just put a noose around her own neck than to set off another Kenny-tirade.

Then Brad's mind began to cut and paste.

"But, wait, wait. That won't work. I'll miss my bond return date in court on Tuesday," Brad said. "Don't you think *that's* going to set off bells and sirens with the cops?"

"Don't worry about it. I'll pay a lawyer to go in for some kind of continuance or something. They may look, but they won't find you. You're going to be *hiding,* remember? Broadman is booking you both under false names."

"But our passports—" Traci began.

"I said, don't worry! I'll bring them with me when I fly down on the thirteenth. Broadman has that covered. He's got a friend who can make up false passports in one hour flat. We're stopping off at the guy's place on the way to the airport. You'll be Mr. and Mrs. Hawkins in Jamaica. Honeymooners." He gave them the look again. "Just don't rehearse the roles too far."

He laughed mostly to himself, thinking that could never happen anyway. Traci was his. He knew it. She knew it. Brad certainly knew it.

And they were, after all, his best friends.

"Whatever," Traci said, disgusted with Kenny, but mostly with herself. She stared out the passenger window as the bright yellow street lights strolled by. It wasn't raining, but it should have been, she felt. A gloom hung over her and, it seemed, over the entire darkened city.

She turned back and looked at Kenny. She was mad at him, yes, but she did still love him. Through foolishness, she had almost destroyed his whole plan and all the hours and money that he had poured into it so far. She stared down at the floorboard. She had just spent several hours at the police department, about a sixteenth of an inch away from three life sentences for a double homicide and robbery. Kenny had gotten her and Brad out of the mess, clean as a whistle. She hoped.

But she could still smell the foul breath of that horrid dog.

Twenty-One

The Reporter

The elaborate plan for Kenny's invasion of Grand Cayman was moving, but almost too quickly, now. After five days of practice runs in south Florida, the Cayman assault teams and all their equipment had been flown to Kingston, Jamaica for final staging.

The story gets complicated here and begins to sound a bit disjointed. That's because it was. In order to piece the events back together, I had to talk with dozens of different players after the fact—both from Kenny's crew and the Cayman authorities—and then thread together a narrative of how the attack actually went down. As you'll discover, recreating the sequence of things was not easy.

KENNY HAMILTON was obviously psyched-up. Everybody around him at the hotel in Jamaica on the morning of May 14th could see it. If he had ever experienced a completely "manic" episode in his life, it was now. He had slept little in the last two weeks, perhaps four or five hours a night, often interrupted by an hour or two being up and at his computer, sweating over lists of team assignments and equipment for the assault.

His Grand Slam plan had fallen together and he felt it was superb. Everyone had arrived in Jamaica on the private charter flight from Miami yesterday. Early this evening, the four team leaders and their minions would hop two yachts and sail, or motor, toward Grand Cayman. The day after tomorrow, May 16th, the assault would be launched.

"And they have no idea what's coming," Kenny bragged to Rick Kell and Ronnie Vaughn at lunch time, a smug swagger in his voice.

He was already relishing his coming victory over the little island nation, and already planning how he would conduct business as the new governor of the Cayman Islands.

THE SUPPOSED Mr. and Mrs. William Haskins had successfully completed their honeymoon of six nights and five and a half days at the same plush hotel in Kingston. They were successful mainly because both had managed to be faithful to Kenny's wishes, only pretending to be married, and had kept their hands off each other completely. Traci had claimed the opulent, oval, king-sized bed in the extravagant Honeymoon Suite. Brad had taken the "full-sized," pull-out double bed in the living room, undoubled. Its size, he found, was suitable for a ten year old.

Brad had always prided himself on his willpower, but for a couple of weeks before leaving Philadelphia he had begun to doubt that he had the will to carry through on the Grand Slam plan with Kenny. Now, though, after having spent six nights with Traci Dennison alone in their luxurious suite, with a huge walk-in shower, and a private hot tub on the suite's lanai—and both of them somewhat short on clothing—Brad had discovered a greater force of willpower beyond anything he could have believed of himself. Traci, like the room service, kept looking more and more delectable each day. Especially in the evenings, when she would put on something thin and frilly that really showed off her lovely figure, Brad had to talk himself over and over into his loyalty to Kenny.

"I talked myself to sleep every night—reminding myself that I was doing all this for my best friend," Brad later told me.

I could see the pained expression in his face as he recounted his feelings several weeks after the whole thing went down, and went sour. After being forced to share the hotel suite with Traci, Brad had already begun to doubt that the whole plan was worth it. He was actually glad when Kenny and the others finally arrived in Jamaica. It felt to Brad like a huge backpack full of wild monkeys was lifted off his shoulders.

"And you know, I was glad that I could smile when I greeted Kenny in the hotel lobby—a smile without any hidden guilt."

He was even more elated to learn that Kenny had now rented for Brad a private room of his own. Brad's eye narrowed as he talked with me.

"As much as I loved her—maybe because of that— not having to spend another night alone with Traci was like being let loose from a torture rack," he confessed.

Surprisingly, Kenny also rented a private room for himself, leaving Traci alone in the Honeymoon Suite. Brad had been sure that Kenny would check into the suite with her as soon as he arrived from Florida. He didn't.

"But then, Kenny was always full of surprises," Brad said as he stared at the wall of his cell in George Town. "I was glad to see my good friend again. But friendship—for me at least—always seems to come with a lot of personal pain."

Not surprisingly, over those days and nights alone in the Honeymoon Suite, his friendship with Traci had grown into something even more outrageously difficult than his loyalty to Kenny.

"It was—I don't know—really peculiar. How could my time with Traci—who is *so* enamoring, so wonderful to be with—how could it be such a damned nightmare? I'd just lay there and wonder about it at night, trying to fall asleep on that stupid couch. The thoughts spinning through my head—it was like being stuck on an amusement park ride after the operator has gone home."

What he didn't realize—and what I learned from talking privately with Traci—was that she had struggled staying faithful to Kenny, too, maybe more than Brad had. It wasn't easy because she had begun to have real feelings for Brad, too. It didn't help that they were forced to act out the playful role of newlyweds around the hotel. Each day was devoured trying to figure out something fun to do, when underneath they both felt miserable. Just sitting in one of the restaurants, poor Brad would almost melt onto the floor every time Traci smiled at him—which she did more and more.

Brad put it perfectly.

"I've always heard misery loves company. But I never knew the company of someone you love can bring such misery."

Separately, a week or so later, Traci drew out her

feelings for me.

Ever since that night at the Philadelphia Police Department, Traci had felt drawn closer to Brad. She had developed a deeper respect for him as a man. Then, after nearly a week thrown so closely together in Jamaica, she began to feel an unexpected desire to just stay close to him.

This surprised her, yet it didn't.

"Brad is a lovable guy," she told me, "and an incredible friend. You know, despite his failings. And one thing I learned—by watching how he acted toward Kenny—is that Brad is loyal to a fault."

That, from Traci's perspective, was nothing but positive.

Her own faithfulness to Kenny, though, was just as important. It was one of the few virtues she had left to cling to, and she didn't want to relinquish it. All right, she was now a murderess, and she had agreed to take part in an outrageous plan to steal an entire Caribbean nation. The least she could do, considering, was cling to this last fragile virtue, her faithfulness to the one man she had ever felt really in love with for more than two weeks. And that was Kenny Hamilton.

"I can tell that wasn't easy," I said to Traci as we chatted.

"Well, there *were* a couple of goodnight kisses between me and Brad," she confided, "and a lot of fawning over each other around the hotel. But we had to be convincing honeymooners. You know?"

I watched the puzzling expression that crept over her face. It was that of a child overwhelmed in a candy store who can't quite make up her mind.

"But the kisses were always in our room," she added hastily, "and they were very careful kisses. If you know what I mean."

I did.

"We didn't let it go too far. A sweet kiss from a friend, then off to our separate beds. It had to stop there." She was silent for a moment. "That's what we told ourselves, anyway."

Her expression shifted. It said the candy store was now permanently closed.

JASON BROADMAN had rented a well-sound-proofed banquet room at the hotel that afternoon for a final briefing, so Kenny could give the whole crew one last pep talk. There was no going back, once they boarded the two yachts that evening.

Broadman several times during the meeting dangled the promise of lots more cash under everyone's nose, and each could smell it. Most everyone was half-listening to Kenny and half-daydreaming about the beautiful tropical island that would soon be their home, and under their control. The taste of power was already in their stomachs.

Brad had special trouble paying attention. Traci's tan had deepened remarkably over the last few days there in Jamaica and she just seemed to be exuding warmth through her radiant skin. He found it hard, more than ever, to keep his eyes off her.

"I guess Kenny knew what he was doing when he put Traci and me on different landing teams," Brad begrudgingly admitted to me. "If she had been with me all the time, heck, I wouldn't be able to concentrate on the task at hand—even a little."

This time, Kenny didn't belabor things. He wrapped up the meeting quickly. All their equipment had already been stowed onto the yachts earlier in the day. Kenny himself had all his stuff loaded onto the high-tech-equipped catamaran that he had purchased for his command post. It's most recent owner was an NBA player who overextended several of his secret, tax-sheltered bank accounts—two of them on Grand Cayman—and was forced to put the cat up for sale. It was built as a racing craft, so the cabin area and facilities were limited, but it would suffice for Kenny, the pilot, and the two-man crew while he oversaw the landings on Cayman from offshore.

As the meeting ended, everyone headed to another ballroom next door, which Broadman had also rented, and where Kenny had a fabulous, late lunch waiting for them all.

"Eat up," Kenny told his little mercenary army. "Can't steal an island on an empty stomach!" he laughed.

He went straight for the head of the food line, Broadman in tow, still discussing last minute details.

Brad lagged back toward the end of the line, feeling like a used piece of furniture.

THEY LEFT Jamaica right on time just before sunset. The first yacht, heading northwesterly, would cut across south of Little Cayman and head offshore along the north coast of Grand Cayman, reaching their anchor spot sometime during the early morning hours of the 16th. The second yacht would follow roughly the same route, but would then veer more westerly to come in along the south coast of the island.

Both yachts would anchor about five miles off the coast and wait for daybreak. The teams would then load into their assigned inflatable speedboats for the final sprint ashore.

All went perfectly and on schedule that evening. Kenny met up with his catamaran pilot, Linford Reid, about 7:30 p.m., several docks down from the hotel. They chatted, verified their own later departure time, then Kenny walked back to the hotel. The cat would clip across the Caribbean much faster than the two larger yachts, so Kenny was in no hurry.

He had other business at hand.

Once he was sure Traci had boarded her yacht and it had departed, Kenny grabbed his large duffle bag and headed for the catamaran. On his other arm, also retrieved from his private hotel room, was an exceptionally beautiful, brown-skinned brunette who had been one of three stewardesses on their chartered flight from Miami to Jamaica the day before. Without anyone else knowing, he had invited her along "for a little ride" on his new catamaran, promising her some "unexpected excitement."

As she herself would later tell me, "I knew it was nothing serious. For Kenny, I was just an evening or two of entertainment. We would have two long nights crossing over to Grand Cayman. It sounded like fun."

The young woman called herself Kylaia. When she first told him her name, Kenny looked doubtful that it was her real name—but it didn't seem to matter. When she told him she was half Hawaiian, Kenny looked even more doubtful. Her rich, dark skin certainly spoke of a tropical origin, but since her present home was in Kingston, he no doubt figured—correctly—that she was actually part native Jamaican with an Anglo-American father.

Whatever her origins, she could see Kenny didn't really care. She was beautiful and very friendly, and for Kenny that was all that seemed to matter.

Kylaia grew up poor and could smell money from a hundred miles off. She could just about taste Kenny's money, she told me, judging from his demeanor, his clothes, and the hotel suite he snagged for them. But he kept her away from the meetings and meals with his friends, for obvious reasons.

"I didn't care. I realized soon enough—on the second morning out of Jamaica—what he and his people were actually up to."

I have no way of knowing for sure, and Kylaia wouldn't say, but I wonder if maybe Kenny was thinking he could keep her. A kind of side girlfriend, a mistress on Grand Cayman, once he was settled there with Traci. From what I've learned about Kenny Hamilton's character, I bet the idea would have thrilled him to death.

ABOUT 2:15 a.m. the first night at sea, Kenny was awakened from his half-slumber next to Kylaia by a quiet knock on the door of the single, tiny guest cabin on the catamaran.

"Go away," was his wish, as he was still mostly asleep.

"Need to talk to you, sir. Urgent," said the voice of Linford Reid, the captain.

Kenny emerged from the cabin door in boxer shorts. His tussled hair looked like he had spent several hours next to a hurricane.

More or less true.

Reid was brushing his own long, sun-washed-blond hair back along his head in a nervous manner.

"Yeah. What?" Kenny asked.

"A problem, sir. On one of the yachts."

"Which one?"

"The one heading to the south shore. For Pedro Saint

James."

"So? What's wrong?"

"Well, they're adrift at the moment, sir."

"What are you talking about? It's nearly a new boat! How can they have problems?"

"Well, not exactly new, sir. Just a new paint job. Anyway, ah, it seems their electrical system has failed. A dead short somewhere. And it's not only killed the engine but their navigational computers, too."

"Can't they put up sail?" Kenny asked, still sleepy and foggy, a look of bewilderment masking his drawn face.

"There's not much wind tonight, sir. And they're without running lights. Couldn't legally move if they wanted to."

"Are you kidding me?" Kenny griped, though he realized Reid had absolutely nothing to do with it.

"I think we can catch them sir, and lend help," Reid went on, "I mean, they are dead in the water. And we're pretty fast."

"The south yacht," Kenny confirmed.

"Yes, sir."

Kenny looked distracted, staring out across the dark, starlit waves.

"It's the one with your Number One and Number Two teams onboard," Reid said, which Kenny knew. "And Miss Dennison."

"Yeah, yeah." Kenny obviously knew this, too. He shook his head. "No point in us trying to catch them, Reid. I know nothing about ships, or boats—whatever. I'd be no help."

"But, sir, actually, I know quite a bit about marine wiring and—"

"No," Kenny said abruptly.

His gaze pulled back from the distance and bored into Reid's eyes. It was perfectly evident to Reid that Kenny did not *want* to catch up to the disabled yacht. It was equally obvious why. Reid glanced at the cabin door behind Kenny which Kenny had discreetly held nearly shut.

"There must be someone on board the yacht who can fix the problem!" Kenny said, getting more agitated. "How could something this stupid happen?"

"Well, yes, I'm sure the captain has a couple of good maintenance crew on board. And, well, maybe I could talk to them by radio, sir. Help walk them through some diagnostics. If their radio's battery holds out."

"Brilliant, Linford. Thank you. That's a really good idea. Get on the horn with them. I really need to get some more sleep," Kenny said drowsily, drawing a slow agitated breath.

I can imagine, Reid thought as he walked away back toward the even smaller helmsman's cabin.

TWO HOURS had been lost by the time Reid was able to talk the crew aboard the south yacht through possible problems and probable fixes for their electrical system. The culprit ended up being a main supply bus fuse that was nearly buried in a small wiring tunnel deep amidships.

One of the younger crewmen, with very thin but muscular arms, was able to reach it without tearing out half the underside of the main deck. They had only one spare fuse that was close to the size needed, although it was rated at a lower amperage. The yacht captain radioed Reid that they were underway again, and praying the replacement fuse would not blow like its predecessor. Because if it did, the yacht could be stranded indefinitely in the waters south of Cuba, far east of Grand Cayman.

"I'm fairly certain Mr. Hamilton would not be happy in that event," the yacht captain told Reid over the radio.

Reid looked up at the array and brilliance of the stars peppering the night sky, like tiny phosphorescent creatures clinging to the ceiling of a pitch-black cave. He thought about waking Hamilton and his friend a second time, but then thought better of it. He realized that it would be, for Kenny, a short night.

Drowsy now himself, Reid reached down and kicked up the throttles of his two large outboard motors nearly to their limit and pushed the catamaran west toward the spot where they would eventually anchor off the northeast coast of Grand Cayman. From there, Kenny Hamilton planned to command his grand invasion of the helpless little island.

V.
CAPTURE THE
FLAG

Twenty-Two

The Reporter

At 8:35 on the morning of May 16th, Brad Schott and Arielle Kemper strolled through the front doors of Comptrell Trust and Savings Bank in George Town. Brad carried a large, leather folio case with copies of the blue prints for the building that Bryan Cantor had stolen off Comptrell's website. Arielle carried a smaller, brown leather folio case with dummied up notes about the supposed plans they were about to finalize to fix the water leaks in Comptrell's basement and vault.

Arielle was instantly recognized by the bank's Senior Vice-president, who promptly escorted the pair into the office of Frank Bennington, Chief Operating Officer of Comptrell. Bennington greeted them both warmly, offering them coffee or tea, and sweets. Brad and Arielle indulged the offer for only about five minutes. They were anxious, they told Bennington, to get started downstairs, rechecking their dimensions and the existing wiring and plumbing. Once these were verified, they could finalize the remodel plans that their engineers back in the States had sent along with them.

Bennington was anxious for the work to go forward, too. The chairman of the bank's Board of Directors had been pressuring him for the last year to fix the water problems, because the resulting dampness in the basement was driving off potential customers who wanted to use Comptrell's highly secured vault for certain unnamed valuables. This little-noted detail about seepage at Comptrell had shown up in a Cayman news account several months earlier, an article which ended up online and became the germ of Kenny Hamilton's idea on how to use the leaks as his "in" to the bank.

After pleasantries and a second Danish, Brad asked Bennington to escort them downstairs to the vault. Unexpectedly, Bennington excused himself to get to an important client meeting and turned them over to the bank's senior security manager, Jim Cartwright.

Brad grabbed up his large blueprints case, which also carried one of the SIG assault rifles that Broadman had bought for the teams. Arielle, in her smaller folio case, had one of the shorter assault pistols, and two extra clips of ammunition loaded to capacity—with blanks. As sophisticated as Comptrell's internal security was, they did not have metal detectors installed by the front doors, as Arielle and Bryan Cantor had discovered on their earlier trip. So Brad and Arielle were able to smuggle the concealed weapons in without triggering any noisy, troublesome alarms.

They followed Jim Cartwright down a wide, marbled staircase into the lower hallway of the bank. Cartwright had no sooner unlocked the outer gate leading into the vault cage when Brad and Arielle both produced their hidden weapons.

"Sit in that chair, there!" Arielle commanded him.

Her beautiful features normally hid her naturally brusque demeanor which she now unleashed. She gave Cartwright a forceful shove toward the metal-framed chair.

Either she had been watching too many recent adventure movies with female heroines, Cartwright thought, or she was genuinely not a nice person underneath her lovely facade. Facing two assault guns, he didn't want to explore which it was. He moved quickly and sat. Arielle trained the barrel of her machine pistol at his head.

"How the hell did you get those guns onto the island?" Cartwright asked indignantly.

"Shut up," Arielle told him.

Brad grabbed the small ring of keys from Cartwright's hand and quickly relocked the outer gate of the vault cage that was composed of reinforced, vertical steel bars like a prison. He pulled two sets of handcuffs from cases hidden under his sports jacket and cuffed each of Cartwright's arms to arms of the sturdy chair. Brad could see that Cartwright might be able to move the chair, and himself, to try to escape or to summon help, but Arielle's assault pistol pointing at the security man convinced Brad that Cartwright was not anxious to test her seriousness, or her resolve to use the weapon.

Cartwright, of course, had no way of knowing both weapons were loaded with blanks.

Brad patted around some more in Cartwright's jacket and slacks pockets.

"I have no weapons," he informed the pair. "You, on the other hand, seem to have come for more than measurements." He gave Arielle an emotionless stare. "Though it seems you already have the basic measurements you need for your kind of work," he said with a not-very-subtle sneer.

Arielle sneered. Brad didn't get it.

"Enjoy them while you can," Arielle scowled at Cartwright. "I might be the last woman you ever see in this life." She walked calmly to the seated, well-restrained man and slapped him hard across the face.

Brad saw it and grimaced, as if sharing the pain. He had never imagined that sweet little Arielle Kemper would suddenly get so rough or mean. He quickly grabbed her free arm, which seemed poised for another strike.

"Come on, Arielle, work to do," he told her, coaxing her away from Cartwright.

Arielle blew Cartwright a mock kiss. Cartwright's expression never changed from one of deep irritation and defeated anger.

Brad reached down and followed a small wire that ran from an earpiece Cartwright was wearing down to a small two-way radio that was hidden in his inner suit coat pocket. Brad yanked both the radio and earpiece away. He flicked the radio's power switch off and stuffed them into his own jacket.

"Don't want you chitchatting with your helpers upstairs," Brad grinned. He had a sudden feeling of power.

He had just taken over a bank.

With two more large rings of keys that he pilfered out of Cartwright's coat, Brad began experimenting until he found the one that opened the main vault door. The door had a combination lock, too, that overrode the simple key lock system, but he and Arielle knew that the combination mechanism would already be unlocked, another detail she and Cantor had discovered on their previous "inspection" visit. The combination system was routinely unlocked early each morning just before the bank opened, to speed up customer service throughout the day. Bank personnel could then enter the vault with a simple, large key—kept by Cartwright or one of his men.

At the instant Brad turned the key in the lock on the massive door, an ear-blistering alarm horn began to yelp loudly throughout the lower hallway.

"Oh my, I'm sorry," Cartwright glowered, "did I forget to disarm the alarm? Well, gosh darn." He glared at the two intruders. "Look, kids, I don't want to sit here and get a massive headache. That keypad there, Mr. Schott. Four-seven-eight-two-nine will silence it."

Brad punched in the code and the alarm went quiet.

"But don't worry yourselves," Cartwright added with the tone of an undertaker, "it will continue to sound at the Central Police Station a few blocks from here. I hope you won't mind some uninvited, uniformed company." He gave them a forced smile.

"Glad we guessed that one right," Arielle told Cartwright. "Your friends upstairs should be greeting a bundle of police officers any second," she glared. "We've counted on that. Your life is our insurance plan—to keep them upstairs. We thought it would be Bennington. You're not worth near as much, of course. But I figure you'll do." She turned her back on him as if he was her latest jilted boyfriend.

Brad stepped to a phone handset that was mounted on the wall near the gate they had just come through. He waited only a few seconds before someone upstairs picked up the intercom.

"Hi, yes, by the way, we really aren't measuring anything down here. We're robbing the vault. So, just let all the arriving officers know that we are heavily armed with assault weapons and a half-dozen grenades, and the moment we see a face on the stairs, Mr. Cartwright will be shot several times in the back."

Brad knew that he and Arielle had nothing but blanks in the guns, and he made up the bit about grenades on the spot. But he, Arielle, Kenny, and everyone else on the Grand Slam crew were counting on the bluff working.

"And the elevator doors over there," Brad added, "better stay shut. Because if those doors open, whoever appears will not get through them alive."

Brad clipped the handset back into its cradle. With Arielle's help, they took hold of the heavy chair that held Cartwright and dragged it to about eight feet away from the steel-barred gate that led back out into the vault foyer. They positioned him facing the gate, his back to themselves, so he couldn't watch them. They made sure he was far out of reach of the gate and the phone, just in case he tried to get brave while their backs were turned.

Armed with the two rings of Cartwright's master keys, it was now a simple matter for Brad and Arielle to start trying the keys on the safe deposit boxes inside the vault itself. Brad began flipping through the keys, looking at the number stamped into each one, and looking at numbers on some of the safe deposit boxes.

"I always used to think that a bank kept only one key for each box, and gave the second one needed to the renter," Arielle told Brad. "But good old Mr. Bennington let it slip on our last visit that, actually, the bank always keeps a copy of the renter's key, too. Because people always lose theirs, then they show up whining and demanding that the bank open up their box for them." She laughed. "Our good luck, huh?"

"Works for me," Brad chuckled as he started trying various keys in different boxes.

It took him several minutes to figure out that the key and box numbers were not just a simple match. There was some kind of coding involved. He could have asked Cartwright for help, but he could see from the inflamed and disgusted look on the security man's face that it would be pointless to ask. Cartwright was not about to help facilitate a robbery of the bank he was very highly paid to protect, even though he thought his life was on the line.

After just a few minutes, Brad deciphered the numbering code. It was a simple matter of matching the letter prefixes on the keys and boxes, and then reversing the last two of six numbers on the key, which then matched the numbers on its box.

"Not very brilliant, Cartwright," Brad called as he unlocked the first box. "A six-year old with one of those toy computers could have come up with something better than this," he added as he explained the trick to Arielle.

Cartwright made a grunt.

Arielle took the second ring of keys and went to work, unlocking boxes as quickly as she could. She was not tidy. She yanked the inner metal containers out of the security boxes and tossed them down noisily onto the marble floor, creating a terrible racket.

"Are you this messy at home?" Brad asked jokingly.

"Are you my mother?"

No, nor your father, thank goodness, Brad said to himself.

RICK KELL was yelling across the parking lot of the soccer field at Old Man's Bay along the north shore of Grand Cayman, trying to get Anson Dahlgren's attention. Dahlgren frowned back at Kell, pointing to his own radio that was clipped to his lightweight, black windbreaker, which was now soaking wet.

Kell felt foolish having to be reminded, but he was very queasy from the choppy surf coming ashore in the inflatable boats and still felt disoriented. Like Traci Dennison, Kell was one of those people who could develop seasickness just standing on a beach watching the waves. But he wanted to appear tough for his men, so he had refused the motion-sickness pills the yacht captain had been handing out that morning just before the teams boarded their boats to come ashore.

Kell reached and keyed his radio.

"Dahlgren, where're your other boats?" he demanded.

Dahlgren, who didn't like being yelled at, answered with a sharp edge in his voice, "How the hell should I know? We got separated about two miles out—in that black rain squall that blew up out of nowhere."

"Yeah, well I've lost track of one of mine, too," Kell hollered over the radio, the stiff and steady wind still blustering around them on shore. "I thought these kind of squalls weren't supposed to happen down here this time of year."

"They're not! Don't worry. The others'll find their way ashore pretty quick," Dahlgren predicted, though not convinced himself. "They sure aren't going to stay out there in that deluge we just came through. Not if they can help it!"

The teams were dressed in dark assault outfits, but no one planned on rain. Everyone was soaked through to the skin from the sudden, powerful storm that had caught them unaware.

Kell worked his way along the shoreline, collecting his teammates who had made it ashore in a second boat just behind his. His third boat was still missing. As best he could tell, two of Dahlgren's boats were still out.

He switched to a master channel and radioed Kenny Hamilton who was somewhere offshore on his catamaran.

"Commander, we're ashore, some of us, but some got tossed off course in a rain squall that hit us out of nowhere."

Kenny came on the air.

"Yeah, we saw the black clouds. Not supposed to happen. Damnit!"

"Well, my team's here, most of us. But only part of Team Four is ashore. Dahlgren is searching. I think they're short two boats. We're assuming they'll make it in pretty soon. But we can't spot them, so we've no idea where they might come ashore."

"Send a couple of your team out in the vans—check along the coast, east and west of your position."

"Likely west of us, sir," Kell replied, "the wind's pretty strong from the east out there."

"Do it, then—do it!" Kenny called, his voice riled, and his nerves already fraying.

After the breakdown and delay on the other yacht the first night out from Jamaica, this was the last thing Kenny expected, or needed. He knew Brad and Arielle were already at the bank. They had called in on Arielle's radio just before entering the place, right on time.

"Sit tight!" Hamilton ordered Kell over the radio. "You, too, Team Four leader," he ordered Dahlgren. "Let me know as soon as you have the rest of your teams found."

"Yes, sir," Dahlgren responded, the frustration in his deep voice obvious.

"I need both your teams ready to move out at a moment's notice," Kenny went on. "If I need you to go,

I can't sit around here picking my nose and waiting. Understood?"

"Yes, sir," both men answered over the top of each other.

Kell scrambled and grabbed a young but hyped-up member of his team named Justin, shoved him into one of the rented vans, and sent him off west down the coastal road, hoping to spot their stragglers coming ashore.

BRAD SCHOTT stood in the bank vault like a statue, dumbfounded, staring down at an open security box on the floor, its long, metal lid flipped open.

Arielle, who had just opened it, also stood frozen— after taking a very large step backward as if it was a rattlesnake. Her mouth hung half-open. She was unable to speak.

It was one of the largest boxes they had pulled out so far, about sixteen inches wide and at least twenty inches long. It was as deep as a kitchen sink and was piled completely to the rim with clear, sparkling gems that glittered explosively even under the dull fluorescent lighting of the vault. Several of the pea-to-marble-sized stones had spilled onto the floor.

"Holy crap . . . ," Brad managed to say.

Arielle took a deep breath and pulled her mouth shut. When she was able to open it, her voice was hushed and frightened as she whispered, "Diamonds?"

"Uncut. Oh man, Kenny is not gonna believe this."

His partner in crime's face revealed the stunned sensation she felt tingling throughout her body.

"What do we do?" she asked Brad.

"Do? You kidding? We're taking as many of these as we can carry." He knelt down and ran his palm under a small portion of the uncut diamonds. They felt like large chunks of rock salt, but heavier.

He looked at another nearby box, the one they had opened just before this one. It was slightly smaller but held a four inch deep stack of commercial bonds that appeared to be worth somewhere in the neighborhood of five-hundred-thousand dollars each.

"Did you read that little slip there, on top of those bonds?" Arielle asked him, still almost whispering, afraid Cartwright would hear.

"Yeah. We're looking at a pile of negotiable bearer bonds."

"Meaning?"

"Meaning whoever has them in hand can cash them out—with no record of the transaction."

"How much is in there?" she asked, afraid to hear the answer.

"Can't tell. But guessing from the ones on top, something in the many-many-millions."

Arielle suddenly didn't look so tough. She had played a good part with Cartwright, but she was, after all, a pretty simple young woman from Philadelphia. Her legs began to look as steady as those of her over-sized teddy bear back home, and she wobbled slightly as if dizzy. She had obviously never seen these kinds of valuables, or this much solid wealth. To Arielle, money was probably nothing more than a few computerized numbers in her online bank account ledger.

She started shaking, but there was no chair in the vault to sit in. She licked her lips as if a horrid, sour taste had vaulted up her throat.

"There's so much," she told Brad, as if he couldn't see. "There's no way we could carry all this."

"Yeah. And what about all the boxes we haven't even

touched yet?"

Brad was stunned, too. His head had not completely cleared. He had never expected to stumble across this kind of stashed wealth, either.

"Call Kenny," Arielle said, at the same time watching through the vault door to where Cartwright sat cuffed to his chair.

"I can't," Brad said. "I tried earlier. Too much metal around us down here. Radio's not getting out."

"You're kidding," Arielle said. "Did you try your cell?"

"Same problem. It's just a radio, too."

"We're on our own?" she asked, a shadow of fear clouding her face. She sat down in a heap on the floor. "We're sunk," she muttered. "How can we possibly get this stuff out of here?" She thought about what might come next. "And if we can't get out—then we're really sunk!"

Brad walked to the vault door, then just beyond, listening. He could hear the sound of a muffled commotion upstairs, through the wide, open stairwell that led down to the vault. But, so far at least, no cops had tried to brave the stairs.

Apparently, his threat to shoot Cartwright was working.

So far.

Suddenly, Arielle's voice caught him from behind. She was still plopped down on the floor, but was looking up at him with an ill-defined terror in her eyes.

"No way," she said sharply, as if Brad had said something. "This stuff stays here. Can you even guess how many pissed off people there's going to be if we try to take any of this? They're probably all gangsters! And politicians!" She looked down at the floor, lost in thought. "Screw this. I'm not getting involved in this!"

Brad turned back to her, even more dumbfounded.

"What are you talking about?" he stammered. "Involved?" He erupted in a poorly-controlled laugh. "Arielle, sweetheart, you are involved way up over the top of your beautiful little head! If you're going to walk out of this vault at all, you might as well walk out fabulously rich!"

"Yeah? Well how? How do we get out? What, we just walk upstairs and breeze out? With all this stuff?"

"You know the plan. We hold tight down here until Kenny has the rest of the island secured. Then one of the teams comes to escort us out."

"Oh sure, I know the plan. Great. Well, what about a bathroom? Huh? Was there a bathroom in the damned plan?" she jabbed him with an almost guttural voice.

Brad wished she had not brought the subject up. But with the emotional surprises of the last few minutes, they both now felt a sudden urgency that could not be ignored, for long.

"We'll figure something out. Don't get excited. It'll just make it worse!" Brad said, trying to calm her.

Arielle sat pouting. She seemed to consider everything for two seconds, then shook her head like a flag flapping in the wind. Brad could read her expression. She knew what lay before them could make her and Brad—and the entire Grand Slam crew—rich beyond their dreams, but she balked.

"No! We can't take this stuff," she repeated, trying to hold her voice down. "We're supposed to be a distraction. Remember? Just a diversion. You kept saying it yourself. No real robbery." She was breathing harder, and from the look of the veins pulsing in her neck, her heart rate had jumped to a dangerous level.

"I'm not doing it, Bradley!"

"Look," Brad argued, trying to keep his voice low, too, "if they get—*when* they get us out of here—and you know Kenny will—if the main plan doesn't work out, I don't know, for whatever reason, well, at least with all this stuff we could sneak off to some Pacific paradise somewhere, right? And hide in luxury. Don't you see?"

Arielle was frowning, deep furrows creasing her forehead. The wheels seemed to be turning madly in her head. She knew full-well there would be no safe or easy way out of the bank, not with all this loot, unless their teammates arrived to rescue them. She and Brad were in the midst of a pretended bank heist, but as far as the police upstairs could know, it was a real, deadly-serious bank heist. They had already threatened to shoot one man. And just having a gun on the island was against the law.

Arielle was clearly agonizing over what might happen next. There might be a small army of George Town police upstairs by now. How were she and Brad going to get out of there—let alone, carry out all those diamonds and bonds? It would take more than ten or twenty of Kenny's mercenaries to spring them now.

Arielle started rocking from side to side, the anxiety obviously overwhelming her. But she caught herself, forcing herself back under control. She said it again. "What do we do now?"

Brad looked out again at Cartwright.

"We wait."

RONNIE VAUGHN and Jason Broadman had gotten all the members of Teams One and Two ashore safely in their six inflatables. It was windy along the south coast, but not like the fury that had hit Teams Three and Four off the north coast.

Vaughn and Broadman's people landed as planned along the rocky shoreline just a few hundred feet west of Pedro St. James Castle. Several teammates ended up with scrapes and minor cuts to their arms and knees from scrambling up the sharp rocks, but no one was seriously hurt.

The breakdown of their yacht the first night out of Jamaica had cost them several hours delay, but they had made up that time with ease last night while finishing the crossing. This morning's problem was more serious. Their cook on the yacht came down with some sort of stomach virus and couldn't even get out of his rack to feed them. None of the teammates wanted to spend the entire day starving, so they had to scavenge in the galley and fend for themselves, scraping together cereals or the previous night's leftovers to put food in their growling stomachs. Everyone got a little bit of food, but no one was happy. The episode caused a forty-five minute delay in launching their small craft toward shore.

The brisk wind slowed them down once in the water. It was ten minutes before 9:00 when they finally hauled their gear and weapons up from the boats. Jason Broadman called in to report their arrival to Kenny Hamilton. He could tell from Kenny's voice on the radio that he was boiling.

"The good news," Broadman reported, "there's not a cop in sight. Apparently Brad and Arielle's diversion down at Comptrell is working great."

"I couldn't tell you," Kenny replied angrily, "I haven't heard a word from them since just before they walked through the door."

Broadman and Vaughn's teams stormed the small compound that encompassed the ancient Pedro St. James house and the modern museum and gift shop. Team One, led by Ronnie Vaughn, took on the museum office and shop that sat alongside the parking area. Team Two, under Broadman's command, headed straight for the main house.

As Broadman's team hustled past a large side building in between, a door swung open suddenly as an elderly tour guide ushered several tourists out of the movie theater housed there, where they had just watched an historical film about the St. James House property.

Broadman, startled, turned and fired two shots from his assault rifle. One caught the tour guide in the upper leg, and he went down hard, bleeding from just below the bottom of his white shorts.

Broadman lurched to a stop, overwrought and cursing himself for his reckless, unthinking reaction. The unobtrusive door from the theater building had opened unexpectedly, and his peripheral vision told him the man was pointing a rifle. Broadman reacted out of gut instinct. Now, with time to look, he realized that the old man had simply been pointing toward the historic mansion with his cane.

Broadman was cursing loudly, beside himself. He had not meant to shoot the poor man. He launched an angry shower of gravel with the toe of his combat boot, kicking himself inside at the same time.

Several of his teammates stood around him, stunned, unable to take in what just happened. They were all carrying blanks in their weapons. They had checked. They were sure.

Why was the old man bleeding?

What none knew, except Broadman and Ronnie Vaughn, was that Kenny Hamilton had made a last minute decision just before leaving Jamaica to have the four team leaders—but only them—carry live ammunition in their weapons.

"Just in case," Kenny had told the four men confidentially. "You know, in case things get hairy—and you need to protect yourselves—or your team."

The rest of the team members had been kept in the dark about this. Kenny never expected that live fire would actually be needed, because he was so certain that no one on the island would be armed.

This far, Kenny had planned. What he had not expected was that his new buddy Broadman was more of a loose cannon than he ever imagined.

Fortunately for the loose cannon, Kenny didn't know about the incident yet, and Broadman gave quick orders to his men to make sure Kenny would *not* know about it anytime soon.

After ordering his men to "stay off the damned radio," Broadman ordered two of his team to attend to the wounded tour guide, who lay on the gravel walk helpless, bleeding badly from his leg. The bullet had apparently severed a main artery.

The cluster of tourists who had emerged from the theater behind their guide were horrified, standing like a small forest of petrified trees mounted to the ground. The exceptions were two small children who burst into tears and were wailing like banshees. Broadman and one other man herded them back through the open door and threatened to shoot anyone who showed his or her face.

The members of Team One in the store building heard the two shots and poured back outside, weapons raised, looking for who had fired their weapons. A frightened clerk in the gift shop, trembling all over, took the opportunity to slip through a narrow door into the office and quickly dialed the Bodden Town Police

Station.

Ronnie Vaughn came running up to the back of the theater.

"What the hell happened?" he demanded of Broadman, who was still visibly shaken.

"Damned gun went off," Broadman said nebulously. "I hit a guy. Didn't mean it."

Vaughn could see his buddy was covering for his own stupidity, but he said nothing.

"Well, your guys look busy. I'll get some of my guys out to the road and set up defensively. Call me if you need help back here," Vaughn said in a rushed tempo.

Broadman didn't respond.

"Did you hear, Jason? *Call me* if you need help!"

Broadman finally nodded. The tone of Vaughn's voice implied he probably *would* need help, a tone which Broadman resented, but he let it go.

One of Broadman's team jerked his shoulder.

"We're gonna need an ambulance for this guy," he said, a shaky arm pointing to the injured tour guide. "It's like he's bleeding from a firehose!"

Broadman was still just reacting, numbed by the sudden turn of events.

"Well, we're damned well not going to call one! Just do the best you can. If we call an ambulance, you can bet there'll be cops right behind it!"

Broadman was starting to panic. He had done the one thing he could not afford to do, which was call attention to their presence the instant they landed. If anything could derail the whole Grand Slam, this was it.

The rest of his team members seemed at loose ends, watching Broadman whose eyes looked like glazed donuts. Finally, Broadman turned, realizing they were waiting on him for direction.

He started shouting, ordering them into various defensive positions around the grounds and inside the old governor's mansion itself. Everyone jumped at his commands. Broadman began to feel a sense of control wash back into him. He took several deeps breaths and tried to shake off the anxiety that had quickly overwhelmed him. Things were going to be all right, he tried to assure himself.

No sooner had this thought zipped through his mind than he heard in the not-far distance the unique sound of an Island police siren. Then two. Then two more from a different direction.

His boot launched another, larger spray of gravel across the pathway that led to an outbuilding by the mansion. He ran toward the big house and its thick, ancient stone walls. It would offer him the best protection from whatever the cops might throw at them.

And his own skin was his only concern right now.

ANSON DAHLGREN was cursing himself for a different reason.

He and the small remnant of his Team Four, all of whom made it ashore in the first boat, were standing close behind the rented vans pre-stationed at the soccer field by Kenny's advance team, trying to be less visible. He and his team had nothing to do and nothing to keep their minds busy, except to stare aimlessly at each other or the surrounding scenery.

There was a fuel station close by. Dahlgren watched it carefully for any sign of a police car that might pull in for fuel, or a snack. Or coffee. Did the cops here drink coffee? He guessed they did, but he didn't know.

There was an awful lot, he had just begun to realize, that he didn't know about this island, or its people.

What a stupid thing to focus on right now, he told himself. Still, he knew that the queasy feeling in his stomach signaled something, something his mind didn't want to consider. They were all on foreign soil, they actually knew next to nothing about this little nation, but in just a few hours they would be in charge. How was that supposed to work? Dahlgren had to assume that Kenny Hamilton had all those details planned out, too. But he himself knew nothing about it.

Dahlgren looked around the area again, getting more and more anxious. Their large SIG MCX assault rifles were slung over their backs, but were in plain view for any passerby to see. Already, a number of cars had slowed to make the tight corners at the three-way intersection adjacent to the field. There was no way, Dahlgren realized, that someone had not noticed the weaponry. He was hoping the locals would see them and just assume it was some police training exercise taking place at the field. Then he remembered. That wouldn't wash, because the police didn't carry any weapons. Hadn't Hamilton assured them of this?

Rick Kell rushed over to Dahlgren. Kell had been on the radio with Justin, his man who had been driving back and forth along the north coastal road for twenty minutes, trying to spot their three missing boats. Justin had just found one group of Dahlgren's team whose boat washed in by the waterfront of a very luxurious coastal mansion.

Anxious to collect the group before anyone spotted them, Justin drove across the stringy looking grass and loaded the soaked men and one woman into his van, leaving deep ruts in the yard because of the heavy, morning rain. Fortunately, nobody appeared to be at home in the magnificent house, so their trespassing went unreported.

The bad news Justin relayed to Kell was that there was no sign yet of the other two boats.

"Look," Kell said to Dahlgren, "we need to get orders from Hamilton. We can't just hang around here anymore. It's getting too hot," he said, and he didn't mean the sun.

"Agreed. Get him on the horn."

They knew Kenny was ticked off about the lost boats. At least they now had some good news.

"Commander, good luck," Kell said, "we just found one of the missing boats. We're still searching, but the rest of us can't just keep standing around here like a bunch of lost ducks."

"Have you looked toward—?" Hamilton began to say.

"Yes, damnit!" Kell answered impatiently, angry at Hamilton constantly second guessing him. "We've got the one bunch in a van, but no sign of the other two boats. So what do you want? The longer we stand around here, the more visible we are—and that's getting to be a problem."

"I know, I know," Kenny fumed.

Dahlgren was getting exasperated, too, partly because the wind-driven saltwater that doused him on their way ashore had badly irritated his skin condition. He was annoyed by Hamilton's apparent indecision.

Stomping one foot on the short grass like a penned stallion, he prodded Kenny, "Look, how about we move both teams—what's left of us—to Rum Point? There's a bar or two out there. Maybe we'll luck out and one'll be open this early. We can hide the weapons in the vans and just try to blend in."

"Blend in? In black commando outfits? Come on,

Dahlgren, open your brain for business. The day's a-wasting!"

Dahlgren could sense that Hamilton was getting angrier by the moment, so he didn't dare reply. There was silence for several seconds.

"All right, damnit. Do it!" Kenny ordered. "Take who you've got left to Rum Point. Except I still want four or five people sent to that strip mall on the east end. They should have been there already. We need that other diversion fired up!"

"We know, commander, but all five men who had that assignment are still lost out in the waves somewhere!" Kell said.

"I don't give a crap who was assigned! Come on, for cryin' out loud! Reassign! Use your heads. Get some people over there—and do it a half-hour ago!"

"What's the word from the bank downtown?" Dahlgren wanted to know.

"I can't reach them. Radio isn't working or something. I don't know if they need you yet or not. We'll have to wait till we hear something."

Kenny's voice was ragged, and sounded higher pitched than usual, a sign of serious stress.

"All right, I'll get part of my team over to the strip mall," Kell said. "The rest of us will move to Rum Point."

He didn't say it, but it felt to Kell like the whole plan was already in shambles. He also knew they couldn't retreat. The yacht that delivered them offshore would have already pulled off and headed toward Little Cayman. There was no chance of them catching it. They were here, and they were stuck.

They needed to quickly retool the plan. Kenny sounded like he was in a tailspin and wasn't going to be any help.

"And a simple, damned rainstorm throws it all into the toilet," he cursed to Dahlgren.

"You didn't bring your umbrella?" Dahlgren teased in a girlish voice.

"Wise up before I smack you!" Kell said, not in a joking mood. "Come on, let's get people moving."

Dahlgren nodded, equally as frustrated. He just hid it better.

One of Kell's men came running toward him.

"Rick, did you get that last transmission?"

"What! No, I was on with Hamilton."

"Justin radioed from the van. He's spotted another one of the missing boats! They're just off shore near some restaurant," the man said panting, bending a little at the waist. "Down that way," he added, gesturing west along the coast. "They're still fighting an undercurrent—can't reach the shore."

"All right, everybody in the vans," Kell shouted. "We're heading out. There's a boat launch down that way. We'll try to get them in there!"

Dahlgren snagged Kell's jacket sleeve.

"The strip mall?" Dahlgren reminded him.

"Darn it. Wait, everybody—you five, you're taking a van to the strip mall at the east side. The grocery store. You remember what to do?"

The five men stared at him blankly.

Kell fumed. "Hamilton went over it all, step by step, at your briefing! You don't remember?"

One fellow stood looking muddled, an eye squinting, and four shook their heads.

"It wasn't our assignment! Why would we pay attention?" the one replied.

"Oh, man!" Kell seethed in disgust.

"I'll go," Dahlgren finally hollered. "I'll take four of my men, we'll handle it. You take the rest of my crew with you. Keep in touch on the radio. Once we do the store thing—and the ATM—we'll come your way, if you need us."

Dahlgren raced toward a van. His short hair was still damp, his skin itched, and his head felt muddled. He was fighting a terrible headache from lack of caffeine this morning, but he was tired of just standing around looking like expensive rent-a-clowns in black. He pointed individually at four of his men and jerked his head toward the van. Without a word, they followed and loaded in.

"Load up!" Kell yelled at the rest.

Unseen by the Grand Slammers, two little Caymanian boys had snuck up behind a low chain-link fence at the far corner of the field. They had been crouched down there for over half-an-hour, watching and listening to all this with great curiosity. Their squat, rusting dirt bikes lay flat on the ground behind them as they used their eyes and ears to scope out what was happening at the head of the field.

They whispered excitedly back and forth, trying to figure out who these strangers were, and who they needed to tell about everything they had just heard. They had seen such big guns in movies, but never at their soccer field.

One boy's mother had a new cell phone. They knew it would reach the police station at East End because it had worked three nights before, when the mom's ex-husband came by in a drunken and foul mood.

If the boys were quick, they could warn the police in time. It was still a ten minute drive for the strange men in the grey vans to reach the shopping mall on the east end of the island.

At that moment, the two little Caymanian kids with their dirt bikes were probably the clearest thinking commandos at the soccer field. Keeping low to the ground, they dragged their bikes back through the tall weeds behind the fence and hustled toward a graveled side road. They hopped on their two-wheeled road hazards and, gulping air, peddled toward the mom's house with every ounce of energy they had.

Twenty-Three

Kenny

What the *hell* is going on?

I gave everyone simple orders—clear orders! How could things get this screwed up? A simple plan, and they're running around like a flock of headless chickens. Damn!

"Do you want me to take you ashore now?" Reid, my catamaran pilot hollers.

"No! Not yet. I'll let you know."

I'm not going near the stupid island until I know everything's nailed down!

Where's Kylaia? She was just there a second ago, tanning on the forward deck. Where the hell did she go? Probably hiding in the cabin. Gutless. Not as adventurous as I hoped.

Radio's chirping again. What now?

"What?" Cheap piece of crap! Nothing but gargling static. "Who is it?"

"It's Team Three Leader, Commander. We found another missing boat—it's my bunch. Just got to their location."

"What about the third one? Dahlgren's."

"Don't know. It's still lost out there somewhere. Maybe they tried to pull out of the storm and get back to the yacht."

"No, they didn't. I talked to your captain. Nobody came back before the yacht headed off for Little Cayman."

"Then I don't know. We can't find them. But we've got to move on to Rum Point. We're still too visible here, too exposed."

"Yeah, I get it," I tell him.

"Sorry, boss. That last boat's just on their own. Maybe they made it ashore further west. We'll keep our eyes peeled."

"Screw 'em—let them worry about themselves. I've got bigger fish." I shake my head in disbelief. What a bunch of worthless buttheads!

Wait a minute!

"Kell—did you cover that strip mall like I told you?"

"Well, not me. We got the call from Justin about this second boat. So Dahlgren took part of his crew over to the east end. They'll be there by now."

"Well why the hell hasn't he called in then?" The wind has picked up again and I have to shout into the radio.

"He'll call, don't sweat it. Probably got his hands full, with staff at the store or something. You know what a hotdog he is."

"Whatever." Kell's probably right. "So, you're heading toward Rum Point now?"

"As soon as we get these guys ashore. There's a boat ramp here. I got some guys out in the water, trying to drag the boat in. With the waves that storm churned up, these bouncy inflatables are too squirrely!"

"Come on Kell," I yell, "nail 'em down! We can't afford to lose any more people!"

"We're trying! It's like trying to steer bumper cars on a sheet of grease!"

"Get that boat in, Kell, we need every one of those guys!"

"I know, I know. Keep you posted."

You better, you moron!

I can't lose any more hands. And why haven't I heard from Brad and Arielle? Why the silence, Brad? You of all people! I better get someone moving that direction. I've got to know what's happening at that bank.

And Broadman—why hasn't he reported in? He and Vaughn should have Pedro Saint James nailed down by now!

Where the hell is everybody?

Stupid Kylaia, I told her to stay close and let me know if anything turns up on the local radio stations. Where the heck did she go?

"Reid, where'd the girl go?"

"Not sure, sir."

Crap.

"Maybe she's in the head, sir," Reid says. "Looked a little pale. Maybe it's the rough ride. Kind of like breaking a bronco today, with these waves!" he laughs.

Kylaia, seasick? After last night? I don't think so.

Well, maybe she is. I'm not feeling the best, either. Whatever sea legs are, I sure don't have them.

But I will *not* let myself puke. Not in front of Reid.

"Reid, can you take us a little further west? Parallel the northern coast?"

"Yes, sir. Do you want to head to Rum Point?"

"No!" Calm down, Kenny, you're overreacting. "No,

I just want to get a little closer, so we don't lose Kell and them on the radio. Not *too* close, though."

"Right, sir. I get your meaning. Can you pull the forward sea anchor for me?"

"Whatever." Man, do I have to do every damned thing myself?

Twenty-Four

The Reporter

When Justin, the driver Rick Kell had sent out, radioed that he had found the first missing inflatable, it was the best news Kell had heard since landing. Justin loaded the drenched group from the boat into his van and resumed his search.

Not long after, Justin spotted the second of the missing boats and called in again.

Kell and the rest of his teammates drove frantically west along North Side Road, one leg of the highway that runs along the northern coast of Grand Cayman. About a mile west of the soccer field, Kell spotted Justin's van. It had obviously pulled off the road in a hurry and skidded to a stop in a small gravel lot near a broken-up, concrete boat ramp.

Several of the group rescued from the first boat were standing around Justin's van. They were still soaked and chilled from their own wild ride and looked reluctant to go back in the water to help this second bunch ashore.

Kell pulled in by Justin's van and discovered Justin

himself, with a panicked look locked on his face, still sitting behind the wheel. He was staring vacantly at the boat bobbing in jagged waves just offshore.

"Why aren't you people helping?" Kell demanded as he ran over to the van.

"How?" was Justin's withering reply.

"How do you think, bonehead? Get off your butt and get out there in the water!" Kell shouted.

"I—ah—I can't swim."

Kell swallowed an "unbelievable," and pounded his fist against Justin's driver's door, leaving a small dent. "Well at least get down to the damned ramp! We need every hand. We can't lose these guys!"

Kell pushed two of the men standing around the van and ordered them into the water to help. He walked several steps toward the beach, radioing Kenny to report that they had found a second boat, the one missing from his own Team Three. Kenny demanded to know what happened to Dahlgren's third boat, but Kell told him they hadn't found it yet.

Then Kenny went nuts on the radio because Kell had not sent part of his team to shake up the grocery store out on the east end of the island. Kell was getting more and more irritated with Kenny's erratic commands from offshore.

"To be honest," Kell eventually told me, "I was getting pretty fed up with Commander Hamilton at that point! I was ready to tell him what he could do with his whole worthless plan!"

But Kell didn't. Instead, he informed Kenny that Dahlgren had taken several men to the strip mall. When he got off the radio with Kenny, he himself tried to reach Dahlgren, but got no response.

Then Kell looked around at the mounting confusion

that surrounded him. Only two men had actually gone to the water's edge, but they were just standing on the ramp. The inflatable was still bouncing offshore, making no progress forward.

Kell turned and once again saw Justin still sitting behind the wheel of his van. Kell strode back, reached through the driver's window, and slapped Justin hard on the side of the head.

"Get your lazy butt moving, you idiot! Now!"

Reluctantly, Justin got out of the van and followed Kell, who commandeered two of his own team and pushed them out into the water to try to help the stray boat ashore. A third man also jumped into the surf and fought the bucking waves, trying to wade out to the boat, which seemed parked about twenty feet out.

Just as one of the men reached the boat, he lost his footing on the slimy rocks under the breakers and flipped sideways into the water. The inflatable boat slapped over him, hammering him underneath its heavy load. Another of the three men lost his footing at the same moment and was swept further out by the violent undertow that lurked just beneath the surface like a squad of ravenous alligators.

One of Kell's men in the boat dove after the fellow who had disappeared underneath them. Another in the boat, a trim, muscular, former competitive swimmer named Corlin Vollane, also leapt into the surf and did his best to swim after the fellow who was being sucked further out by the treacherous water as it washed seaward with amazing fury.

The third rescuer was still trying to get his footing in the large, uneven rocks about fifteen feet off the boat ramp. He managed to grab a rope dangling from the front of the inflatable, looking like a man trying to drag an angry bull out of a rodeo ring. Despite all his effort, the current was too strong and he wasn't able to pull it toward shore.

After a few seconds, Kell's man who had been knocked under the boat popped out from the other side, a rubber duck bobbing up in a giant tub. His cheek was bleeding badly from a scrape with the rocks. The man who had leapt after him from the boat also popped up and was able to grab the injured man in time, just before the undertow took him, too. Looking like twice-drowned rats, they trudged into shallower water, winded, their chests each heaving like a blacksmith's bellows. Both collapsed onto the rocky shoreline as Kell and the others ran to help them.

Kell's third man was still tugging at the thick rope on the front of the boat as if wrestling a python. His strength nearly spent, he persevered and managed to get his footing back onto the edge of the concrete. With a final effort, he dragged the nose of the boat onto the submerged foot of the ramp. Everyone in the boat—most of them seasick—bailed out.

The fellow who had been swept out to sea by the undertow made only brief, spasmodic appearances as he bobbed in the waves. Corlin Vollane swam hard and finally reached the man about forty feet out. The fellow was struggling violently, weighted down by his soaked gear and clothing, completely exhausted. With a look of dread as if he had seen the very eyes of the devil, he swung his arms wildly—smacking Vollane right in the chin—then went under. Vollane spun around in the turbulent water, but could no longer find the man.

Despite being an expert and superbly conditioned swimmer, Vollane, too, was nearing exhaustion from fighting the waves and the undercurrent, his gear and clothing waterlogged. He could feel the undertow like a spectral shark biting hold of his legs, trying to pull him down as well. Fear forming into a thick, black serpent rose from his subconscious, arching up into his less-and-less rational mind, as his eyesight went ten shades darker.

Corlin's vanishing rationality told him that he was not willing to drown trying to save the other man, who he could no longer see. He managed to overcome the powerful drag of the current and stroked as hard as he could back toward shore. He paused briefly, managed to shed the soaked windbreaker that was weighing him down, then forced himself forward, the muscles in his arms and shoulders vibrating from fatigue. He finally reached the boat ramp on his hands and knees.

His dazed teammates, having pulled their boat ashore, just stood there dumbly watching Vollane, looking like the Keystone Cops at the moment the movie film broke.

Vollane tried to stand but vomited up a mouthful of salt water he had swallowed, feeling like his whole insides came up through his mouth. Sweat poured from beneath his clothing along with the bath of saltwater, and even the cloud-covered sun felt as if it might melt him. He managed a shaky stance and one of his buddies finally lunged to give him a hand, helping him to the parking area where Vollane collapsed and vomited again, more violently. Everything he had eaten for breakfast, and a residue of last night's supper, pooled into a sticky, yellowish-green puddle on the rough gravel.

As all this happened, no one noticed that the other missing inflatable from Dahlgren's team had appeared in the spray about thirty feet offshore and a hundred yards further west, where it appeared to be stuck in an invisible traffic jam. The blades of its motor revved and re-revved wildly as the back of the boat bounced in and out of the water, but the pilot could make no headway against the impossible current rebounding off the shore.

Then, with no warning, the back of the craft was violently thrust upward by an eight-foot-high breaker that came up behind it like an angry linebacker and tossed it shoreward where it slammed nose-first into a contour of jagged rocks. Jets of air hissing as from a nest of baby vipers escaped from a dozen holes in the ruptured nose pontoon.

Miraculously, the eight men in the craft managed to hang on. Looking like amusement park patrons coming off a wild coaster ride, they each lurched for the shore as their boat began to sink.

Kell, cursing nonstop through the whole ordeal, worked furiously to get all the men corralled. He sent a van to retrieve the men from the third boat which had just crash landed. After several minutes of confusion, some pushing and shoving, and a lot of angry words, the men from both boats managed to transfer their drenched gear and weapons from the two boats into the vans.

Kell was so upset that he hopped into the front passenger seat of his van, ordering another man to drive. As he closed his door, Kell shot a final glance out to sea, to where the one hapless mercenary had disappeared. Still no sign of him.

Kell barked out another angry, vile curse and told his driver, "Go!"

They had not gone a quarter mile when Kell remembered Kenny's demand about the team leaders regularly checking in. He really didn't want to talk to Hamilton anymore, but keyed his radio anyway. There was no answer, just static. Kell let out an audible sigh of relief.

He switched channels back to the team frequency again to talk to the vans behind him.

"All right, Bozos, we're headed to Rum Point. Ditch what you can of the commando look. Strip to your swimsuits if you have to. Plain T-shirts, if you have one. Leave weapons in the vans. Try to look like tourists."

Several laughs came from the men behind him in his van. He turned and scowled.

A guy in one of the other vans looked at his buddy.

"You wear a swimsuit under this?" he said with an embarrassed look.

"Nope," the other fellow said. "Didn't know we were 'sposed to. You?"

"Nope."

"Skivvies will have to do for swimsuits, I guess." He thought. "You wearing boxers?"

"No," his friend said, his face turning a darker shade of red than his Florida sunburn.

The other young man cackled. "Sorry about your luck." He laughed even louder. "Yup, we be tourists!"

AT COMPTRELL Trust and Savings, Brad could see that Arielle was battling a vicious panic attack, and it was starting to rattle Brad. She had so disheveled her hair with worry that she could have auditioned for any B-grade horror flick without further makeup.

"We guessed—correctly—that the bank turned off the air conditioning system to try to flush us out," Brad recalled during an interview. "Poor Arielle was sweating buckets—said her panty hose felt like they'd been pasted to her legs with shop glue."

Brad wasn't much better. His nerves were as frayed as the wiring in an antique lamp. They had heard nothing upstairs but a low commotion over the last hour. What Brad *could* hear told him there were probably fifteen or more Cayman police officers up there by now. He had no idea if they had a plan.

He had none.

Brad tried repeatedly to raise Kenny by radio but the thing just answered with a somber hum that meant its battery was hot, or nearly fried. The lack of radio reception could have been because of all the metal around them in the vault, coupled with the steel reinforcing bars in the poured concrete walls—not to mention the fact that they were eighteen feet underground. But Brad suspected—and I later verified this—that the Cayman police were jamming his radio signal, hoping to force he and Arielle to give up.

In desperation, forty minutes earlier, he tried the intercom phone on the wall that was connected directly to someone upstairs. The line, which had worked before, was now dead.

"Why would they kill the intercom line?" he demanded of their hostage, Cartwright.

Cartwright looked at him with patronizing disgust.

"Figure it out, son. You're a smart kid, right? That's why you're here, isn't it? Because you're so damned smart?" he said with a tone of ridicule.

Brad felt like giving him what Arielle had given him earlier, but resisted the urge.

"We have *got* to get out of here, Brad!" Arielle said in a loud whisper as Brad stepped back inside the vault. "I'm getting claustrophobic! And if I don't get to a bathroom pretty quick—it's not going to be nice," she moaned, the physical agony working its way up into her voice. "I think my eyeballs are about to turn yellow."

"Just shut up about the stupid bathroom, will you?"

Brad pleaded. "I'm telling you, Kenny will get us out. He planned on this, OK? You heard it in the briefings. We make a commotion, build a big distraction while the main attacks go forward. Pretty soon they'll have everything under control, and come get us out. All right?"

Arielle gave him a pained scowl.

"Just hold it!" Brad grumbled.

Arielle wasn't having it. What began as simple panic was turning into a much blacker fear. It appeared to Brad that her ability to reason had been whipped into banana pudding. She squinted at him as if strange snippets of unreal, disconnected images were plaguing her mind.

Then she began to pace the perimeter of the vault, making a hard left turn at each corner, apparently trying to shake off the apprehension that had imprisoned her.

"That sure as heck isn't going to help your bladder, woman. For crying out loud, sit down and sit still! *Please?"* Brad begged.

She seemed deaf. Brad kept fuming. Arielle kept marching, one wall, the next, then the next, until the rectangle began to spiral. In the small reception area outside the vault door, Cartwright was trying to figure out his own plan. It had been nearly three hours since they cuffed him to the chair, and he had wolfed down far too many cups of coffee that morning.

Simple biological pain was beginning to drive all three of them toward doing something really foolhardy.

TRACI DENNISON and Bryan Cantor, along with five other members of Team One, were driving quietly up a side street through George Town in two cars they had stolen from the parking lot of Pedro St. James. Their minds were not all that coherent, either.

Just after Jason Broadman shot the tour guide on the Castle grounds, Ronnie Vaughn, leader of Team One, had rounded up Traci, Bryan, and the other five near the gift shop.

"You guys hear the sirens?" Vaughn asked them.

"I'm not a guy," Traci spat, "and we're not deaf." The sirens had already rattled her. Her voice was starting to shake.

"Yeah, well, Jason had a little accident. Here, Randy, you take my rifle," Vaughn said, shoving his MPX into the hands of Cantor's friend, Randy Ballard. "It's loaded hot. Here's two extra clips."

Ballard, also part of Team One, balked and said, "What do you mean, hot?"

"No blanks, OK, dummy? The real stuff."

Ballard's eyes grew large.

"Can you handle this?" Vaughn snapped at him.

"Ronnie, we're all supposed to have blanks!" Traci almost shouted, grabbing him by the sleeve. "What are you doing with live ammo?"

"Look, yesterday Kenny changed it. He just didn't tell you. All four team leaders are carrying live ammo."

"What in the world for?" Traci demanded angrily. "Somebody'll get hurt!"

"Somebody already did," Vaughn slowly confessed. "Broadman accidentally shot a guy over by the theater."

"What? That was those shots?" Traci said with a look of horror.

"Yes! All right, look, it's too late to stand around crying about it! You and your task group here have got to get to Government House—now! Ballard goes with you. Just take the damned gun, in case!"

"In case of what?" Traci demanded.

Vaughn stared her down, crowing, "You hear those

sirens, right? Getting closer? You either go now—or you won't get through!"

"Damn it all!" Traci bellowed, looking at the machine pistol in Ballard's hands. "Keep that safety on, Randy! You hear me?"

Traci, Bryan Cantor, and the other men piled into two unlocked cars that belonged to the gift shop staff, both of whom watched helplessly from inside as their cars were stolen.

"You call the police station, Reena?" the head clerk, Ethel, asked her assistant.

"Yes, Ma'am, and I'm praying they'll be here any minute!" Reena whispered, pattering her fingers nervously on the glass counter. "Taking my car! How can they do that? I still owe money!"

She almost cried.

Bryan Cantor and Randy Ballard made short work of jimmying the steering columns with large screwdrivers and forced the ignition switch of each car on. They flew out the driveway leading from the Pedro St. James complex, passing several members of Broadman's team who had hunkered down on one side of the roadway waiting for the approaching police cars which, from their sirens, sounded like they were getting very close.

Cantor and Ballard gunned the cars down the narrow street at almost sixty miles an hour, then jammed the brakes and hung a left just before they reached a fast food restaurant by the main intersection at Shamrock Road. They spun quietly into the hamburger joint's small parking area and shut off the engines. Everyone except the two drivers hid low in their seats.

No sooner had they gone quiet than two white Cayman patrol cars came screaming toward them from the east and swung rapidly off Shamrock. Without so much as the squeal of a single tire, they flew south toward Pedro St. James, their engines sounding like mother bears protecting their young.

Barely a half minute later, three more police cars came from the direction of George Town and roared south, sirens blaring. A white EMS ambulance lit up like a Christmas plaza followed close on the bumper of the third patrol car.

As the last of the sirens went silent, Cantor and Ballard restarted their cars. Everyone else leaned back up, each imagining what was about to happen down at the Castle. The remaining members of Teams One and Two were all in position, armed with blanks, ready to make a good show of an armed invasion. Broadman, on the other hand, was apparently going nuts and—as far as they knew—was still wielding his MPX loaded with live ammo.

What's going to happen when the cops roll up? Traci agonized.

As if he read her mind, Cantor put their car in reverse, saying, "No time to think about it, Traci. We've got our own assignment. Let's get our butts over there!"

Cantor drove slowly out of the burger joint lot, followed by Ballard and the rest of their little squad in the second car.

"I'm just freaking a little," Traci said. "I always worried Broadman was too wild to be part of this."

"Look, he's a friend, he brought me in on this little party," Cantor reminded her. "Yeah, he's a little wild, but believe me, he can handle himself."

"That's kind of what I'm afraid of."

They turned west and headed toward George Town, folding easily into the rest of the traffic. As they reached a traffic circle to merge onto the East-West Arterial, two fire trucks came racing toward them from the west right down the middle of the four-lane street, their lights and sirens running, and loaded with full fire crews. The two engines skated through the tight quarter-circle onto Shamrock and rushed on.

"That's not good," said the guy in the backseat behind Traci.

Traci just moaned. Cantor ignored them and drove.

After cruising quietly up through the back streets of George Town, they cut across to the heavily-trafficked Esterly Tibbetts highway, then wound their way north. They looped another traffic circle and drove toward the western shore that formed the beautiful, watery edge of the city, where Government House, the governor's home, sat facing the beach.

The street side of the house was protected by a high, white wall with steel gates, but the wall ran just so far. Cantor followed the frontage street north a little way and pulled off the road into a sandy area where he managed to hide their car among a group of thick trees and bushes, just across from the elaborate Governor's Square shopping center. Ballard slowly pulled his car in behind them and swung around the first car, further hidden from sight.

They could not easily get past the large, iron gates in front of Government House. They saw no guards as they drove past, and Kenny had assured them there was no security around the governor. Still, they didn't want to chance it.

Instead, they worked their way through the underbrush easterly toward the shore, where they were able to hike back south along the beach a few hundred feet to the back of the property. Despite the huge wall along the front of the residence, laws being what they are, even the governor could not fence off the beach. Access to the back of Government House would be easy.

The little task group—all except Traci—had rehearsed their roles in Florida, and had browsed over detailed sketches of the house and property on their way over from Pedro St. James. As Traci, Cantor, and the first two men crossed the seaside yard and approached a back door of the house, Ballard and the two guys with him hung back in the bushes.

Cantor and his two men had their machine pistols shouldered over their backs so only the narrow sling strap was visible. Still, it was evident to anyone who would take a second glance that they were carrying weapons.

Traci intentionally left her gun in the car. With Ballard now carrying a live weapon, it seemed pointless to her to be walking around with a gun full of blanks.

Quietly, and as unobtrusively as possible, Traci and Cantor walked politely up to the back door. She knocked firmly, trying to maintain a fast-fading air of authority.

A young, dark skinned Caymanian woman peeked her eyes out through some loose drapes covering a window near the door. Her eyes got big, and a look of confused suspicion followed.

Her face disappeared. Nothing happened.

Traci rapped again with more force. This time, part of the young woman's face appeared behind the opening door, but so did two large, muscular men who looked as if they might at one time have wrestled alligators for entertainment.

Cantor didn't hesitate. He pushed past Traci and burst through the door with his machine pistol already flipped in front of him, pointed at the two men. Both backed away quickly, their hands whipping into the air, without so much as a blink or a whisper from Cantor.

As if on cue, Randy Ballard and his two backup men leapt from the underbrush and were at the door almost instantly, also forcing their way through into the back hallway of the house.

Traci, caught off guard by the sudden moves, was still out on the small concrete porch and had to catch her breath to collect herself. She was supposed to be in charge here—or so Kenny had told her—but apparently Cantor was not going to leave anything to chance. He wanted to feel like he had controlled the situation before Traci did her little act.

The two guards behind the house girl were clearly unarmed and acted compliant. Cantor and the others, weapons pointed menacingly, were making sure of that.

Traci took a deep gulp of air and stepped inside.

"We're here for Governor Edwards," she said in an authoritarian voice.

The young woman looked up at one of the two guards, then cautiously said to Traci, "Ma'am, he does not accept visitors without an appointment."

"Do we look like visitors?" Bryan Cantor snarled, already impatient and feeling very insecure with their exposed position in the expansive hall.

"No, sir," she replied carefully, "No, you don't."

"Then bring us the governor—now!" Traci barked.

"I am his wife, Miss. Can I help you?"

Traci and the others lurched, looking toward the sound of the pleasant, female voice.

It came from a narrow doorway to their left, where a very lovely, later-middle-aged woman in a casual but beautiful island dress appeared as if from a magician's box. She took a step forward hesitantly, but if she was frightened by the sight of so many guns, she didn't let on. She advanced with authority into the hall. The two guards moved toward her, keeping themselves between her and the assault weapons. She stopped and smiled at both men.

"Thank you Frederick, thank you Daniel. But I think I'll be fine. I'm sure these very decent young people have no intention of hurting an old woman like me."

Both men nodded doubtfully, then back-stepped ever-so-slightly. Unnoticed by anyone, Daniel reached calmly into his left pants pocket and pushed a small battery-powered remote control.

Cantor adjusted his positon to keep an eye on both guards and the governor's wife. His teammates adjusted too, though they looked uncertain about what they should be doing. They had not planned for a nice, little old lady to appear in the middle of their attack on the governor's home. It shattered their concentration. Randy Ballard seemed at a loss. Traci eyed the gun he held—Ronnie Vaughn's gun with the live ammo—and her heart pounded. She uttered a silent, fitful prayer that Ballard would not prove as trigger happy as Jason Broadman.

Traci stepped toward Mrs. Edwards.

"You're his wife?" she asked, trying to remain calm, but hoping to break the impasse.

"Yes, dear, for over thirty-two years now. I'm sorry. I didn't properly introduce myself, did I? I'm Theresa Edwards."

"Well, that's nice. But I need your husband, *here, now!*" Traci almost yelled. She wasn't sure how to handle what was going down. Her eyes scanned the hallway and its occupants, unsure what she might be looking for. She suddenly realized she had no idea what the governor looked like. He might be one of these men standing here who they had taken for guards.

"Oh, I wouldn't worry too much, miss," Mrs. Edwards said. "Whatever you're after, I doubt the governor would be much good to you, really. He pretty much counts for nothing, to most folks. He's much more important in London, where he's recognized as part of Her Majesty's government," she added, as if teaching a group of fourth graders. "He does all the public appearances and such. I do the housework."

"Housework?" Traci asked, confused and balking.

"You know, all the day-to-day work, the actual governing," the woman said more brusquely, her patience beginning to strain. "He is just window dressing, you might say."

Traci, Cantor and the others continued to stand there, feeling their toes in their shoes, trying to adjust. Traci was prepared to manhandle an old man. She was not mentally prepared to manhandle an old woman.

She glanced at Bryan Cantor, who looked suddenly hollow. She turned toward Randy Ballard, who was standing only three steps behind her, still holding the loaded MPX assault rifle. His hands shook noticeably. Traci felt sick. She gave Ballard a *please calm down* look. She didn't want to provoke the situation to where it might over-test his nerves.

She looked back at the governor's wife and said the only thing that she could pull out of her staggering mind.

"Where is he?" she asked, trying for a tone of politeness.

"Oh, well, he's on vacation, actually. In Las Vegas at the moment. Flew straight there from London after some very taxing and terribly useless meetings last week," Mrs. Edwards told them, mustering a feigned smile.

From her tone, they could tell Mrs. Edwards had

graduated them all to sixth grade.

Traci cursed under her breath. She would now have to use this woman in her husband's place as a hostage, and she didn't want to start off on a completely bad footing. She leaned toward Bryan Cantor with a quiet, "What do you think?"

"That we're wasting a hell of a lot of time," Cantor replied impatiently.

"Do we take her hostage, then?" Traci whispered.

"No choice, Traci. Me and Ballard will deal with the guards. You and the other guys go get the wife settled somewhere. Make sure she's secure. No phone close by. No cell phone, or tablet, or anything she can use to call for help," he reminded her, assuming the role of leader as if it was his second nature.

Traci would have known all these things, had she not been arrested with Brad in Philadelphia and missed all the run-throughs in Florida. Plus, Cantor could see from her expression that she was shaken by the sudden curve ball they had been pitched and wasn't thinking clearly. He hated leaving anything to chance, but he had to deal with the two guards.

Taking another deep breath, Traci nodded.

"Do you have an office in the house?" she asked Mrs. Edwards.

"Of course. Would you like to follow me?"

Traci nodded again.

But Mrs. Edwards didn't move. She nodded toward Cantor and the others holding their weapons.

"Are you planning on using those stupid things?" she asked Traci.

Traci had prepared herself for this question, at least.

"Only if necessary. You won't *make* it necessary, will you?"

"Oh, goodness. Not me. I'm planning on living to ninety," Mrs. Edwards said with a cheerful smile. "How about you, dear?"

Traci almost lost it. "Just lead us to the office!" she ordered firmly.

They began to move down the hall toward an adjoining but longer hallway when noises came from behind them. More commotion leaked from a wide archway to their right. As if by another trick of magic, eight more gigantic guards materialized and were on top of Traci, Cantor, and the rest in hand-to-hand fighting.

Fortunately—for Mrs. Edwards—Randy Ballard was one of the first tackled by a mammoth, dark-complected Caymanian man before Ballard could even think about squeezing off a shot. This guard and two others, summoned by the remote alarm in Daniel's pocket, had sprinted from a nearby restaurant in Governor's Square. Finding the front of the house secure, they rushed to the back and burst through the open door like three bulldozers. No one on Traci and Bryan's team had shown the sense to keep a watch on their rear ends.

The five other guards had been in their nearby sleeping quarters, not sleeping but watching reruns of *Voyage to the Bottom of the Sea*. They were summoned over their radio by the three guards racing back from the restaurant. The five off-duty guards rushed the house through a side door and erupted into the hall at almost the same instant as the first three.

It was like a bar brawl for the next minute and a half. None of Traci and Bryan's team were able to even crank off any blanks. As Mrs. Edwards gracefully disappeared through a doorway, the assault rifles were arm-chopped from the men's hands like rotten tree branches.

The brawl ended badly for the Grand Slam team.

Before they could even begin to react, they found themselves empty handed and on the floor, arms pinned painfully behind their backs, and cuffs being snapped on. There were a number of grunts and several pained screams—one from Traci as a thick, heavy knee landed squarely into her back—but the guards didn't slow down in pummeling them into submission.

Traci ended flat on her stomach with the Caymanian giant kneeling over her, his knee still in her back and his fist raised. She knew that fist could shatter her jaw—and maybe her skull—if it came down suddenly. She cried out in pain from his knee gouging into her ribs, but swallowed the cry as quickly as she could. She didn't want to appear weak. She was in such fantastic physical condition that with any smaller man she could have put up a respectable fight. But this guy's fists looked as large as her head. She twisted her face away, and braced for the blow.

But the man didn't strike her. He lifted her into the air like a Raggedy Ann doll and placed her down onto her feet, whipping out handcuffs that locked her arms behind her almost as quickly as her feet settled onto the floor.

"What the *hell* do you people want?" Frederick demanded angrily. "Who in the world would be stupid enough to try to kidnap our governor?" he asked, confounded.

The heads of the other guards were wagging in unison with the same disbelief, each panting from the fight. It looked like a puppy dog convention.

"Yeah, well just wait," Bryan Cantor said in a strained, muffled voice, his own face wedged against the hardwood floor. "You haven't seen the rest of us yet," he added, attempting smugness. He tried to laugh but couldn't take a deep enough breath. Someone's knee was still in his back, too, holding him like carpet to the bare floorboards.

"Call Central Police Station," Daniel said to one of the other guards. "Tell them we have some heavy-duty trespassers here. Oh—and mention that they have guns," he said ominously.

Traci said another heart-sinking prayer, thanking God her weapon was left in the car.

Not that it would matter.

As Traci's teammates were dragged helplessly to their feet by the burly guards, Mrs. Edwards reappeared as quietly as she had before. She looked at Traci with a sad, bitter expression, shaking her head like a very disappointed track coach Traci once had in high school.

"What is your name, miss, may I ask?" Mrs. Edwards said. "I introduced myself, but you failed to introduce yourself."

Traci shook her head with self-loathing, pain ripping at her shoulders from her arms handcuffed tightly behind her.

"Just call me Imbecile. I think that'll do from now on."

Mrs. Edwards studied Traci closely, a vague sympathy forming in her eyes.

"Oh, perhaps not an imbecile, dear. But you are a very, *very* foolish young woman to gang around with the likes of these men." She examined Traci's companions as if they were weeds growing up through rotting waste in a trash dump.

As Randy Ballard was handcuffed, he started shaking violently, letting out hiccupping sounds like a frightened young chimpanzee that has just lost its mother.

Twenty-Five

The Reporter

The Grand Slam plan was unraveling like a cut piece of cheap nylon rope. Having isolated himself offshore on the catamaran, all Kenny could do was to pace the deck, and spit, and fume.

In protecting himself from any actual danger, he had also cut himself off from being able to take direct charge of anything. His four teams of mercenaries on the island were looking like the rookies they were. Every pitch was a curveball, and Kenny—struggling just trying to communicate with them—was powerless to help.

If he had planned any way to call things to a halt, he might have. But it apparently never occurred to him the attack might somehow fail. Now, events on the island were happening faster than he could react to them, let alone stop them.

The Grand Slam ball had been pitched and batted. All Coach Hamilton could do now was watch where it might land.

AT PEDRO St. James, the remnants of Teams One and Two were under attack. Three fire trucks had showed up and the firemen and police were using the high pressure hoses as water cannons to keep the invaders pinned down.

Doing one of the few smart things he had done all day, Jason Broadman ditched his loaded assault rifle and the spare clips into a wooden cupboard in an antique, outdoor kitchen near the main house. He hoped and prayed the Caymanian police would not find it because it was covered with his fingerprints. If they uncovered it, they would easily identify it as the weapon used to shoot the tour guide, not only because the ballistics would match but because it was the only remaining live-ammo weapon at the crime scene.

Broadman had finally called Kenny by radio and was frantically trying to talk his way out of what had happened. Shooting the tour guide had destroyed any hope the Grand Slam crew had of capturing the island in a quick, bloodless coup.

Kenny, still a safe distance off the north coast, was pacing the small deck of the catamaran and going ballistic himself, raging at Broadman for his stupidity. Broadman, always one to pass the buck, kept trying to defend his defenseless actions.

"Well, stop crying over spilt milk, damnit!" Broadman shouted at his radio. "What are we supposed to do now? I don't see any way out of this place. There's only the one single road in and out of the area. We've blocked the cops out like we planned, yeah. But now they've got us blocked *in!*"

"Don't panic, Jason!" Kenny ordered him. "Just shut up and let me think!"

Kenny's brain was already stretched out of shape

trying to figure out what to do with his other two teams, most of whom had fled to Rum Point, giving up their original strategic position at Old Man Bay. Worse, he had never anticipated that Broadman would not be able to take, and hold, Pedro St. James.

"Did Traci and them get over to Government House?" Kenny demanded of Broadman.

"How the hell would I know that?" Broadman responded, his irritation growing. "All I know is Ronnie sent them. Whether they made it, I have no clue." He tried to collect himself, peering out through the railing of the third floor balcony of the main house where he was holed up. "I figured you'd be in touch with them by radio."

"Well, they're not answering their damned radios!" Kenny swore.

"You make it sound like that's my fault!"

"No, no. Maybe I'm out of range," Kenny said in a calmer voice. "You try it," he ordered Broadman, "you're closer."

Broadman hunkered further down behind the railing, out of sight of the police just a few hundred yards up the road. He made several attempts to reach Traci and Bryan Cantor at Government House. There was only static.

He switched back to Kenny's frequency.

"Nothing," he told Kenny. "Nobody's talking!"

"Damnit, what's going on? The whole plan's falling apart! We had this plan down perfect, Jason—every "i" dotted and every damned "t" crossed. How could it all get so screwed up?"

"Maybe fate has *double*-crossed you, boss. Don't ask me! I don't run the world!"

"Shut up! You're starting to sound like Traci," Kenny groused.

Broadman could tell from Kenny's voice that he was boiling over, and he was glad he was not out on that catamaran with Hamilton. But then, he was not happy about being cornered at Pedro St. James, either.

"So I'm asking again, you're the boss, what you want me to do?" he called to Kenny. "I don't see any way we can break out of here. And we have no change of clothes, so even if we did, we'd stand out like a bunch of sore thumbs!"

"Just hold tight!" Kenny warned him. "I'll figure it out. I'll get you out. OK?"

"Right. Well you better make it quick! They're pumping tons of water down our throats, but I have a feeling they're not just going to keep soaking us all day. A couple of new cops showed about a little bit ago. And they look pretty pissed off."

Kenny nodded to himself. "All right! I'm working on it. Anybody else hurt?"

"One of the guys fell, barreling up the stairs here into the house. Fell over the second floor railing. He landed on the concrete pretty hard. Hasn't moved. I think maybe he broke his neck."

Kenny shook his head violently as if it were about to burst.

"Dead?"

"Can't tell. Maybe he's just knocked out," Broadman answered. "At least, I hope. Don't really know, Kenny."

"No names, idiot! No real names on the radio!" came Kenny's angry rebuke.

Linford Reid watched from the pilot's chair as Kenny did a kind of spastic dance on the deck of the catamaran, anger beginning to consume him.

"All right, look," Kenny finally said into his radio, "I'm going to send Kell and Dahlgren and their people down into George Town. We've got to get control of the main police station—and knock down their communications. Once we've got it locked down, I'll have them send a rescue party after you guys."

Broadman did not reply.

"Did you hear me, Broadman?" Kenny shouted, nearly in a rage.

"Yeah. I heard. Thanks," Broadman said, chewing every word. "But they better move quick, Kenny. Cops keep piling up out here like cats around a rat's nest."

"You'll be fine," Kenny tried to assure him, also trying to calm himself back down to some level of clear thinking. "Give me some time."

"I'd give you some—if I had any."

UNFORTUNATELY, JUST when it seemed to Broadman that things could not possibly get worse, one of his team, a fellow named Mark Gillman, upped the ante.

Gillman had seen Broadman stash the hot-loaded MPX in the cupboard of the old outdoor kitchen. Realizing from the earlier shooting that Broadman's weapon was actually loaded with something other than blanks, Gillman decided to swap his rifle for Broadman's.

Gillman had trained in Montana two years earlier with a white supremacist mercenary group, and he was anxious to be part of some real action. He took up a sniper position on the second floor of the main house so that he had a long view of the approach road where the cops and fire trucks had pulled in. From shouting back and forth, Broadman knew Gillman was one floor below him, but he had no way of knowing that Gillman had snagged his live-ammo MPX from its hiding place.

Kenny had been absolutely no help, and Broadman was not a patient person. Besides, Kenny sounded like he was losing control. Broadman quickly concluded that it was time to make an executive decision. He switched his radio onto a common channel that would reach both Teams One and Two.

"OK, people, listen up! It's time to scare these pea-brains off! Everybody crank off a few blanks—in their direction!"

He didn't have to ask twice. All the men, and the two women who were part of Vaughn's team, fired off several shots. The noise was sudden and ear-piercing.

Mark Gillman, not wanting to look like a weak sister, took aim out toward the cops, too, and fired three random shots high over their heads.

Though trained in firearms, he had never actually trained with this weapon. He also had no idea of the powder load or velocity of the ammo Broadman had loaded into it. Since neither Kenny nor Broadman ever expected any actual firefight, Broadman had put very lightly-loaded, short-range ammo into his rifle and spare clips.

Gillman didn't know this. Because of the distance between him and the officers, and the weak ammo in the rifle, none of his rounds made it over their heads as he expected. One shot caught a fireman in the chest. The second shattered the windshield of a police cruiser, and the third struck a police officer in the neck.

An outraged cry went up from all the police and fire personnel. Everyone dove for cover. Without hesitation, several dashed to help the two wounded men.

At the same instant, the trunks of several police cruisers flew open. Officers reached in and pulled out a small armory of shotguns and scoped rifles. A commander shouted a single order and they quickly opened fire on the old house and its surrounding buildings, all except the store where they knew some employees were hiding. They were careful to miss the theater too, since staff had informed them by phone that some tourists were still trapped there.

The return fire caught the Grand Slam crew completely off guard. Broadman, Vaughn, and the others were—literally—thunderstruck. Cops in the Caymans had no guns. That's what Kenny had assured them over and over. Suddenly they were ducking a barrage of very real bullets.

The firing went on for several minutes in carefully aimed, short bursts.

A burly police officer in a dark brown suit—who Broadman would soon learn was Detective Sergeant Dane Marketta—waved his hand at the other officers. The guns went silent.

Gillman was panting hard and wanted desperately to fire back, but realized he was severely outgunned. Plus, he was a coward at heart and didn't want to call attention to his position. He had meant to miss—he was *sure* he would miss. And he believed he was an excellent shot. But when he saw the two men go down, it was like he himself had been shot. He was nearly certain he was the only one shooting live ammo from their side.

He began to feel sick. He laid his head down on the cool, wooden floor of the balcony, shoved the MPX as far away as he could, and started shaking.

One floor above, Broadman was going berserk.

"We're screwed, Hamilton!" Broadman bellowed at Kenny over the radio. "They're shooting at us!"

"They're—?" came Kenny's stunned reaction.

Reid was still watching him from the wheel of the

catamaran. "I think Hamilton's brain skipped a beat," Reid would one day tell me. "He shook his head like it was on fire, like he must have misunderstood—or didn't want to believe what he just heard." As Reid watched, Kenny tried to grab a piece of air in front of himself.

"They're what?" Kenny cried. "What the hell are you talking about?"

"*Shooting* at us! Are you deaf?" Broadman screamed.

"They can't, stupid! They've got no guns, remember?"

"OK, butt-brain, I'll remember that when the first slug hits me!"

"Broadman—have you lost your mind?"

"Get off that damned boat and come in here and I'll show you what's in my mind!"

"But you—"

"Then you can also tell me what these long metal things are that're spitting fire and lead at us!"

Kenny grabbed the railing of the cat and leaned hard against it. "Guns? No way," he muttered. "I was sure—" Reid overhead him start to say before he swallowed the words.

Reid could tell Kenny's mind was on overload, in part because Kenny had just downed his second bourbon in less than half-an-hour.

"Hang on, Jason! I'll get some help coming that way."

Broadman was hunkering down more tightly on the balcony floor. He didn't answer.

"LOOK—LISTEN to me!" Kenny hollered at Rick Kell over the radio. "Just do it! Now! Half your men to the main police headquarters, the other half to Saint James. Get moving!" Kenny ordered.

Rick Kell was getting furious. Nothing was working as planned, and several of his men had just filled themselves with greasy hamburgers and various beverages. This was no time to launch another sudden move, or throw another wrench into the shambles of their original plan.

But Hamilton was not politely asking.

"Some of our people are still out at the east end, remember? At the store?"

"Have you been able to reach them?" Kenny demanded.

"No report, here," Kell answered, "unless you've heard something. I figured maybe we're out of range of their radios."

"Dahlgren called me once, then broke off," Kenny said. "I can't reach him, either." He let out a loud, frustrated curse. "Look, just go do what I told you! Half of you get downtown and get that police station secured. The other half—whoever you've got—get them to Pedro Saint James five minutes ago. Move!"

Kell didn't want to upset Kenny any further, so he started rounding up his people. He couldn't believe what Kenny had just told him, that there was shooting going on at the old St. James House. He handed off his live-ammo MPX to Larry Pinter and sent him with several others to their vans, ordering them to Pedro St. James. The men piled in, awkwardly but quickly trying to change back into their commando gear, which was scattered around the interiors.

"And you need to try to raise Dahlgren on your way," Kell yelled at Pinter as he climbed into the driver's seat of one the vans. "We need their help. Kenny says they're shooting the place up!"

"At the strip mall?"

"At Saint James, moron!"

"We're shooting it up?"

"Couldn't tell. Kenny sounded frantic. Just go, would you? Stop asking so many stupid questions!" Kell jeered, waving his bulky arm. "And don't forget Dahlgren and them. You've got to reach them. Kenny wants them to pull off the east end and head down to the Saint James with you guys!"

"Well, you call him!" Pinter yelled back, waving his radio as if he was explaining modern technology to a three-year old.

"Tried. Can't reach him. We're probably out of range. Hell, I don't know! Just do like I said! See if you can raise him on your way over—when you get closer."

Pinter and half of Team Three in two vans headed back east along Rum Point Road on their new mission. They would catch Frank Sound Road near the soccer field and head south. Pinter knew it was only a short, four mile jaunt to cut across the center of the island and connect up with Bodden Town Road along the south shore. From there, they could make it to Pedro St. James in just a few minutes.

What, exactly, they would do when they got there, Pinter hadn't yet figured out. He had Kell's hot MPX, but he had no desire to use it. And he had no clear idea of what was happening at St. James, nor how many cops might be there ahead of them.

In any event, it wouldn't matter. Pinter would never reach Dahlgren—who was no longer at the strip mall. Pinter and his crew were about to be snagged by four patrol cars and a large, mobile-police-communications truck set up as a roadblock on the south highway— waiting for any newcomers—just west of Bodden Town.

Pinter's mission would be short, leading straight to a

jail cell.

RICK KELL gathered the rest of Team Three and what was left of Team Four in a parking lot at Rum Point. They would split up into the six, pre-stationed speedboats, three from Rum Point dock, the other three from Water Cay dock which lay about a mile south of Rum Point along the east edge of the huge western bay that nearly severs Grand Cayman into three chunks. The speedboats could fly across the big bay in about twenty minutes. From there, it would be a quick trip down into George Town to capture the island's main police station. The most urgent thing, Kell realized, was to take down all the police communications, to hinder the police response to their attack.

Once they made it across the bay, they would have to find the rental cars Kenny's advance team had pre-stationed north of George Town. The information was all in Kell's big folder—which he had forgotten on the yacht that morning.

He could not let this slow them down. They certainly weren't going to walk to George Town. Kell would have to think of something else—in a hurry—as they raced across the bay.

Twenty-Six

The Reporter

I probably don't need to point out that Kenny Hamilton's spectacular, well-planned Grand Slam operation had morphed into Murphy's Law on steroids. Actually, it was more like Murphy's Law on steroids, crystal meth, and crack cocaine.

I'm almost embarrassed narrating all this. It feels like I'm rubbing salt into the wounds of the ill-fated, luckless people who tried to pull this idiotic thing off. But I committed to telling the full story, as far as I've been able to piece it together, so I'll push on.

The reason no one had heard from Anson Dahlgren for so long was because he and his whole squad had been promptly carted off to the Bodden Town Police Station shortly after they arrived at the east end strip mall. Worse, their radios had been confiscated by the Cayman police who had since been listening in on the various Grand Slam team frequencies, trying to piece together exactly what was going on.

How did *that* happen? It wasn't complicated.

DAHLGREN AND crew had arrived at the small grocery store at the east end of the island about fifteen minutes after leaving the soccer field earlier in the morning. What neither Dahlgren nor anyone else knew was that the two little Caymanian boys by the soccer field who overhead Kell, Dahlgren, and the rest talking had peddled back to the one boy's house doing double-time, grabbed his mom's new cell phone, and called the police. The youngster who made the call was very colorful in his description of the foreign men in their strange, dark clothing and their "big—*really big*—evil-looking guns."

It also happened, as things sometimes do, that two police officers from the Bodden Town station were just then at a resort office across the road from the grocery store. As the boys' call was coming it at the station, one of the officers was setting up his wedding anniversary with the manager of the resort, planning an intimate—and hopefully fruitful—evening with his wife at a nice little table set out on the beach.

Being alerted by radio from their station of some armed men heading toward the strip mall, the two uniformed officers left their unmarked car in the resort lot and ran across the road, where they concealed themselves in a small alcove by one of the shops in the mall. They were in place, waiting, when Dahlgren and his men arrived.

While the two cops dashed across the roadway, the communications officer at Bodden Town also called the grocery store, warning them of possible trouble. He ordered the staff to bolt the doors from inside and not to open them except to a police officer.

Just minutes after the store was warned, the attackers

arrived. When Dahlgren and his crew came roaring around the bend on Queens Highway in their rented vans and skidded into the parking lot of the little mall, they were met by several surprises.

First, they found the front door and the steel security screen of the grocery were locked up tighter than Ft. Knox. When they pounded on the screen, they got no response. They peered inside and could see several faces of staff hovering low behind a counter near the rear of the store, but no one would come near the door.

Dahlgren, as the team leader, had live ammo in his weapon, but he was not about to start shooting into the store. It would cause damage but do no good, and it would make those inside even less likely to approach or open the door.

The next surprise was the sound of two sirens rapidly approaching along the highway from the south. Bodden Town had dispatched two more cars with two officers each after the little local boys called in.

Dahlgren was a brawler, but he had slim choices. They could stand their ground and wait for a fight with unarmed local cops, they could pull out and try to get by the approaching patrol cars and head south, or they could retreat back toward the soccer field at Old Man Bay. None of the choices sounded any good, except to stand and fight. All his team needed to do was fire several blank rounds from their assault rifles and the arriving officers would hop like rabbits for the closest cover. Dahlgren felt confident he would not have to resort to the live ammo in his own gun.

As he was making his hasty decision, the two patrol cars slid to an angled stop at the edge of the highway in front of the mall, noses toward the parking lot. The trunks flew open as the four officers rolled out the far side of their vehicles.

Dahlgren was just about to order his men to send a volley of blank shots that way when he saw the next surprise. The four officers each grabbed a long-barreled shotgun out of their trunks, took defensive positions behind their cars, and leveled the guns at Dahlgren and his men.

Dahlgren's jaw opened, but his command to fire never came. He was stunned to see the shotguns but was certain they were *not* loaded with blanks. In half-a-heartbeat, he realized that a command to fire would get them all killed.

Where the hell did they get all the guns! Hamilton promised—they'll have no guns, Dahlgren cursed silently. Deep regret set in as his now-ashen-gray face fell, regret that he had ever listened to a single word from the mouth of Kenny Hamilton.

The final surprise was that the first two officers who had hustled over from the resort had—as quietly as cats—snuck out from a passage between the grocery and the south wing of the mall and were now standing only twenty feet behind Dahlgren and his men.

"Do not move!" said the threatening voice from one of the two unarmed officers.

"Lay down your guns or we will fire!" ordered the second.

Dahlgren was now cursing very much out loud, and very profanely. His men all stood frozen in place, even afraid to move to lay down their weapons.

Dahlgren robotically keyed his radio. "Hamilton!" he called in a hushed, desperate voice.

He was answered with some garbled words broken by short bursts of static.

"Do as commanded!" hollered one of the armed

officers behind the patrol cars. "Point your weapons to the ground—then slowly lay them down."

"You have five seconds!" shouted another. "One . . . two . . ."

"Dahlgren?" came Kenny's voice over the radio. "Dahlgren!"

Dahlgren didn't dare try to answer his radio. He knew they were in deep trouble. He also knew, as the only one carrying live ammunition, that he was in the deepest.

On "four," he very slowly pointed the barrel of his rifle at the asphalt, nodded to all his men, and set his MPX gently down on the pavement. The others followed suit. Still afraid of any sudden move, Dahlgren slowly glanced over his shoulder at the two men who had snuck up behind them. He saw that their hands were empty, and began cursing loudly once again.

"You cheating bastards!" he yelled, "You can't even lie honestly?"

It made no sense even to himself as the words came out of his mouth, but he was so upset that he had become irrational.

"Dahlgren?" came another garbled plea from Kenny on the radio. "Say something, damn you!"

Dahlgren cautiously reached for the radio's power switch and shut it off.

While the armed officers approached and held Dahlgren and crew under guard with their shotguns, the two unarmed officers collected their assault weapons. They handcuffed Dahlgren's crew one by one, also confiscating each one's radio.

It was like free prize day at the fair.

"You're not supposed to have those guns, you know!" Dahlgren snarled at the officers. "They're illegal down here, you idiots!" he added loudly, making an even greater fool of himself.

One of the Caymanian officers glanced at another, wondering what moon Dahlgren had landed from.

His buddy nodded, "Dang tourists."

KENNY HAMILTON was striding wildly up and down the deck of the fancy catamaran, as it lay sea-anchored several miles off the north coast. Two and a half hours after failing to connect with Dahlgren, Hamilton was visibly shaken, mumbling to Linford Reid that it looked like his Grand Slam might become a Slam Dunk—for the Caymanian authorities.

Agitating him even more was the fact that no one was reporting in. Not only was Dahlgren off the air, Kenny hadn't been able to raise Broadman either, not since Broadman reported being shot at by the police. Kenny had no clue what was happening at St. James now. He couldn't raise Traci or Cantor to find out if their group ever reached Government House and captured the Governor. Then there was Kell, who had not called in since Kenny gave him the order to split up the men hanging out at Rum Point.

"Kell, come in! Answer me!" Kenny blabbered into his radio, frustration and warm bourbon rising up like the taste of garbage in his throat.

He got no reply.

KELL WAS busy. Not only had he found himself literally up to his ass in alligators, he had feared he would end up being their lunch.

Having crossed from Rum Point, his lead boat slowed into the no-wake area of Governor's Creek cove. Kell spotted the large dock of a luxurious property at the water's edge that seemed a perfect place to tie up their three craft. As they approached from the east, though, they discovered a low, steel fence protruding just out of the water, preventing them from reaching the dock.

Kell, being the impatient person he was, tied off the bow of the boat to the fence and jumped over it to wade ashore. His men were about to follow when they saw something else splashing around not fifteen feet from their hot-dogging leader.

Kell had jumped into the underwater pen of two pet alligators owned by the elderly couple who leased the expensive home. The water was three feet deeper than he had estimated from the boat, reaching his chest. Soaking wet, he was forcefully wading along the mucky bottom when the two alligators surprised him from behind.

He was certain they wanted to borrow his legs.

Kell was nothing if not lucky. Both of the six foot gators had been around their owners since infancy, so were fairly tame. Even then, the sight and sound of a big, wet human in black thrashing around in the shallows of their home was awfully tempting. They slithered around Kell, dragging their tails in the mucky bottom, stirring up a cloud of silt that made it impossible for him to track them.

They kept circling the screaming, terrified man as he frantically slogged toward shore.

It was a good thing his pants were already soaked.

With his feet finally on land, he barreled over another fence that kept the gators from chewing up the expensively maintained yard. He sprinted faster than he knew himself capable to a parking area by several shops across the road from the mansion.

The sight of Kell running for his life caused muffled laughter among the men on his boat.

"That would have been great on video," joked the

pilot as he untied their line from the fence.

"Yeah, you see guys do crap like that in the movies," chuckled another, "because it's only a movie. I'll just watch, thanks."

They, along with the other two boats from Rum Point, judiciously decided to stay onboard until they reached an adjacent dock jutting into the cove. The equally expensive looking place appeared to be vacant at the moment, so no one noticed them docking.

They caught up to a still-winded Kell as he sat in a patch of brownish grass by one of the shops. No one dared say a word to him.

"All right, clowns," Kell finally said, standing, "let's find us a ride."

THE OTHER three boats were running ten minutes behind this first group because it had taken that long to drive from Rum Point down to Water Cay where their boats were docked.

"Why didn't the moron put all six boats together at Rum Point?" one of this group asked his buddy as they untied their craft from the Water Cay dock and headed out into the huge bay.

"Why does anyone do anything stupid?" his buddy frowned. "Because it's stupid."

This second bunch, the remainder of Kell's Team Four, shot across the bay as fast as the boats would carry them. The three craft each had a 5.7 liter inboard engine powering twin jets and cruised along at what seemed a breakneck speed, covering the roughly six mile distance across the bay in just over fifteen minutes. The bay was calm, nearly as smooth as a mirror, so the ride was exhilarating after their dead time in the bar at Rum Point.

The only problem was that the compass in the lead

boat was miscalibrated and pointed them too far northwest. They missed Governor's Creek cove completely and ended up coming ashore almost a mile further north.

"Where the heck are you guys?" Rick Kell's exasperated voice called over the radio as he and his men prowled around for cars. "We saw you shoot by heading north! What gives?"

Marty Watson, the pilot of the lead boat, radioed back.

"Sorry, Rick, something's off with the electronics. The compass, I think. We're coming in by a big restaurant up here. You want us to head back south?"

"No! No time," Kell called. "Just get ashore! Head toward the west shoreline. Whatever main road you hit, follow it south. It'll eventually get you down into George Town."

"Have you found the cars Hamilton pre-stationed around there?" Watson asked.

"No! And I'm not even gonna look. I forgot to bring the stupid folder!" He was so upset with himself, he was ready to explode. "We're looking for alternatives. Just find yourselves some wheels! You know how to do that, right?" Kell asked, not really needing to pose the question.

"Sure. No problem."

Kell didn't know the area well enough to realize that his directions would send the group too far west, adding almost another mile to their jaunt into George Town, and delaying them even further.

The men and one woman in Watson's group found two large sedans sitting unlocked in the parking lot of the restaurant. They were planning to hotwire them but were delighted to find that both owners had left the keys hanging in the ignition locks.

"Friendly natives," Marty Watson laughed to a sidekick.

The group packed into the two large cars and headed west along a skinny road that snaked away from the restaurant.

They were lost after just five minutes in the maze of winding roads and streets that wove through abutting neighborhoods on this part of the island. The woman in the group was trying to follow their positon on her cell phone GPS, but the signal was poor because she was roaming on a foreign system and the phone couldn't keep up with their rapid movements.

Suddenly, Rick Kell's radio crackled again.

"Boss, you're not going to believe this!" Marty Watson called, his voice a mix of humor tinged by anxiety.

"What's wrong now?" Kell replied as he and his own team headed south into George Town in three other stolen cars.

"Well—don't laugh—but we just passed a big sign that said 'Welcome to Hell'!"

Kell was in no mood for jokes, trying to find his way through the unfamiliar streets while driving on the "wrong" side of the road.

"If you're trying to be funny, Marty, you failed miserably."

"No, Rick, I swear! We just passed a little shop place with a huge yellow sign, and it said 'Welcome to Hell.' You sent us this way on purpose, didn't you?"

Kell shook his head, convinced Watson was losing it.

"Will you just get your worthless butts to George Town and stop screwing around!" Kell yelled into his radio.

Watson was watching the large Hell sign recede in his mirror and didn't respond.

AT COMPTRELL Savings and Trust, the hours-long standoff was about to come to a harsh, unexpected end.

Arielle Kemper, having ditched her woolen suit jacket, had paced the perimeter of the vault for over an hour, then collapsed in a pile on the hard, marble floor. She sat moaning, and hurting. Brad came over and knelt by her.

"Come on, Arielle. Buck up, will you? Everything'll be OK," he said in a soft tone meant to pacify her. "It can't be much longer."

It had an opposite, explosive effect.

"Damn you, Bradley! Damn you—and Traci—and all your stupid friends! Why did you guys drag me into this mess? We're screwed. Don't you get it? We're totally, permanently screwed!"

She violently shoved Brad away and was on her feet.

"Give me the key," she growled at him like an angry hound.

"What?"

"To the security gate—the key. I'm getting out of here!"

"Arielle, no! Think! It'll only make it worse. At least we're safe in here. They haven't bothered us, right?"

Her face became as hard as a statue's. He could see the muscles under her shirtsleeves tightening like over-twisted winch cables pulling too heavy a load. She suddenly lunged at him, and ripped the key ring from his grip, the ring that held the key to the security gate in the vault foyer.

She shoved Brad violently again, her strength now built to a peak by fear, anger, and desperation. "Don't you dare try to stop me," she glared at Brad. "I *will* hurt you," she snarled.

Brad stood still, icing up. He had no idea what she might do. Beautiful, smart, lovely Arielle was suddenly like a caged, hungry animal bent on getting her own way. The poisonous look in her eyes telegraphed that she was deadly serious, a serpent wound up and ready to strike him.

Before Brad could react, Arielle grabbed her leather folio case and ripped the assault pistol out. Brad rushed at her and grabbed her arm that held the pistol.

"Don't!" he warned.

She pointed the pistol at him.

"Blanks, Arielle?" he reminded her, his teeth clenched.

"I don't care!" she shrieked.

She wrenched her arm free and bolted out of the vault toward the security gate that led into the lower hall, shoving past Cartwright on his chair. Out of control and trembling, she barely managed to unlock the steel gate. Brad raced up behind her and tried to grab both her arms this time, but she spun and whacked the hardened-plastic pistol grip across his chin. Brad twisted like a broken sapling and fell to one knee, his back to the gate.

Throwing the gate open, Arielle screamed like a madwoman, "Everybody get back up there!"

She took one step through the gate and sprayed half a clip of blanks into the lower hallway, creating a cacophony of explosive blasts that echoed repeatedly around the basement like firecrackers inside a steel drum. The unbearable noise seemed amplified a thousand times as it reverberated off the marble walls.

Arielle never took another step.

Before she could turn her head to look up, two

uniformed police officers and two plain-clothed bank security men suddenly descended from the top of the stairs, just far enough to get off a clean shot. All four were armed with shotguns loaded with buckshot rounds. Four blasts came simultaneously, sounding like cannon fire in the enclosed, marble stairwell and basement.

Two rounds struck Arielle directly in the head and chest. She flew backward against the wall by the gate and dropped like a bucket of rocks, blood bathing the pink marble floor. The other two rounds didn't hit her squarely but still peppered her body with buckshot.

Two pieces of shot ricocheted off the floor and splashed through the open security gate, striking Jim Cartwright in the right knee. He let out one angry yelp, and flipped his chair over onto the floor, biting hard enough on his tongue to make it bleed.

Brad was still on one knee, his back to the gate. Three more pieces of ricocheting buckshot caught him in the back of his left shoulder. Pain seared down his spine through his whole body like a cascading waterfall. He felt blood start to trickle down his back just as his nostrils caught the smell of burnt gunpowder that was clouding the lower hallway and vault.

No more shots were fired. Brad had left his rifle laying on a table inside the vault, which saved his life. After shooting Arielle, the four officers, followed by six more, swiftly descended into the vault and were ready to kill anything that moved behind their friend Cartwright.

"On the floor, monkey!" one of the police officers cried.

Brad, already halfway there, reached out his arms and lowered his face onto the cold marble. The thin stream of blood began to pool in the hollow of his lower back.

As he lay there being handcuffed, a very thin trickle

of water leaking up from the floor sill in the corner reached his cheek. Cartwright, also from floor level, could see the faint glistening water wetting the floor and Brad's face.

Cartwright laughed as two of his security men released his handcuffs and lifted him off the floor.

"They really should fix those darned leaks," he smiled toward Brad. "A guy could catch a cold down here."

Out in the hallway, an officer and a paramedic went to the crumpled pile that was Arielle Kemper. The medic raised her head slightly, her face horribly disfigured by the shotgun blast. He felt her neck for a pulse. She was dead.

"HAVE YOU reached the Central Police Station yet?" Kenny Hamilton was yelling at Kell.

The battery in Kell's portable radio was running low, but the transmission made it through.

"Not far now," he assured Kenny.

"Make it fast. If we don't shut down those police radios pretty quick, they might get a leg up on us," Kenny said, trying to sound as confident as he could.

Kell pushed the gas pedal of his stolen car a little harder. He had not seen a police car since coming ashore. He was hopeful that by now they were all preoccupied downtown at the bank and out at Pedro St. James.

He radioed Marty Watson and his men.

"Are you guys going to join the party anytime soon?"

"Yeah, we made it to the west shore, we're working our way toward you now. But these streets are crazy, man, they zigzag all over the place. Looks like some drunk laid them out," Watson replied with an edge of frustration. "I keep forgetting to keep to the left. Almost smacked a trash truck head-on!"

"Well hurry it up! I can see the police station. It's just a couple of blocks. I'll hang back till you get here."

"Yup, going as fast as these stupid local drivers will let me," Watson said. "I can't believe the traffic! No way there can be this many cars on such a tiny island!"

Watson tried to pass a small, battered sedan and almost struck a woman and her two little girls who were jaywalking. He started to curse out the window but was silenced by the petrified look on the girls' faces.

After the near miss, he and his following car navigated south. Ten minutes later, he radioed Kell.

"OK, where are you? We're about two blocks west of the cop shop. We're—" He looked around. "What street are we on?" he asked his man riding shotgun.

"Here, turn right—there!" the other fellow said.

Watson made a slow, careful turn, hoping their car and the one following would be invisible.

"Kell, we're a block west of the station," Watson radioed.

"OK, we're right here. Pull in anywhere you can. We all hit the front doors at the same time. Got it? Watch for me."

Kell and his two following cars sped up, cruised around the end of the police station and pulled into the lot near the front entrance. Watson and his crew poured out of their stolen cars across the street and ran across to meet them. Everyone had their assault rifles in hand. Kell now had Larry Pinter's original gun, so they were all carrying blanks. Kell hoped the bluff would work.

The crew of nineteen men and one woman marched like a riot squad through the doors of the station looking as threatening as they could manage. Scowls and sneers wrapped their faces and they walked with a swagger that said they were ready to take on the largest army in the world.

What they found looked bleak. The reception area of the station was empty except for one female officer who sat behind an information desk, a look of feigned panic on her face.

The look was forced. She was a highly trained, iron-willed officer who had faced lots of firearms during her former career in the British navy as part of a UN peace keeping force in the Middle East.

She sat passively, making her eyes wide but otherwise sitting perfectly still.

She was just the bait.

No sooner had Kell's crew stopped at her desk than they heard the sound of at least forty pairs of boots running at them from three different directions. The men and women rushing at them had been hiding behind doors and partitions—and they were ready for a serious fight. Their own weapons were levelled at the intruders, ready to fire.

Without so much as a word or command from the oncoming police, Kell slowly bent down and set his rifle on the floor, confirming his essential cowardice. He just as slowly stood, his arms rising toward the ceiling.

Kell's crew watched him, then turned their attention to all the uniforms that surrounded them. Eight or nine of the officers had shotguns, the rest held handguns. But there were so many of them, they could have taken down Kell's people with a fistfight.

The rest of the intruders placed their weapons on the floor and took a step back.

Kell knew he and his team were not getting back out the door. Nor were they getting anywhere near the communications center that held the police radio and dispatch system, along with the other high tech research and surveillance gear the Royal Cayman Police Service was so proud of.

Kenny Hamilton could not have timed things better. His voice crackled over the speaker of Kell's radio like a soccer game announcer calling a big play inside a huge stadium.

"Is everything under control at the police station?" he hollered, his loud, digitalized voice bouncing off the walls like the ricocheting bullets at the bank.

Kell slowly twisted his neck from side to side like a giraffe stretching for leaves that were too high up. He grimaced at the officers, then keyed his radio.

"Yup, Kenny—I think it's fair to say things here at the station are definitely under control," Kell replied grimly.

He looked at the floor, shut off the radio, unhooked it carefully from its holder, and handed it to a uniformed sergeant whose face was now about four inches from his own. The smell of hot sauce from the sergeant's late breakfast attacked Kell's nostrils. He winced.

"It is really so nice of you to all come turn yourselves in like this," the sergeant said to Kell. "Yes, you've saved us a great deal of trouble. I will be sure to tell that to the judge," he smiled. "Next week."

Another officer bent and picked up Kell's rifle, simultaneously clearing the chamber and ejecting the clip. She picked the cartridge off the floor with a curious expression, then examined those in the clip.

"My, my. Look at that. Can you believe this? These folks are carrying blanks," she grinned, her perfectly whitened teeth glistening.

The sergeant eyed Kell from head to toe.

"Actually, that does not surprise me," he laughed. "I bet their heads are loaded the same way."

Laughter erupted all around.

"Tell me, Mister . . . ?"

"Kell, Richard."

"Mr. Kell, tell me, why were so many of your people carrying blank ammunition around our island today? Is this a new technique to win a war?"

The sergeant's eyes glistened. The curl of his lips showed how much he was enjoying the moment.

"Because we are all idiots."

"Oh, is that it?" the sergeant chuckled. "Yes, I think you're right," he added very seriously.

He turned to his other officers who had joined in the laughter. It sounded like a pleasant evening in some local bar where everyone was half-stewed and someone had just told a really bad joke.

"Actually," Kell said, angered by their laughter, "maybe you should ask our fearless leader."

"Who is your fearless leader, Mr. Kell?"

"Kenny Hamilton," Kell said, more than happy at this moment to incriminate the mastermind of the whole stupid scheme.

"And I might find Mister Hamilton, where?"

"Probably hiding under a rock somewhere," Kell sneered.

The laughter died out and all the officers were serious again. It was plain they were very upset about this band of outsiders disrupting the serenity of their island home.

"We'll talk more later," the sergeant abruptly informed Kell.

The intruders were marched through several corridors to a large bank of holding cells. With no booking, or further questioning, they were stripped to their undergarments, men and women, and locked into four large cells.

The cells were not empty.

"Welcome home," Bryan Cantor said as Kell came through the steel door.

Kell stopped short and stared at him. Cantor was laying on a steel bed with no mattress. Two others of Cantor's squad were standing against a far wall, stripped to their undergarments. Kell turned his head and saw Traci Dennison curled up in a ball on the floor near the steel toilet fixture.

"Oh," said Kell, making a wide, pained grimace. "Home, and family."

Traci looked up at him briefly, absorbed the wounding sarcasm, then turned her head back toward the cinderblock wall. Kell thought she might melt herself into the concrete if it were possible.

DURING THE foreshortened fracas at the George Town Police Station, everything had unwound even further at Pedro St. James.

Broadman and his team, who were still trying to hold defensive positions on the road and grounds around the old estate, had been soaked by the firehoses for so long that they were ready to surrender. Even in the moderate, eighty-two degree weather, they were beginning to chill from the damp clothing clinging to their skin.

"Where the heck are they getting so much water?" crowed one soggy man to his buddy.

His friend gave him an "Are you really that stupid?" look, and nodded toward the ocean waves lapping up against the nearby shoreline.

"Oh. Yeah," came the lukewarm response.

Up on the third floor balcony of the house, Jason

Broadman and three other men from Team Two were hunkered down below the balcony railings that overlooked the beautiful, scenic yard and shoreline.

"Damned-fine place to spend a pleasant aft'rnoon," one of the men quipped sarcastically at Broadman. "How much'd you say we're gittin' paid?" he asked with his home-grown Tennessee drawl.

Broadman scowled at the man, a fellow named Brock Quisler, whose name seemed to fit his personality well.

"Not nearly enough," Broadman answered acidly.

"Kin we make it back to the boats, ya thank?" Quisler asked.

"Don't be a moron," Broadman replied, nodding behind himself. "Go look out from the balcony on the other side. There's already six police boats parked out there. How far do you think we'd get?"

"But would they be armed?" the imbecile pressed him.

Broadman scowled again, saying, "Well, apparently every damned cop on this island is packing. Contrary to the claims of our brilliant Mister Kendall Hamilton."

"The Fourth," Quisler added, as if the word had a putrid taste to it.

One floor below them, Mark Gillman had not changed position in almost an hour. After shooting the police officer and fireman, he shoved Broadman's rifle with the live ammo away and just laid there on the floor, wondering why in the world he had ever agreed to Broadman's bribe to become part of the Grand Slam. If he hadn't owed Jason nearly three thousand dollars in gambling debts, he would have begged off. But Jason was the kind of man who made backing out of anything nearly impossible. As long as he had known Broadman, which was eleven years, Jason always had a threatening, overbearing quality of personality that made it hard to say no and not end up looking constantly over your shoulder.

As the minutes wore on, Gillman was half-tempted to grab Broadman's rifle again and use it on its original owner.

Gillman didn't know the condition of the two men he had shot. He saw them both drop like lead weights from a shelf, but he wasn't sure how bad they were. He worried, but refused to accept, that he might have killed them.

In fact, he had.

"Let's give it up," Gillman moaned up to Broadman from one balcony below. "This is pointless, man! We're trapped."

As water continuously dripped on him from the balcony ceiling, Gillman was about five seconds from breaking into tears. He had wounded—maybe killed—two innocent people, both uniformed officers. Whatever happened next was going to be very bad, not just for him, but for everybody involved in the whole operation. He could feel the anxiety vibrating in his chest and was afraid to stand for fear his legs would not support him.

It would be worse, Gillman speculated silently, for Kenny Hamilton. This whole thing was his brainchild, after all.

Up on the third floor, Quisler looked over at Broadman with a pleading eye.

"He's rawt, ya know. Ya know we're not gitten outta here."

The police had stopped shooting a long time ago, but another thirty or so reinforcements had shown up, all armed with handguns, shotguns, or scoped rifles. Broadman was not stupid enough to try to go up against that force with the few people he still had—even if they had not all been carrying blanks.

"Yeah. Guess that's right," Broadman said after several moments of slow thought. "Let's just hope they're not all so pissed off that they just blow us away for the fun of it."

He keyed his radio on a common team channel.

"All right, people. Weapons on the ground. Stand in place. Do *not* move, 'cause you may get shot. We're giving it up."

Broadman dug in his back pants pocket. He always carried a handkerchief. It wasn't white, it was the color of blood. He stood slowly, held the hankie up high, and waved it slowly anyway.

"I hope they get the message," he said, mostly to himself.

OUT ON the catamaran off the north coast, Kenny's radio was scanning all their channels. The catamaran captain, Linford Reid, could hear brief bursts of static from time to time.

Reid was just able to make out Jason Broadman's last transmission as it came across the air. He could see that Kenny heard it more plainly. Hamilton grabbed the steel bow railing with both hands as if it were a snake and he was about to wring its head off.

Hamilton stood there, bracing himself. He seemed dumbfounded. He turned and stared toward Reid, who had been hovering near the wheel for the last hour, waiting for an order from Kenny to move in for a landing.

Then Kenny turned away from Reid and stared across the waves, which had calmed since morning. His vacant eyes, Reid guessed, must have been picturing Jason

Broadman's large, reddish face.

"You dumb, stupid numbskull," Kenny said, but not keying his radio. "You bastard!" he cursed louder at the waves. "Claimed you were so tough! And now you chicken out? *Now?*"

He switched his radio to the Team Three channel.

"Kell," Kenny yelled into the radio, "answer me!"

Only silence.

He switched through the other channels.

"Traci, Bryan—anybody? Where the heck is everybody?" Kenny demanded, his voice tearing at his vocal chords.

Silence again, chased by static.

He stormed toward Linford Reid, waving an arm and yelling, "Get us out of here, now!"

"Where do you want to land?" Reid asked.

"Land! Are you *kidding?* Get us as far away from this place as you can! Head us east—back toward Jamaica!"

Reid was disconcerted. Kenny was obviously losing it, but what could he do except follow orders? Hamilton still owed him a great deal of money for this voyage and he didn't want to jeopardize that by getting mouthy.

"Yes sir. East it is."

Kenny went to the small cabin, where he found Kylaia napping. He shoved at her shoulder hard, and she stirred.

"Move over, you stupid woman!"

She rolled toward the wall as Kenny sat heavily on the narrow bed, crunching her hand under his leg.

"Ouch!" she cried, pulling her hand free. "What's wrong?"

I REMEMBER how Kylaia described those moments, when I finally tracked her down and interviewed her.

"It looked like he was about to disintegrate, into little pieces," Kylaia told me. "He looked like a frightened boy. So I asked him again, 'What's wrong?' He glared at me, like I should know the answer. Then he gave me the coldest stare. 'What's wrong?' he said, 'the damned world! My chicken, supposed friends. You,' he said. At first, I thought it was regret he felt. But then I realized, he was mad at the whole world."

I thanked Kylaia—whose real name is Esme—for the insight. Hamilton had seemed like such a blank piece of paper to me for so long. Her few words rang true, and helped me make sense of what drove him.

In many ways, Kenny had it made. That's what others saw, at least. But I think he was deeply unhappy, and he blamed everything—and everyone—but himself. His obvious blindness about himself must have prevented him seeing it.

Esme left me with another tidbit that really stuck.

"I could see something else in his eyes," she told me in our first and only interview, "that afternoon, in our little room on the catamaran. I don't know what emotion to call it. But I could see it. It kind of horrified me. He badly wanted to escape—and leave the others behind. Without a thought. His friends be damned."

"What do you mean?" I asked, puzzled.

"Well, I said, 'Can't we help them?' There was that awful look again, and he just said, 'They're not worth it.' It was terrible. But *nothing* would turn him back."

THE GRAND SLAM had hit the wall.

Jason Broadman, Ronnie Vaughn, and their remaining teammates at Pedro St. James were corralled, frisked, and loaded like cattle into the back of two open, stake-bed trucks that were brought to St. James after the remnants of the Grand Slammers surrendered.

"Take them to Bodden Town Station," Detective Dane Marketta ordered the officers in charge of the new prisoners. "Sounds like we're getting pretty full up downtown."

"Right, sir," the lead driver answered. "Say—if the Bodden Town cells fill up, can we just put them out in that little pig sty at the next-door neighbor's house?" the officer laughed.

"Nah," Marketta said, looking up at Broadman sitting on the truck bed, his back against the cab, looking downcast. "They don't deserve food that good."

Twenty-Seven

The Reporter

It ended up being a very long day, especially for the Royal Cayman Islands Police Service. They did a superb job—an incredible job, really—of derailing Kenny Hamilton's planned coup. It didn't hurt that early in the day the Cayman police got ahold of the radios from Dahlgren and his little bunch. By late afternoon, they had all the attackers inside a cell.

Well, all except two. Arielle Kemper, and Kenny Hamilton.

Luckily for me, I have several buddies on the police force who were willing to fill the many blank spaces I ran into as I did my research in the weeks that followed. They even let me read the official statements from Traci Dennison, Bradley Schott, Jason Broadman, and many of the others. Without those, I could never have pieced this story together.

One thing that especially bothered me for the first couple of weeks was that I couldn't find out anything about the secret advance team that Hamilton had sent in before the assault. It was this group who had lined things up, like the rented vans and speedboats. They also managed, on Kenny's last minute orders, to smuggle in a small boat load of extra live ammunition two days before the attack.

Apparently Kenny wanted to hold onto the place for a while.

That ammo stash has long since been tracked down and confiscated by Detective Marketta's men.

I also learned, after weeks of digging, that the advance team also made month-long reservations for Kenny, Traci, Brad, and the rest of the crew at several of the big resorts along Seven Mile Beach. It seems that Kenny planned to house everyone in hotels while they settled in and took command of the islands, and confiscated what would become their permanent homes.

According to Traci, Kenny himself was going to move straight away into the governor's official residence.

So, I was stuck. Who was on this advance team? More importantly, what became of them? Without Kenny around to explain this, I started checking for hotel records, rental car receipts, or anything else I could get my hands on, looking for clues. This part wasn't easy. The main problem was that I had no idea *who* I was looking for. I was getting nowhere.

The stroke of luck came when one particular restaurant receipt fell into my hands from a very popular place by one of the big hotels on Seven Mile Beach. It was brought to me by a young woman I know, Julia Hyde, a native islander who waitresses at the restaurant. She had seen a couple of my earliest write-ups in the newspaper, so she knew the names of some of the key Grand Slam players. Julia has this photographic-like memory and—luckily for me—she recalled serving an older man and woman one evening not long before the attack. The woman's maiden name was Hamilton.

Bingo.

Julia persuaded her manager to let her dig through piles of credit card receipts from the days leading up to the now notorious attack.

"Why did the name Hamilton jump out at you?" I quizzed Julia, staring down at the receipt she had just handed me in my office cubicle, after my weeks of dead-end attempts to identify the advance team.

"Well, it's been kind of a major name in your newspaper stories," she said, looking at me like I had a mind on the level of an iguana.

"Yeah . . . ."

"But it was something else, too," she admitted, smiling. "My best friend in secondary school—Regina—she used to talk till I was nauseated about the famous Alexander Hamilton."

"Why was she so interested in Alexander Hamilton?"

"You know, in school we used to daydream about our own futures, maybe someday being famous, or rich. Regina thought it was fascinating that Alexander wasn't actually from the United States at all. He was an orphan from the Caribbean."

Anyway, when Julia saw the name of Kenny Hamilton in my third article, she instantly remembered this old couple she had served one night. The man had run off to the restroom, so his wife signed the check, and she used a hyphenated name, "Susan Hamilton-Briggs."

With Julia tagging along with me, we hit the streets. In just two hours, we were able to find out that a Franklin Briggs and his wife Susan had been registered, during the right time frame, at the pricey hotel next to where Julia works. We gave this tip to a buddy of mine in the police service and it didn't take them long to find nearly a week's worth of hotel, restaurant and shop receipts from a Frank or Franklin Briggs, or his wife Susan.

Then the Briggs name started to pop up other places, as well. Three more people, who turned out to be the two adult sons and adult daughter of old Frank and Susan, had also been on the island during the same period, but they stayed at two other hotels. John, Barton, and Anna Briggs—apparently she was either unmarried, or divorced—had been running around the island for three or four days with their parents doing the usual touristy thing, while also secretly lining up vehicles, boats, and hotels for Kenny's planned overthrow of the Cayman government.

Susan, it turns out, is one of Kenny's aunts, on the Hamilton side. And if she had just not signed that restaurant receipt with her name hyphenated, the cops— with some help from Julia and me—would never have gotten on to them.

The question still haunted me, though, when and how did they disappear? Obviously, they were long gone before I ever stumbled onto the name.

What they learned—my police buddies—was that all five Briggs had flown out of Owen Roberts Airport the morning after the attack since, as far as anyone knew, they were unconnected to anything that had transpired the day before.

The police and customs, of course, had locked down the whole island, including the airport, the morning of the 16th, shortly after trouble broke out at Comptrell, and then at Pedro St. James. The Cayman authorities weren't stupid. They knew very quickly that the assailants had come in by watercraft, but they also knew perfectly well that they might try to escape by aircraft.

The Cayman police were not about to let that happen. Everyone who had already reached the airport the morning of May 16th was turned back to home or a hotel, outbound flights were grounded, and inbound flights were diverted. This caused major anxiety for several airline pilots who were no doubt looking forward to a couple of layover days on Cayman, enjoying—as they like to put it—some of the local scenery.

Having tied down all the Grand Slammers around the island by suppertime on the 16th, the police made a decision to reopen the airport early the next morning. So, when the five Briggs showed up at the airport about 10:00 a.m. on the 17th, Mrs. "Susan Marie Briggs" was able to waltz away unscathed, along with the rest of her now-criminal family. While she liked, on a lark, to sign things using her hyphenated maiden name, her passport and driver's license bore only her married name.

She lucked out. For a while.

As things now stand, the Cayman police are working on arrest warrants, as I write this, to have all five Briggs picked up in the U.S. and extradited as accessories to the Grand Slam attack. Justice grinds slowly, but it does grind.

All five Briggs, by the way, will also be accessories to the attempted robbery of Comptrell, and to three murders. Because not only did the police officer and fireman who were shot out at Pedro St. James both die, the elderly tour guide there—the one Broadman blasted—bled to death because Broadman wouldn't let anyone in to help him. It had been a reckless, un-aimed shot but the slug punctured the man's femoral artery, causing massive blood loss. Despite a valiant attempt by one of Broadman's men to stem the bleeding, the poor fellow was dead in just over half an hour.

So I was elated when my friend Julia found that receipt. The police spread the names around to businesses across the island. In just two days, they found evidence that all the vans and the six speed boats had been rented by one or another member of the Briggs family, who did relays dropping and positioning the equipment where Kenny had dictated.

It amazes me how foolish people really are, and what they'll do for a little cash.

THE OTHER thing that bugged me even more was this: how did Kenny Hamilton manage to get away from the island that day?

The first part of the answer, of course, was that he was never *actually on* the island. Through several weeks of planning, Kenny had tried to convince his people, especially Traci, that he would come ashore just as soon as things were under control on the island. He said he just wanted to float and to stay loose, so he could command the broader situation from the catamaran, without getting snagged down at any one hot spot.

Traci though, as she later admitted to me, suspected Kenny's motives even at the big briefing up in Philly. Brad, too, thought it was odd. Ever since conceiving the Grand Slam, Brad said, Kenny had talked big, and talked tough. But Brad was his best friend. He realized that Hamilton was simply a chicken-heart and was afraid to come ashore until everyone else had taken all the real risks.

How, then, did Kenny manage to escape? And how did he make it back to Jamaica so quickly, where I encountered him barely forty-eight hours later?

This took some real digging, and frankly, I should get a Pulitzer for this part. It baffled me, so I starting burrowing deeper, like a mole in search of grubs.

As soon as I got back to Grand Cayman—after my aborted flight out of Jamaica two days after the attempted Grand Slam—I started talking to anyone the police would give me access to, making lots of notes. I was just going to put it all into a short series of articles for the paper, until I realized I had this book on my hands. But I couldn't tell the story without the answer to this key question: how did the mastermind of the whole operation, Kenny Hamilton, elude capture that day?

None of his friends had any idea.

I started with the obvious possibilities. I took the shuttle flight over to Little Cayman and snooped around. From there, I ferried over to Cayman Brac and snooped some more. I came up empty. Kenny's catamaran, as far as any of the locals knew, never came near either of the other two islands that day, May 16th, or the next.

So, was Hamilton a new David Copperfield who could make himself and an entire catamaran and crew disappear? Surely that catamaran didn't carry enough fuel to make it all the way back to Jamaica without refueling, not after their trip over. Yes, they had sails. But I doubted, checking the wind conditions, that they could have made sufficient speed to get Kenny back to Jamaica in time to board a plane on the 18th.

I spent a whole day in a dinky motel on Little Cayman scribbling down theories until I thought my head would split from too much thinking and bad coffee. Finally, I called my boss and got him to extend my expense account a few hundred dollars more. He wasn't thrilled about that, but he agreed. He's a cheapskate, but he trusts me.

I caught the shuttle flight back to Grand Cayman, then flew directly back to Jamaica. There, I worked a kind of magic. I'm not sure, still, how it worked out as easy as it did. Some would say *karma.* I'd call it Providence.

Following one of my many theories, I popped my head in at the general aviation building, across from the commercial terminal at Norman Manley International Airport in Kingston. There was only one guy on duty that day, and his English was pretty weak. He was a native Jamaican, tall, lanky, with rich, dark skin and almost black, tightly curling hair.

After some small talk, I got him to understand that I was interested in chartering a small airplane, but it had to be a pontoon.

He looked at me curiously. I'm sure, from the look he gave me, that he had dealt with a lot of crooks.

"No pontoon, mon."

"What?" I asked him to clarify.

"We have no pontoon planes," he explained slowly as if I was not quite all there. "Only wheels," he said with a squinting look, "you know, how like you land on the regular ground."

He looked pained to have to tell me. I got his meaning. I turned to leave.

"But, hey mon," he said to my back.

I stopped and turned. His expression telegraphed that he had just had a major brainstorm.

"You know what we do got? We got the helicopter. That one got the pontoons you want."

He gave me a toothy smile, part of which was missing.

My eyes lit up. He was sure he was about to earn a great rental commission. When I asked if he could look back and see how many times the helicopter had gone out in the last few weeks, his face fell.

"Sorry," I said. "Look, I'm a reporter, OK?"

He suddenly looked as if there was something dead down near his feet and it had begun to really smell. Some of his three-day-old whiskers needed itching, too.

"Look, I'm working on what happened over on Grand Cayman. You've heard, right?" I asked him nicely.

"No, mon. Hear nothing. Something happen, you say?"

I couldn't believe it. The guy must have worked, eaten, and slept behind this sales counter, and his television must have been broken.

"Don't worry about it," I said. "I just need to know exactly which days the copter went out, and where. Since about May tenth. And—if you can tell me—who paid for it."

He still seemed to be smelling the same foul substance, but then, just as suddenly, because I was just a no-good, low-life, newspaper reporter, his expression changed and he looked like he felt a strange kinship with me.

"OK, mon—for you, anything. But you're gonna have to buy me a beer when I get done with work."

I couldn't believe he ever actually got off work.

"Sure. I'd be delighted."

Nodding to some tune that was dancing around in his mind, he pulled out a red register book, ran his fingers up and down the pages for half a minute, then tapped the keys on his computer.

"Shouldn't be too hard. It's *old,* mon. Hardly ever leaves the ground. Unless people are pretty brave."

He tapped the mouse as if it was an electric hotplate and bounced through a couple more screens.

"Yeah mon, well look there." He swung the computer screen so I could see, too. "You see? There. It only went up once since then. On the sixteenth."

I knew I had hit the jackpot. I'm sure the guy could see triple sevens glistening in my eyes.

"Who went out?" I prodded him.

"Funny, that one," he said, pulling an ear lobe to help him remember exactly. "Nobody went out. Just the pilot. And he brings just one back."

"What did he look like?"

"He has kind of peppery looking grey hair, moustache, white pilot shirt, you know—"

"No, no, I'm sorry," I broke in, "I meant the passenger. Who did he bring back?"

"Oh, mon, it was long hours that day. Long. I don't remember exactly." He found one whisker that had been ignored and must have itched. "The man he brought back, let me see him . . . he was in shorts, I think. White shorts, a soft blue shirt."

He continued to describe the passenger, and I realized it fit exactly the description given to me by the friends of Kenny Hamilton.

So that's how he did it. Whether it was plan C, or plan D, or maybe E, I have no idea. Kenny Hamilton may have been a chicken, but he was a crafty and devious chicken. Not only had he arranged for the catamaran to take him separately and safely over to Grand Cayman, he had also back-planned his very own, private escape route.

IT TOOK me two more weeks to track down Linford Reid, the captain of the catamaran. I had to figure out who the previous owner of the catamaran was—the NBA guy—first. He led me to Reid, who had been his captain, too.

Kenny's escape was really quite simple, Reid told me.

"Once Hamilton realized everything had gone south on the island, he ran and hid in the cabin for about half an hour. I didn't want to knock on the door—not after what happened the night before. So I just left him alone, him and the girl.

"Finally, the girl—Kylaia, she called herself—she stormed out of the cabin in a big pout. I wasn't surprised she was pouting. I was mostly surprised she was fully dressed. 'Take me home,' she demanded. 'Sorry, miss. I have to wait for orders from our boss.' 'Your boss, not my boss,' she snipped. 'That man's insane, I think. And he's ruthless,' she almost hollered.

"Pretty quick, Kenny comes out of the cabin. His face was still red, but he seemed to have calmed himself down. He was putting a small phone back into his pocket. 'Sorry, sir,' I told him, 'you won't get reception out here.' 'Well, there you're the one who's wrong, Reid. It happens to be a satellite phone.'"

"He came prepared, huh?" I asked Reid.

"For certain. So I stuttered, 'You called someone?' Yes, it *was* a dumb question," Reid admitted, "but I was very curious. Who'd he be calling on a phone, when he'd been communicating with his people all day by radio?

"'Don't let it worry you, Reid,' Hamilton said with a sarcastic tone. 'We'll just keep heading east. We're going to do a rendezvous in a few hours. I'll let you know when I think we're close.'

"'All right, sir,' I told him.

"'Make on a straight line toward Jamaica,' he added. 'And when you can tie off the wheel, get me and Kylaia some food, would you? I'm starving.'"

"Kind of demanding, wasn't he?" I commented.

"Oh, you cannot begin to imagine." Reid went on with his story. "So after several hours, Kenny comes to the helm and tells me to keep an eye peeled for a helicopter coming up from east-southeast. Sure enough, before long, here appears the copter sporting big, orange pontoons. I brought the cat to a slow crawl, then halted her and dropped our stern sea anchor. The copter—slick as can be—drops right down beside us, about sixty feet off our port side, so as not to swamp us with the downwash of the blades.

"Kenny had already packed what few things he brought on board. He rechecked his shorts pocket to make sure he had his satellite phone. Then I helped him drop down into the little inflatable raft we carry as a life boat. 'What about me, Kenny?' Kylaia squawked as soon as she realized he was about to leave her behind. 'Hey, babe, you get a free sail back to Jamaica. Don't worry, I'm not going to charge you for it,' he laughed.

"I thought the girl would go berserk. I have never— and me, an old sailor—I've never heard those kinds of words come out of the mouth of any female—even these young ones! I even turned a little red. It took me nearly an hour and several mixed drinks to calm her back down. Oh, she was a spitfire!"

"And he just left her?" I asked, baffled.

"Oh, yeah. Cold as any fish down there in the sea, that was Hamilton. He started paddling hard toward the helicopter, so I called after him. 'This will cost some extra, sir. You realize, I don't have enough fuel to motor back to Jamaica.'

"'It could take days, right? Is that what you're telling me?' he hollered back.

"'Likely so, sir. Likely so.'

"'Well, you've got sails, right? And now you've got Kylaia. What the hell more could a man want in the middle of a beautiful, open sea?' Hamilton laughed.

"A couple more minutes and he struggled out of the raft and into the chopper.

"'I'll just add it into your bill,' I called, as he closed the chopper door. But I'm sure he didn't hear me over the rotor noise. And that's the last I ever saw of that little son of a mother dog."

Reid scowled at his cup of coffee going cold on his beat up dining table. He got stiffed for the entire bill, he said—several thousand dollars, if he didn't count the food he himself ate, or his own drinks.

"But lucky I didn't get arrested with the whole lot," he added with a pained smile.

"Yes, you are," I told him. "The Cayman police have gone after just about everybody who was anywhere near to this bunch."

"Well, believe me, I paid. That little Hamilton gig cost me my meager profit margin for the whole darned year," he said with a sour expression, as if I might help him out.

Then he remembered I was a reporter. And based on what I had already told him, Reid knew there was no way he would ever get to take Kenny Hamilton to court.

LOOKING NOW through the deep piles of notes scattered on my writing table, I realize there is so much I could add. I could keep writing about the Grand Slam for the next two years and probably still never cover all the craziness. But life goes on, as do the demands of each day, so I've got to draw this to an end.

I've covered the key events, as best I've been able to

reconstruct them, up through "the big day" of the failed attack. So it's to that day that I now want to return, to try to bring this to a close.

As the day wore down, Brad Schott, Traci Dennison, Jason Broadman, and other Grand Slammers were plucked one by one out of their jail cells at the George Town and Bodden Town police stations and were being interrogated by Dane Marketta and *his* team.

VI.
Back To The End

Twenty-Eight

The Reporter

The afternoon had worn itself out. As evening crawled into nighttime, Detective Dane Marketta and his staff were feeling drained. But no one was going home until they were sure they had a solid handle on what had happened on their island that day, and until they were reasonably certain they had every one of the attackers under lock and key.

AFTER THE disaster at the bank, Brad Schott was brought to the George Town Police Station but was placed in a different cell than the one Traci Dennison was already in.

Once Marketta figured out that Brad and Traci were key players in the whole scheme, he placed them into separate interrogation rooms where he and his assistant, Detective Andrew Carden, went to work on them.

Over several hours of questioning, Marketta only became more and more irritated with the pair. It became obvious that Brad and Traci were in on the attack plan from the very beginning, but the harder he or Carden pushed them with questions, the more stubborn they became.

Traci, sweating it out in her interrogation room, was not sure who else the police had in custody, besides the men arrested along with her at Government House. She had not seen Brad, and wasn't sure if they had him or not. But the bigger question she kept asking herself was, *Where the heck is Kenny?*

Brad, isolated in another interrogation room, guessed that the cops might have Traci. He was fairly sure he had heard her voice once in the hall as someone walked her by. Mainly, though, he was wondering exactly the same thing as Traci. What happened to Kenny? Did he eventually come ashore as he had promised? Had he been caught? But if the police had him, why did Marketta keep asking where Kenny was? *Or is it just a trick to get me to talk?* Brad wondered as he sat there feeling like beef jerky drying.

Out at Bodden Town Police Station, Jason Broadman, Ronnie Vaughn, and the others who had been rounded up from Pedro St. James were also being grilled with questions. Several men had already flipped like burgers over hot coals. They were more than happy to turn on their comrades if it might get them an easier time in front of the judge, or maybe a lighter sentence.

Still, as talkative as several of the members of Teams One and Two were, none of them seemed to know where Kenny Hamilton was, either.

Jason Broadman remained tightlipped and said absolutely nothing. He realized how deep he had already dug his own grave. Marketta stayed in contact with his officers in Bodden Town and knew that Broadman was one of the top leaders of the attempted coup. One of Broadman's own team—the one who tried to save the tour guide's life—had already told police that it was Broadman who shot the poor man.

"Have you gotten anything out of that Broadman character yet?" Marketta asked an assistant during a routine phone check-in.

"You joking?" his officer answered, "Broadman's head is harder than eighty-year-old concrete. We're not going to get anything useful from that toad."

"Nothing about this Hamilton guy?"

"Not a word. Not from Broadman."

All afternoon, Marketta had heard the name Kenny Hamilton from different directions, but the man seemed like a ghost. Now, as evening darkened, Marketta was reaching the limit of his usually tempered patience. After hours of he and Detective Carden grilling Brad Schott and Traci Dennison, and managing to get only a vague, preliminary written statement from each of them, Marketta still had few details about the elusive Kenny Hamilton, and no lead as to his whereabouts.

Tired, irritable, and frustrated, Marketta made a very unorthodox decision in terms of interrogation. He decided to throw Brad and Traci together into the same room and press them even harder in front of each other. Over the previous several hours, it became obvious that there were serious emotional ties between the two, revealed by the way they kept asking about the other. Marketta was smart and experienced. He knew he could use their feelings for each other to his own advantage.

He also, though, had a new and even better reason to put them together. One of his staff had just handed him some emailed police reports from a different police jurisdiction, one that had a *very* keen interest in both his prisoners.

Marketta wanted to watch the expressions on Traci

and Brad's faces, and the interactions that might follow, when he shared what he now held in his hands.

"HAVE A seat right there, Miss Dennison. You, Brad, over there, opposite her. Good."

They were no sooner facing each other than Traci was mouthing the words, "Are you OK?" to Brad. Brad looked at Marketta and knew he was watching them intently, but he gave Traci a little nod, *Yes,* that also seemed to convey, *so far.*

Marketta played along, keeping his new information secret from them for the time being. He wanted to let their little friendship bubble swell a bit, before he burst it.

"So, you can see, you're both fine. Well, except for Brad's very minor shoulder wound," Marketta said with a pleasant, fatherly tone.

"What happened?" Traci asked Brad, her eyes getting intense.

"I got hit, at the bank. When Arielle was shot."

Traci's eyes enlarged like those of a school girl watching a frog get dissected.

"Arielle?" she said in almost a whisper. She hadn't heard anything about Arielle, and now was terrified to ask. But she instantly saw the pain and reluctance in Brad's eyes.

"Yeah, well . . . she kind of went nuts," Brad said somberly. "Anyway, she's gone."

"Where?"

Brad looked at Marketta, who refused to rescue him.

"Traci, Arielle's dead," Brad said, forcing the words out as his face tore itself with emotion.

Traci lurched back against her chair as if she were a prize fighter's punching bag. She felt hot needles stinging her all over like a mass of crazed hornets. "Arielle—? *Dead?"*

Traci knew there had been more shooting at Pedro St. James after she and Cantor and their crew left for the fiasco at Government House. But until now, she hadn't heard about the shooting at the bank.

"It has not gone well for you and your little army," Marketta said to them ominously. "You see, we're not just talking about an attempted overthrow of our nation. We are now talking about murder—as Mr. Schott here already knows from speaking with Detective Carden. Your friend, Miss Kemper, is not the only person who died today."

Arielle? Traci mouthed toward Brad, not really hearing Marketta. Her eyes became drizzly wells of emotion as she tried to make sense of the devastating news. "Oh, God," Traci croaked. "Oh, my, God." Her eyes closed tightly, trying to stop the eruption that might come at any moment.

Marketta gave her only a moment to breathe.

"Miss Kemper, I'm afraid, was a casualty of her own stupidity," Marketta said bluntly. "But I'm not talking about her. I have a dead police officer and a dead fire officer on my hands. And there's the man your friend Broadman shot at Pedro Castle. He died of his wound— long before we were able to reach him."

Brad was sure Traci would smash her head down onto the table any second. His heart wrenched because he couldn't stop what she was feeling.

With no warning, Marketta sat down ponderously in the dark, wooden chair at the end of the table, his face a mere two feet from Traci and Brad's. He glared at them, his lips pressed tightly together. The stubble on his face was getting darker, as were his eyes, and expression.

Traci sensed him sit and looked. She looked at Brad. They knew they had pushed Marketta past his limit.

Brad tried to derail Marketta's train of thought. "But neither of us had anything to do with that!"

"Well, I'm sorry, Bradley"—Marketta's eyes became inflamed—"I'm afraid that's not true. You see, all these deaths—and a number of very serious injuries to other *innocent* people—all these things happened because of you and this friend of yours, Mr. Hamilton. I understand enough at this point to know that you two were in on this from the beginning. So that makes you accessories to the killings. And all the other crimes perpetrated against us. Before—and during—the fact!"

He went silent, letting this settle in. Mentally, he was sharpening the pin that would shortly burst the thin bubble of security that each other's presence had furnished.

Brad was desperate to change the subject.

"But how did you take us all down so quick?" It was a back-handed attempt at a compliment for Marketta. Brad hoped to defuse the hostile, bitter look in the detective's eyes. "I mean, we planned this thing out for weeks. Every detail. I—well, I can't believe you could respond with such force. And so quick."

"Well, Bradley, I know I may look like just a frumpy, poorly educated island cop to you," Marketta said, with a certain relish in his voice at what was coming. "What you doubtless don't know—and probably don't care—is that I'm the head of the J.I.U., and—"

"The what?"

"The Joint Intelligence Unit of the Royal Cayman Island Police Service. I was trained in Advanced Police Science at a college in London and I've been doing this for about twenty-three years. And while you are without doubt the stupidest bunch of crooks and robbers I've ever run into—you are certainly not the first."

"But Kenny said there were only forty or fifty cops—ah, police, I mean—on the whole island. And you didn't have guns," Brad said, as if this would somehow assuage Marketta's ire.

"Mr. Schott, look at me. Our Police Service is made up of nearly four hundred officers and support staff. And yes, it's true, firearms are illegal on our islands. But how do you suppose we would be able to enforce that law if we had absolutely no weapons ourselves? You cannot be *that* stupid."

Brad wanted to change the subject even worse, now. He looked across at Traci, whose eyes were scratching the finish off the table top as she sunk in a pit of dark emotion over the loss of Arielle. Brad's insides echoed what she was thinking. It was Traci who had talked her good friend Arielle into being a part of this. Never—never—could Traci have imagined it would lead to Arielle's death.

Brad knew Marketta was right. He himself was just as much to blame as Traci, or anyone else. He wanted to crawl into that pit with Traci and sink into oblivion.

Marketta turned his gaze toward Traci, too. While the last thing he would ever do would be to show this, he was beginning to feel real sorrow for this attractive young woman.

"You still with us, Miss Dennison?"

She looked up, newfound despair in her eyes, which were sopped.

She nodded.

Now it was Marketta whose emotions began to twist. The girl looked despondent and utterly lost. He had learned that she and Arielle had been close friends.

Could he bring himself to say what he was about to say? Brad, he knew, would handle it. Could Traci? She was already facing the funeral of her friend, a funeral she would not be able to go to because she would be locked away in a cage.

Marketta steeled himself. At certain moments, like this one, he really did not like being a cop, or doing what he had to do. He took a deep breath, but very quietly. He did not want to betray to Brad and Traci how reluctant he was to go on.

"I'm afraid there's something more. A completely different matter we need to discuss."

Traci looked at Brad, panicked, then looked back at Marketta. She felt she was about to pass out. Without Marketta moving his lips further, she sensed exactly what was coming.

Brad, naively, did not.

Traci felt that her head was about to explode. She had developed a crushing headache over the last several hours, fueled by stress, anxiety and gnawing hunger. She forced her wet eyes shut again, waiting to hear the inevitable words.

"We found something very interesting among your belongings, Bradley," Marketta said out of the blue.

For a brief moment, Traci thought she might have gotten a reprieve.

"What's that?" Brad asked, staring. A sudden, un-named dread stalked him.

A shudder ran through Traci, the expression of wrestling, conflicted emotions over the fact that it might be Brad who was about to take the brunt of all this, instead of her. She felt a sickening guilt for thinking this.

"Well, you had your credit card wallet on you, in your little blue fanny pack," Marketta went on.

"Uh-huh."

"There was some cash, too. Eight one-hundred-dollars bills folded up in there, in fact."

Marketta opened a file folder in front of him, whisked out one of the bills, and ironed it out with his hands on the table, without taking his eyes off Brad.

Brad's heart crashed through the floor. *How stupid am I? To carry any of that cash down here!* he realized far too late. Of course, he had never expected to be sitting in a police station that evening.

Traci gave Brad a horrified look. Her mind whirled as she began to grasp it. *One-hundred-dollar bills.* She remembered the party, the laughter, as the men counted all that soggy cash in Kenny and Brad's hotel room at the High Point.

She looked down at the bill Marketta had laid before them, then at Brad. Her eyes dried as if they had been hit by a blast of desert wind.

Brad replied with a grimace and a hesitant nod.

"You didn't," Traci whispered, her teeth locked.

"I thought we'd need a little cash. You know, to help us get started here," Brad told her with the look of an abandoned puppy that had just been hit by a car.

Traci looked like a rock had struck the back of her head. Her eyes went to the floor, as she shook her head very slowly. The stinging headache exploded into something twenty-times worse, and it now had a name. It was called Brad.

"It seems," Marketta said as he watched them both intently, "that the serial numbers from those eight bills happens to match up with some cash taken in a recent robbery. Up in Philadelphia." He made a false smile, and waited.

Traci and Brad sat like ice sculptures. In whatever way they might try to beg out of responsibility for what had happened here on Cayman, Traci knew she could not beg out of what had happened that day on the bridge. She was guilty as sin—and apparently Detective Marketta already knew this.

Brad watched her expression fade from shock, to numbing pain, to the blank look of the dead.

After several beats, the dead face spoke.

"How did you find out?" she asked Marketta, both hands massaging her forehead.

"Well, there were those serial numbers. And it just so happens, doesn't it, you two hale from Philadelphia. The world is just full of these amazing, little coincidences, isn't it?" He arrested his sarcasm. Traci was already bleeding, though there was no physical wound. "And as you know very well—*both* of you," he said, drawing Brad into his lasso, "there was this armored truck robbery. As you also know, two guards died in the supposed 'accident.'"

Brad's eyes winced, though he tried to hide it. Deep down, he had known this would catch up to them someday. He just hadn't expected it to be this day. The back of his throat felt like there was a tree trunk stuck in it. His mind began to spiral, considering all the consequences that were about to parade in front of him because of the reckless decisions he, Traci, Kenny and the others had so foolishly made.

Marketta continued his damning narrative.

"I guess the question they'll want to clear up—up in Philadelphia, I mean—is exactly whether this armored truck thing was just some random robbery, or part of a bigger plan." He paused, for affect. "Like a plan to steal a Caribbean island?"

Traci spoke unexpectedly with a bitter glance at Brad.

"And here I almost thought I was beginning to love you." Her tone held confused anger, and rejection.

Brad's heart recoiled in his chest. If she had only stabbed him with a hot fireplace poker, it wouldn't have hurt so much.

Marketta's voice dropped, both lower and quieter, but it also became harder. He sat back in his chair, straightening up his shoulders, already the judge and jury, and, if possible, the executioner.

"You see, young people, there is no going back on any of this now. The only question I have is, how badly do you want to cooperate with me and the authorities here in Cayman—and how much do you want to try to impress the judge up there in Pennsylvania with how willing you were to help us out down here."

He wasn't begging, and he wasn't manipulating them anymore. He had them pinned to the mat on dozens of criminal charges here in Cayman, but he was also lightly holding a foot on the brake pedal of how badly they would eventually be punished in Philadelphia.

"Of course," Marketta went on, like a doctor trying to ease the pain of a dying patient, "it's going to be quite some time before you ever see the inside of a courtroom in the States. Our legal processes down here tend to move kind of slowly. Island time. You know how that is." He gave them another fatherly smile, which was halfway genuine. "Look Traci, Brad, I *will* help you as best I can on the robbery and murder charges up north—if you are willing to help me. What do you say? It's been a very long day for us all."

Tracy looked like she was already at the bottom of a six-foot hole pulling dirt in on top of herself. Brad was just nodding soberly.

"You told me earlier you hope I catch and punish this Hamilton fellow, Traci. But you haven't really done anything to help me find him."

They all felt at an impasse. Traci was gulping down sobs, feeling again that she was about to throw up. Brad looked at her, unable to speak. She glanced back, her spirit crushed, but just wanting this all to be over. She gave him a defeated, broken-hearted nod. Permission. They were, when it came to it, still in this together. Her heart ached for Arielle, and also for herself. But it also ached for poor, shy, fumbling Brad.

Maybe she really did love the poor soul.

"What else can you tell me about this Kenny Hamilton. Kendall, I think it is?" Marketta asked patiently.

"Well, not to sound trite," Brad replied, "but it was all his stupid idea in the first place."

"I have no trouble whatsoever believing that. What I want to know is, where do I find him?"

"I was honest before. I don't know."

"Traci?"

"I already told you, too. I'm not sure where he ended up. Or where he went. At some point, he was supposed to come ashore."

"Well, you know, I don't want to call you both liars again, but I am starting to think that maybe this Hamilton fellow is just a ruse."

"What do you mean?" Brad asked, alarmed that they were losing ground.

"Well, see, we've done some backtracking on all of you, trying to find some trace of this Hamilton person. But we keep coming up blank. We know you all launched out of Jamaica in the evening day before yesterday. And I happen to know that the two of you spent nearly a week at a hotel there. Together. In the same room."

"Wait, I can explain—" Brad tried to say.

"You don't have to explain your personal lives to me."

"But we didn't—"

Traci reached over and clamped onto Brad's hand to stop him. She shook her head. Marketta rolled on.

"We also found that the plane tickets that got you two to Jamaica were purchased by none other than Jason Broadman. Who also, by the way, chartered the special flight from Florida down to Kingston that brought everyone else to meet up with you. And he made all the hotel reservations. And chartered those two yachts."

"Oh, my God, you know everything," Brad moaned in anguish.

Traci's look of grief and defeat was replaced by one of bewilderment.

"Yes, but then there must have been a plane ticket—or a room—or something in there for Kenny, too," Traci tried to convince Marketta.

Marketta nodded, but it was a probing nod.

"One would have thought that. Except, there wasn't. No such name in the cake mix."

Traci and Brad stared blankly at each other. Marketta continued prodding them.

"There is simply no trace of this Kendall Hamilton, no record of any kind that he's had anything to do with this whole thing." Marketta looked at Traci, then Brad with a strained expression on his face, a look that said maybe he was being bamboozled. "You know, I'm beginning to wonder if maybe this Kenny character is just somebody you made up, to distract us. Somebody, maybe, to take the fall for you two, and the others. A kind of imaginary friend and scapegoat—to blame this whole, idiotic episode on." Marketta seemed to be thinking this over for several moments. "Is that it? Hamilton doesn't really exist, does he? Just a name, a figment—to blame this scheme on."

"Look, think what you want, man!" Brad said, almost spitting the words. "Maybe it's the other way around. Maybe Kenny managed to stay so invisible so that you'd blame the whole thing on us!" He became furious, realizing this might be the truest statement he had made all day. Right then, the mere thought of Kenny Hamilton enraged him.

"Wait," Traci said, feeling exactly the same but desperately searching her thoughts for some incriminating connection. "What about the catamaran?"

"What catamaran would that be?" Marketta asked her patiently.

"The one Kenny's been on all day. He didn't cross with us. He was on his own boat."

"You're saying—what—he was not on either one of the yachts?"

"No. I mean, yes. He was on a catamaran that he bought—or rented. I don't know. But he was on it through the whole thing, giving orders over the radio. He was going to come ashore once we had everything under control."

She gave Brad a hopeful glance.

"And did he?" Marketta asked.

Traci's head jerked slightly as she glanced at Marketta, then turned back to Brad for the answer.

"You think *I* know? I was stuck in the basement of that stupid bank all day!"

"So where was he?" Marketta asked, a light beginning to come on in his head. "On Brac? Or Little Cayman, I'll bet!"

"No, no, he was right here. I mean, offshore, but right here off Grand Cayman," Brad insisted. "I think," he added with gnawing doubt.

"Where, exactly?"

"Well, I . . . I don't know, exactly."

Traci's eyes prowled the wall behind Brad.

"He told me—before we left Jamaica—he said he'd be somewhere off the north coast," Traci said, remembering a brief conversation after their final prep meeting in Kingston. "Or out toward East End."

"Well, we've had our helicopter searching the whole perimeter of the island since late afternoon," Marketta said with disappointment in his voice. "We haven't turned up any stray catamarans."

"Well, then he *must* have come ashore."

"Maybe not, Traci," Brad said, a thought creeping loose in the back of his mind.

Traci stared at Brad.

"You don't think . . . ?"

"I'll have our officers do some further checking," Marketta said, persuaded that Hamilton was real after all. "But no one has reported any unknown craft tied up that we can't account for. Not yet."

Traci looked at Brad with an incensed frown. "Did that rotten bastard ditch us?" she asked, not really needing the answer.

Then something clicked. She remembered the forged passports that Broadman had gotten for her and Brad to fly to Jamaica that night, right after their arrest in Philadelphia.

"Look, detective sir," she said, "couldn't Kenny be traveling on a fake passport?"

"Of course . . . ," Brad added nebulously, taking in her thought.

"Broadman had this friend," Traci was telling Marketta, now as anxious as Marketta to track down Kenny. "This guy—Broadman's friend—he does that sort of thing. Passports, fake IDs, you know. In fact—well, I probably shouldn't tell you this but—oh, screw it. We flew, the two of us," she confessed, gesturing at Brad, "from Philly to Kingston on forged passports."

"Well," Marketta nodded, another piece of the puzzle falling into place, "that explains why your names didn't match up at the hotel. The staff recognized you from pictures we sent over earlier, but they didn't have your correct names."

He smiled at his good luck that Brad and Traci were finally caving in. Maybe his supervisor would actually let him go home sometime tonight.

"So, you think Kenny could have come to Jamaica on a fake identity, too?" Traci asked.

"As slippery as this friend of yours seems to be, I would have to say that's not just possible, it's likely." Marketta looked at his two prisoners, who were beginning to feel like friends. "So, what name would he use?"

Traci and Brad stared at each other. Both realized that as well as they knew Kenny, neither knew him well enough to even hazard a guess.

Traci looked at Marketta for several moments, then back toward Brad. Her eyes brightened with a kind of devious delight at the capture of some memory. "What was the name of that playwright guy you hated?" she asked Brad. "The one they made you read in college English?"

Brad looked blank.

"Come on, you know," she said, "that play about a guy's dead wife, she comes back as a ghost after he remarries?"

Brad remembered. "Oh, *Blithe Spirit* you mean."

"Yeah. The writer, what was his name?"

They remembered in unison, saying, "Noel Coward."

"Try that," Traci said to Marketta. "Mr. Something Something *Coward*."

Twenty-Nine

Brad

I'm back in my cell, with some of our other Grand Slammers. What a miserable looking bunch. Looks like a human garbage dump in here. Smells like one, too, after today.

And there's no shower in here. They must have showers in this jail, somewhere. And somebody's really gotta clean that sink and toilet thing over there. It's bad. They have janitors in jails, right?

Maybe we take turns. Oh boy.

I look around, and it's like I'm seeing them for the first time. They look like refugees from the human race, every one of them. I can't believe we signed this bunch on. Bet most of them have seen the inside of more than one jail.

But then, who am I to talk? Am I any better? Or smarter? I can't believe I ever went along with Kenny myself.

Well, at least Traci isn't stuck in here. I couldn't bear having to be in the same cell with her, watching her put up with its occupants. Like me.

Poor Traci. She's so soft-hearted, under that tough exterior. A tough, *beautiful* exterior. And look what we got her into. I'm such an idiot. It's my fault, probably, that she's in this mess. Kenny asked me, didn't he? Should he ask Traci to get involved? I should have said, *Hell no!*

Great hindsight, Brad. You've always excelled in hindsight.

Why didn't we see the risks—for all of us? It's like we were all blind to the dangers we were walking into. Heads on crooked, eyes firmly shut. I should have said, *Hell no,* for myself.

Why didn't I? I didn't want Kenny to be mad at me, I suppose. That's my biggest fault, probably. I just want people to like me, ever since I was a little kid. I'm awkward around people, and not very swift. I know that. But Kenny acted like a friend, like he cared about what happened to me.

Acted. Maybe that's all it was.

Anyway, if he ever really cared about Traci—or me—he would never have cooked up this whole stupid scheme to begin with. And he wouldn't have asked us to help him pull it off. I can see that so easily, now. Hindsight.

That last hour with Traci and Marketta—oh, man, it was awful. How did the cops find out so much about us, and so fast? Unbelievable. We thought we were so clever, planning everything out.

And the look on poor Traci's face when he laid out that hundred-dollar bill from the armored truck. That's gotta be the stupidest thing I've ever pulled in my whole life, bringing some of that cash along. Why didn't I realize what that could do, the trouble that could get us into?

It looked like Traci would die on the spot. I so badly wanted to grab her, hold her, comfort her. I knew Marketta wouldn't let me. That's what made it hurt so much. Two feet away, and I couldn't touch her. When she grabbed my hand that once, it was like a soothing bandage on a third-degree burn. There's something about her that way. I've never been able to figure it out exactly. But it's like there is some kind of healing power in her look, her touch, that Traci smile.

I think maybe I permanently destroyed that smile today. Look what I got her into. Why the heck didn't I tell Kenny *No!* from the first?

She'll never forgive me.

And my God, I'm still torn up about Arielle. I tried to calm her down. I tried, but she just lost it. I've never seen an animal caught in a trap, but I bet that's the look they have. That terror, desperation—that plea in their eyes to just be put out of their misery.

I guess I'm to blame for Arielle, too. I couldn't handle things properly there at the bank. Kenny said it'd be a cakewalk.

Sure, Hamilton.

Well, he's the one who picked Arielle to go with me. I had no idea she was that volatile. It was like watching a building crammed with fireworks explode—one after another, and you couldn't stop it. It was just plain ugly, watching her go to shambles like that, helpless to control her. My jaw still aches. Maybe I should have bashed *her* in the jaw. Maybe she'd be alive.

I'll never know.

It's strange. Arielle seemed so sweet at first, when Traci introduced us. Why couldn't Kenny or I see what was underneath? But then, with guys, when a woman looks *that* great, it's like, why bother looking deeper? She always looked so calm and confident. Was that an act, too?

Maybe life is an act.

Her interest in Broadman, that should have been a clue, I suppose. A woman who could be attracted to Jason—it should have been a signal.

I wonder what they'll do to Broadman. It sounds like Kenny had him rooted really deep in this whole plan. Deeper than I was, I guess. That kind of ticks me off. Maybe Kenny really didn't trust me—if he'd rely on somebody like Jason so much.

Kenny. He's the one who ought to be sitting here, sweating all this out. Why can't they find him?

Anyway, they're bound to be tough on Broadman. A lot of the blame bricks are going to land on him, now. But I really don't care. The guy is a family-sized creep, if you what to know. Deserves whatever he gets. He was always so condescending to me.

But really, so was Kenny. When I think about it.

I'm exhausted. These last few weeks, it felt like I've been running behind a racing train, trying to catch it, trying to get on board—and then it runs over me. I can feel the wheel marks through my skull.

I've always been a little slow. Mentally, I mean. Slower than most of my friends, anyway. I kind of thought that's why Kenny looked after me. Like he was my big brother or something. But I think I see it now. And I can't hide from it. All the time, he was just winding me up like a dime store watch, getting what mileage he could out of me—and if the watch spring breaks, toss it in the trash.

That's Kenny. That's what he's like. I always knew it, in a way, just tried to overlook it. Because I wanted him as a friend. Him being so rich didn't hurt, either. It sure made my life easier—and a lot more comfortable.

Well, until now.

I look around the cell and there's nothing but miserable faces. And those two poor women from Team Four, Dahlgren's crew. They were with Kell and them, I think, when they got nailed right here at the main police station. You'd think the cops would be considerate enough to put the women in separate cells. Or give them a jacket—something. But maybe this is part of the punishment.

I haven't heard much about Dahlgren. I think he and some of the others are being held at a different police station. Broadman, too. Good. I don't need to see their mean, ugly faces right now.

Traci must be stuck in a cell with Cantor and them. She's probably sitting there blaming me about Arielle. Like I was supposed to look out for her or something. I tried, Traci. I did. But how do you control a volcano once it erupts?

I don't want to think about it anymore.

This is insane. It's truly just insane. All of it. How did I end up like this? My life was on cruise control. Plenty of fuel. Enough friends. Well, a couple. And I go and blow it all to hell.

Yeah, I'm slow, but I never realized I was *this* stupid. Kenny and I are—were—friends. Good friends, I thought. Was that it? I just went along with his hare-brained idea because of friendship?

We all trusted him. I did, anyway—blindly. You never get to see your own blind spots, do you?

Why can't you just stop the clock, or wind it backward or something? Replay certain things, you know, like they do in football games? That's what I want. I want a watch you can turn backward—to make all this crap disappear. Like it never happened in the first place.

You know, if I was God, I would give everybody *that* kind of watch.

Traci, I'm sorry. So, so sorry.

I wonder if she will ever, *ever* forgive me.

Thirty

Traci

Detective Marketta took Brad somewhere else. Maybe back to his cell, I'm not sure. But he made me stay, asked me to write out another statement. A confession, I guess they call it. More details this time. Pull my own noose tighter.

Does he feel sorry for me, even just a little? At least he's going to bat for me. For Brad and me both. Maybe Marketta's got a soft spot in there somewhere. Without him, I'd probably rot in jail here the rest of my life.

What an awful, agonizing day this has been! I feel trapped in the middle of a mine field. Anywhere I step, it's going to hurt. And poor Brad. I don't know why they finally let us see each other. Maybe Marketta figured we'd do what we did do—convince each other to start talking.

What other choice did we have?

They say you always have a choice. Not really. We weren't going anywhere unless we started cooperating. Holding out on information with these guys, it just makes everything worse. Brad knew it. I knew it.

Brad's feeling so terrible, I could see it. He looked like a kid dropped off on the doorstep of an orphanage. I know how hard it hit me about Arielle. I can't imagine how *he* feels. He was there. He had to see all the blood and everything. How gross. I bet he's blaming himself.

I have to stop thinking about her. What I keep imagining it was like, her laying there—it's probably ten times worse than it actually was.

God, I feel so badly for Brad. I wish things were different. Back home, he was sending out hints. I've known he's liked me—for a long time. I didn't give him any real hope, though. Kind of strung him along, so I wouldn't be lonely. When Kenny didn't have time for me.

Kenny wasn't always there, but he was always in the way. That was the problem. I wanted to be faithful. That's so important to me.

Now look.

When I reached over and touched Brad's hand a while ago, it felt so good. I felt I was touching something solid. Because nothing around me feels solid anymore. Except this fear.

I felt better, though, knowing Brad was ready to flip, too, and start talking to Marketta. It was like finally walking out of a dank, dark fog. It was almost funny, the way Brad kept looking at me, like, *Do we turn, or not? Do we help Marketta, or keep our mouths shut?* He wanted to know what I thought. He cared what I thought.

I wonder what he thinks of me now, after what I said. It was so harsh. And I didn't really mean it, about almost loving him. I do. How could I be that mean, that cold with my words?

I wish I could take back what I said. I *do* love him, I've known it for a long time. I just kept pushing him away—because of Kenny.

I am so blind.

Well, it'll be years now. Any relationship I had with Brad—any hope—it's just gone, probably. Marketta says it may be only about ten years, maybe fifteen, since we've decided to help him. But how can I trust that?

Well, better that than the rest of my life. God, what a mess I've made! I'll lose the gym. I'll lose everything.

Kenny, you royal jerk! This was just all about you, wasn't it? You were going to be king, I was just a pawn. All of us were. You never loved me, did you? You used me. Took what you could get, and gave me nothing. Well, you gave me one thing, a future that looks empty.

You're rotten! You're a glutton who feeds on everyone else's misery, Kenny. Worse, I think you love it.

The door's opening, Marketta's back.

"All right, Traci, have you had time to finish your written statement?"

I look down at the writing pad.

"Yeah. Twenty three pages. Is that enough?"

"Oh, it's a start, with what you wrote earlier. And I'm sure we're going to be talking a lot over the next few days. As we piece everything together."

I nod, and try to force a smile that doesn't feel good at all. You shouldn't have to cooperate with cops. You shouldn't even end up in the same room with them.

"Now, one last time," he says, "are you sure there is nothing else you can tell me that would help us locate Hamilton?"

"No, I swear to God. All I know is, he was off shore somewhere on this boat. I—well, I don't even know what it looks like. I didn't actually see it. He just kind of described it to me, before we left Jamaica."

"All right. Well, it's time to take you over to the processing center, to book you in."

That sounds terrifying. Booked in. Locked in. Can't I just spend the rest of my life in this little room? I wish.

"Yeah. I guess," I say. I know he's trying to make this easier. There is just no way it's going to be easy.

Jail. Then prison—for years.

"You look pretty glum," he says. "I suppose I can't blame you."

"Well, I was just thinking about him. Kenny, I mean."

"Hamilton?" Marketta asks, sitting quietly, facing me. I think there's some genuine kindness hidden behind that stiff cop look. "Listen, Traci, I suggest you *stop* thinking about him. And try your best to stop worrying about him. He's not worth your worry. And he'll answer for all this. Someday."

"You really think that?"

"Yes, actually, I do. We're likely going to catch up to him. We're pretty good. Not always fast, but pretty good. And, hey, if he gets away from us, trust me, someday, he'll pay the piper. That may be many years from now, I grant you. But there will come a day."

I stare down at the beat up table. It's a plain, brown wooden table that should be in a closed-up library somewhere. Bleak, and worn down. Like me. "I hope so," I tell Marketta.

Marketta can probably see the new storm of depression clouding up around me. Can he tell how deeply rejected I feel? By Kenny? By Brad?

He's taken young women off to the jail before, I'm sure, but I can see something. There's just a shade of pity in his eyes. I've never wanted anyone's pity before. But to be honest, right now, it actually feels pretty good.

If nothing else, maybe I can get a shower. I sure need it. I feel dirty all over. A murderess. That's what they'll tag me. I suppose some of the other women in the prison will look up to me because of that.

How sick. It'll just make the shame worse.

I glance at Marketta. His expression is part sadness, but there's real sympathy in his dark blue eyes. He tries to assure me again.

"Hamilton will pay. We all pay, Traci. One way, or the other. And every time some dirt bag like your friend Hamilton gets—"

"Please—don't call him my friend."

"Every time some dirt bag like this *jerk* Hamilton gets away from me, that's what I hang on to. He'll answer. If not to us, to someone. Someone with a much bigger hammer."

"I don't know if I believe that or not," I tell him. "But I kind of hope you're right." And I mean it.

Then he says the worst thing yet.

"Let's go."

He walks me from the room, one hand on my arm. Doesn't trust me? Why should he? I'm a killer, and a thief. And a not-very-good liar.

Have a wonderful life, Traci. They're taking you to book you officially into their jail.

"Name please?" someone will ask.

"Traci I. Dennison."

"And what's the 'I' stand for?"

"Imbecile."

I can't believe you, Kenny—getting me into this, then leaving me here. It's so unfair. We all rot in a Cayman jail. You walk away, scot-free.

You pig.

Thirty-One

Kenny

Feels like the air conditioning is broken in this rotten airport. How can people stand it here in Jamaica without air?

Doesn't matter, I've got the perfect escape plan. Fly north from here to Houston, then back south. Zig-zag.

Man, these airport lounge seats feel like a piece of vinyl stretched over a pile of bricks. It's hard to read a newspaper when you've got numb-butt. But there's nothing much in the local papers here yet. It's been a day and a half, now, and so far just one dinky article on the bottom of page one of the paper here in Kingston. Kind of disappointing, really. And strange. I'd have thought the Grand Slam would be all over the place by now.

Well, maybe it's good for me it's not.

I made a pretty slick getaway from Cayman, if I do say so myself. Off the catamaran, zoom back here to Jamaica, hide out in a new hotel that first night, then a different one last night.

You are pretty much a genius, Hamilton.

All I know is, I'm not leaving by that lousy helicopter. You'd never get me back in that piece of crap again. I'm surprised we made it back alive! The engine sounded like it had emphysema. And the pilot had to take a snort before every cloud bank. Said it steadied his hands.

Bank. No wonder I couldn't get through to Brad. The newspaper says the cops whacked Arielle. Wonder what happened? Why would they shoot a looker like her?

Brad, what a dunce! You couldn't handle yourself and Arielle for a couple of hours? How could anybody screw up an assignment that easy? All you had to do was stare at her, for crying out loud, if you needed to keep your mind off the time! How could you get the girl shot?

Maybe she wasn't as tough as she pretended. Traci said she was sharp, and capable. Guess that shows how much Traci knows.

Forget them, Kenny. The new plan. Focus. This is going to work. I backtrack, to confuse the authorities. Up to Houston, then immediately south again to Roatan. It's not Cayman, but still, it'll be a perfect little island haven. And this time I'll just be a tourist again.

Who's ever going to think of looking for me there? I'll buy a speedboat, maybe. Do some fishing, deep sea stuff, spend my time on the water. That was sort of fun the other day, out on the cat—except for all the confusion on the island. If it hadn't been for all my halfwit friends running around screwing everything up, it would have been a really awesome day!

All right, it's settled. Get the tickets. *Why* are these ticket lines always so slow? And it's always the dumb or clumsy ones who end up right in front of you!

OK, that's done. Now, just have to wait for boarding. I'm sure I'm safe. It's going on two days, now, and obviously the Cayman cops haven't tracked me back here to Jamaica. Wouldn't you think this would be the first place they'd look?

But then, why would they? I was too careful. *Nobody* knows where I'm at. Not Brad, not Traci. I even kept Jason out of the loop on this part. No loose ends. That's what I like.

Well, except Kylaia maybe. But she's still out there in the middle of the Caribbean somewhere with Reid. It'll be at least another day—probably two or three—before they make it back. He had to go somewhere to get fuel. Or rely on the wind—and that'd be even slower. Oh well, Kylaia would never talk. What would she say? Anything she'd admit to, it'd just make her look more foolish.

Oh well, a loose end, maybe, but at least she knew what a woman is for. Unlike prim and proper Traci.

Anyway, the tickets have the name from my forged passport, Mr. Jacob Hurlbut. Dummies, they won't even know I was here—or on the plane! They'll never track me now.

I hate this waiting. I need to kill some time. Watch says twenty-five minutes till boarding. I wonder if there's any cops around. Plainclothes guys, maybe?

No, come on Kenny, relax. Nobody's watching you.

It's too bad about Traci and Brad, getting busted. They just weren't careful. But it was their own fault. Obviously, they didn't follow the plan. I told them, over and over, stick to the plan. It can't fail. And look— idiots—they somehow managed to get arrested in Philly before we even left! *That* was real stupidity. Maybe I should have ditched them right then.

I wonder what really happened between them, at the hotel last week?

Come on, Kenny, who cares? If they made out, so what? It's not like you were going to spend the rest of your life with the woman or something.

Kill time.

How?

I'll just hang out here in the lounge at the gate. But those two men by the boarding agent, they look like they're asking a bunch of questions. Cops maybe? Or maybe just trying to figure out their flight home. Yeah, they've got to be tourists. Look at those cheap sandals.

Better to play it safe, though. Maybe I'll wander over to the newsstand. Be cool, browse the books till they call the flight.

Wouldn't you know it? Nothing worth reading. Junk. Who puts all the money into printing this crap? The funny papers are better written.

Wait. The bathroom. That's it. Who's going to search a bathroom? The perfect place to keep out of sight till we board.

VII.
Up, Up, And Away

Thirty-Two

The Reporter

The careless customs agent at the airport in Kingston, Jamaica, distracted by a striking young woman in wild pink, overly-tight short-shorts and a tissue-thin excuse for a sleeveless top, took a scant glance at Kenny Hamilton's bogus passport, stamped it, and waved him through without looking at his face, or his picture.

Just another day, just another stupid tourist.

It was just two days since the attack on Grand Cayman, but this customs guy obviously didn't care less that there was a major manhunt going on.

Looking back, it seems almost comical, but this fellow was a pathetic excuse for a customs official. The Cayman Police had already circulated a wanted flyer to all the regional islands with Kenny Hamilton's photo, which they cloned from his Pennsylvania driver's license. This customs guy in Kingston had a golden opportunity for a big bust, and probably a promotion, and he blew it. A copy of the wanted flyer on Hamilton was posted not six inches from the agent's computer screen, where the public couldn't see it. He had paid little attention to it when his supervisor taped it up, and even less attention since.

The final call had been announced for the flight to Houston, Texas, where Kenny Hamilton planned to reverse direction and fly back down to Roatan, as I would eventually discover from the ticketing records of the airline. On Roatan, if he kept a low profile and had a little luck, he could have hidden from the Cayman Police forever.

How do I know all this, even the details about the customs agent?

Because I witnessed it.

As I hinted at the outset, it was here at the end when I unwittingly came stumbling into this story myself. The end of the Grand Slam was just the beginning, for me. And if I've seemed somewhat invisible throughout my account, by not telling you my name, it's because I was worried about how my version of the events would turn out. Reading back over it, though, I'm satisfied. Someone else might have told it better, but as far as I know, no one has, so I'm all you've got. Anyway, my name will come out eventually, if this ever gets published.

So, the name is Art. Arthur, actually, Arthur McLaughlin. But most everyone calls me Art, except my mom. She always calls me Arthur—Arthur William, when she's mad. But because I loved to write so much even as a kid, she used to joke that she should have named me "Author." Funny.

My sense of humor is a lot like hers.

Anyway, there at the airport in Kingston, I came to be an actual part of the events surrounding the Grand Slam. I stumbled into it by accident, you might say, and I'll never forget the date, because of what happened that day. It was May 18th, just two days after the attempted capture of Grand Cayman by Kenny Hamilton and his gang.

Why was I in Kingston? At that point, I knew nothing yet about Kenny Hamilton, but I had learned that a bunch of the Grand Slammers were from the Philadelphia area. "Young Americans Captured Trying To Capture Island." That was my boss's first headline at home, the morning of the 17th. Pretty lame? Yes, but normal for him.

After me begging for two hours, my boss agreed to fly me up to Philadelphia to do some background on the story, which was only beginning to spread into major papers around the world. I missed the early flight out of Cayman, so I had to shuttle over to Jamaica and head up to the States from there.

Before I go further, though, I need to put that day in Kingston, the 18th, into perspective. Since I've already covered so much about the events leading up to the Grand Slam, and the capture of Kenny's gang, it may be hard to grasp that on that afternoon, the 18th, I still knew next to nothing. I knew some sparse details of the attack and the names of a few key people, but that was it.

It's not that I hadn't tried. I dug for details like crazy that first day after everything went crazy on our island. But the police were staying pretty tight lipped, as you can probably imagine. Dane Marketta, especially, said very little in news briefings because, even with all the Joint Intelligence Unit's fancy information gathering systems, not one of them had picked up a single clue that this thing was about to go down.

That, when you think about it, is pretty remarkable, considering how many real lowlifes Hamilton and

Broadman had recruited into their scheme, not to mention the fact that two of the principals had been arrested up in Philadelphia just hours before they were supposed to leave for the big caper.

Although the Cayman authorities had put out the confidential wanted flyer for Kendall Hamilton, as of the day I flew to Jamaica—the 18th—they hadn't shared much about what they thought his role in the Grand Slam was, or the nature of his relationship with Traci Dennison, Bradley Schott, Jason Broadman, or the others. Complicating matters was one fact they *had* learned. Kenny Hamilton was wealthy and from a very prominent Pennsylvania family which bore a name almost hallowed, by some, in American History. If the Cayman authorities put his name out publicly with criminal allegations and then later had to retract it as an error, they would not only have egg on their faces, it would be scrambled eggs. So they trod lightly around the Hamilton name, still uncertain if he was the right Kenny Hamilton. Marketta, in particular, was very worried about walking on his own Humpty-Dumpty eggshells.

So then, how can I be so certain that it was indeed Kenny Hamilton who got onto the plane to Houston ahead of me that afternoon in Kingston?

Smarts, and a whole lot of digging, and a lot of not worrying about breaking eggs.

Don't think it was easy. It took me a very long time to paste this part together. This, in fact, was the hardest piece of the puzzle, and one of the last that I punched into place.

Ironically, the tight-lipped, muscle-brained Jason Broadman was my key. I interviewed him several times over about three weeks, trying to drag information out of him. It was like pulling teeth from a fossilized dinosaur.

It was only after I threatened to demolish his name even further in the press that he gave up the name of his guy in Philadelphia who did the forged passports.

That, of course, meant another flight up to Pennsylvania, and my boss almost jerked my whole expense account at that point. I've never seen him so red. But in the end, he was glad he let me go, because it brought so many loose ends together.

I managed to track down Broadman's forger, the same guy who dummied up the falsified passports for Brad and Traci to fly to Jamaica ahead of the rest. What I discovered was that Broadman's guy had also made up a fake passport for Kenny, weeks before they left Philadelphia.

The forger was good. I'll just call him Sammy. He had been doing this counterfeit work for years, although he ran a perfectly respectable print shop in one of the suburbs. He specialized in fake documents for illegal immigrants who had just snuck into the U.S., or for others who wanted apparently-legal documents in order to overstay their visas. Anyway, when I caught up to him at his shop—and after a few threats that his real name might end up in several major newspapers—he finally coughed up the phony name that he had used for Kenny's fake passport. The name isn't important anymore, but if you're curious, it was "Jacob Hurlbut."

What *is* important is that I found myself on May 18th standing behind Kenny Hamilton, under this other name, at the boarding gate at Norman Manley International in Kingston. I noticed him mainly because he was so cocky. He was very rude to the woman at the gate.

"Have a wonderful flight, Mr. Hurlbut."

"Sure, whatever you say, lady," Hamilton replied with slight scorn.

Wonderful, I thought, *I hope this guy doesn't act like a jerk for the whole flight.* Oddly, while being so rude, he was also trying to act nonchalant. That snagged my attention, too. It didn't match and that, I suppose, is why I paid attention to him. He stuck out like a sore thumb.

He had also been rude to a fellow in the men's room a few minutes earlier. I happened to be in there, as I usually am before a long flight. I didn't know who Hamilton was, of course, but I do know he caused a long line to back up in the men's room because he hogged a stall, needlessly, for at least twenty minutes. I know. I was one who had to wait.

As Hamilton finished washing his hands, he bumped a distinguished looking, elderly man aside to get at the paper towels. The man frowned at him. Hamilton sneered, "Buzz off, old man."

The gentleman didn't respond, but after Hamilton was a few steps away, the old guy flipped him a very precise finger.

The whole time we stood in the final boarding line, Hamilton was putting on his not-very-good nonchalant act. He was also sweating more than I would have expected, considering that the air conditioning was working overtime that day. He looked back over his shoulder a couple of times, worrying, I suppose, that some customs agent—or somebody worse—might unexpectedly follow him down the ramp.

We reached the plane and ducked through the squat door. The semi-attractive, mid-forties stewardess smiled at Kenny's handsome features as he came through the door. I'm not sure, but I think he gave her a wink.

I have no doubt, knowing now who he was, that he would have preferred to sit in first class. Instead, he was back with us, traveling economy. Maybe he thought he would be less noticeable that way.

Blend in, he was probably thinking.

Hamilton had a window seat to the left of the aisle. I ended up sitting across the aisle from him, four rows behind his.

As it turned out, that was a very fortunate thing.

Being four rows back, I didn't really notice anything Hamilton did. I had lost interest in him, anyway. As soon as I was seated and belted in, I started flipping through my story notes about the Grand Slam—the few that I had at that point. So I've only been able to piece together what happened next with information I got from several other passengers. One in particular was opposite Hamilton in the window seat on the far right, but the same row. I'll just call him "Jack," because he wanted his name kept out of it.

As we climbed through 18,000 feet and banked left, heading toward the gulf coast, Jack, who told me he is a naturally curious person by nature, noticed Kenny lean forward, digging through the magazines in the seat pocket in front of him. What Kenny found, with a grin spreading on his face, was a squeaky-clean, new-looking tablet computer that had been shoved down between two dogged-eared airline magazines.

Hamilton pulled the device out, turned it over, and looked at it. Jack, watching all this, assumed that some passenger probably woke from a nap right at landing, hurriedly collected belongings, but inadvertently left the tablet behind. Kenny probably assumed the same thing. Easy enough to do. How many things have I left on planes over the years?

Instead of calling a steward or stewardess to turn in the lost device, Hamilton's obvious curiosity—nosiness, Jack called it—took over. The plane was not very full and there was no one in the seat beside Hamilton. He casually looked around. No flight staff were lurking nearby. Kenny looked relieved. Nobody watching.

The seat next to Jack was empty, too, which made it easy to see what Kenny was doing. As the plane rocked gently from side to side, Kenny noticed Jack looking at him. Jack looked away, but moments later he looked back, trying not to be so obvious this time.

Kenny glanced around furtively again and decided to turn the tablet on. Maybe he wanted to find out who the owner was, but I doubt it. Based on what I've learned about him since, I think he just wanted to snoop around. Maybe it held some secret, sensitive information left by a banker or an insurance man, something Hamilton could steal and use to bribe or blackmail someone. Or maybe it held the outline of a book or a story, an idea that could be the seed for Kenny Hamilton's next crazy escapade. The way Kenny Hamilton's mind apparently worked, how could anyone possibly know?

With Jack trying not to watch, Kenny thumped the tablet's power switch with the side of his thumb.

The explosion was instantaneous and thunderous, as though catastrophic lightning had struck the inside of a large metal barrel.

In that instant, what Kenny had no way of knowing was that the aircraft had made a short maintenance stop at Raleigh-Durham International in North Carolina earlier in the day, before heading to Miami and then on to Jamaica. What transpired at Raleigh-Durham would only become clear five weeks later when Jamaican authorities, with leads from the FBI up in the States, were able to string together the few clues that existed and decipher what had been done.

What they uncovered was simple enough. During the

stop at Raleigh-Durham, a maintenance worker—who was also a member of a terrorist sleeper cell in Raleigh—slipped the brand new tablet computer undetected into the seat pocket, then walked casually off the plane with her cleaning kit.

Also unknown to Kenny—or anyone else at that moment—was that the innocent looking device had been packed with plastic explosives, its detonator tied to a micro-trigger activated by the tablet's power switch.

The vicious, earsplitting detonation ripped a jagged, man-sized hole out through the fuselage. Luckily, Jack, myself, and most everyone else in the plane were still tightly buckled in because the pilot had not yet turned off those obnoxious little yellow seatbelt signs. We hung on for dear life as the pilot and co-pilot struggled to bring the wounded, shaking bird back under control.

But Jack noticed one other small detail. Unfortunately for Kenny—or maybe fortunately, considering that he had been holding the explosive device in his lap—just before he leaned forward to rummage for a magazine, Kenny released his seat belt.

The sound of the terrible blast was deafening—but "deafening" is completely inadequate to describe the unbearably loud noise. It shook me down to the deepest core of my body. I felt as if the noise alone would rip me into a hundred pieces. A second or two later, I realized blood was trickling out my left ear, the side nearest to the blast. The pillow my head was leaning against saved my right eardrum. I was blinded for about thirty seconds, then my sight began to reemerge as I tried to take in what in the world had just happened.

I looked toward the huge hole where Kenny Hamilton had been. The explosive force of the blast coupled with the instant decompression of the cabin had created a miniature tornado that sucked Kenny out through the hole like a ragdoll, tearing half his clothes away, shredding parts of his flesh that grotesquely decorated the razor sharp edges of the jagged hole, and flinging him violently into the unbreathable, ice-cold nothingness outside.

As the plane was gradually brought back under control by our heroic cabin crew, Kenny Hamilton flew his own path through the frigid darkness, encased during the first few seconds in white-hot gases that roasted him in the cold.

The thick stench of fumes from the explosion filled the cabin, along with dense smoke. Fortunately, the heat and smoke being siphoned out through the large hole in the fuselage saved us all from suffocating in the moments that passed before the dainty little oxygen masks deployed.

Barely stabilized, the plane hurtled on, wounded, lurching, and still shaking violently as the pilot tried to maintain the little control he had regained. He banked harder than he should have, and I guessed correctly that he was turning us around as rapidly as he dared for an emergency landing back on Jamaica.

I can't really describe the resulting scene in the plane. I was stunned senseless by the terrible noise and encompassing flash of the explosion, so I was not very lucid over the next few minutes. I was not coherent enough to take in, let alone remember, all of what I was witnessing until we touched back down in Kingston, rather roughly but safely.

I'm just grateful that I was a few rows behind where Kenny was sitting, or I would probably have spent the next few weeks in a hospital, like some of my fellow passengers.

Jack was not so lucky. His left arm and leg were badly wounded by flying shrapnel and debris. The lower part of his arm had to be taken off, but he survived. So did everyone aboard—if you don't count Kenny.

Call that a miracle if you like, if you believe in such things. By rights, the flying debris should have killed Jack and several other people outright, or at least taken a few more limbs. By some grace or Providence, we were spared that.

Even once we landed, I remained in shock, physically, and emotionally. And I can tell you, it took hours to wear off. Days, really. I don't suppose I will ever get the abject horror of those few moments completely out of my head, or heart. The least little snap or bang, now, causes me to jump in my skin. Don't expect to ever see me again at a fireworks show.

Some things stay with you, despite your best efforts. I've continued to wonder what it was like for Kenny, as he gasped for a final breath. Did he lose consciousness instantly—or outside the plane? What did he feel in those split-seconds? I'm betting the force and speed of being hurled from the plane made sucking in air impossible, so I'm guessing he never got that last breath. He could not have lasted more than a moment or two, considering what the explosion did to him.

I've wondered, too, if what the rest of us saw as the extreme brilliance of the explosive flash also looked bright to Kenny? Or was everything utterly black as he lost consciousness and flew into darkness?

I can't help it, my mind keeps going there. What were his last shattered thoughts? There's no way to ever know, of course. But still, I wonder. Wouldn't you?

It's like a ghostly specter that haunts me. I've tried so hard to understand Kenny's mind and motivations, to grasp what drove him through this whole debacle. As I was thinking about this just last night, I recalled one of my talks with Traci Dennison several weeks ago, as she sat there in her jail cell telling me more of her part of the story. I'm not sure how it came up. Maybe it was after I told her about Kenny's last moments. I don't remember. Anyway, she mentioned a conversation she once had with Kenny. She asked him if he worried about what God would think of what they were planning to do. And she remembered—very clearly—how he answered, how he sneered at her, and at God. He said, "Well, if there is a God, he's nothing but a cosmic clown," or something like that.

Now *that* makes me curious. As I sit here, trying to wrap this all up into a neat little literary package, and looking back on how Kenny Hamilton and his whole Grand Slam team ended up, I can't help but wonder. The world seems so chaotic and cruel, doesn't it? Is there really any ultimate justice built into our existence? Some final "reality check" rendered on each life, on who we became, what we chose, and what we did with it all?

I'm not going to render a verdict on the kind of person I think Kenny Hamilton was. I think you can already tell. But will there ever *be* some final verdict on his life? Has it already been rendered?

In my weak moments, I try to just laugh thoughts like this away, try to bury the whole idea. But then, as I read back over what I've written here, my curiosity gets the best of me. Is each one of us facing an ultimate judgment one day—something we can try to laugh about now, but something we can't actually evade?

All I can tell you is that Traci Dennison, Bradley Schott and Jason Broadman are all sitting in a very small, hot Cayman jail, awaiting sentencing. And

Kendall Hamilton the Fourth? Well, I saw him rocketed out through the hole in the back of that plane like a homerun ball off the end of a perfectly swung aluminum bat.

I guess you could call that a grand slam.

Thirty-Three

Traci

Isn't that how it goes? You never really know what's going to happen. Just when I was reaching the deepest part of my despair, sitting here in jail, Art McLaughlin, that reporter guy, came and visited me again. And he told me—finally—what happened to Kenny at the end, on that plane. I'd heard vague rumors, but Art was there. It's kind of a miracle he's alive, really. Still has some cuts healing up on his face, and a fading-out black eye from some piece of something that whammed him from the explosion.

As Art told me about Kenny, I didn't know if I wanted to cry, or laugh. It triggered so many memories —none of them good. Kenny must have thought he was making his great escape, and leaving the rest of us behind. That's what we all thought, too, that he got away scot-free. He was so cocky, always so sure of himself. So sure nobody was watching.

Art admitted that he held the news about Kenny back from me for a long time because he didn't want to throw my thinking off, you know, about how I was feeling through the whole Grand Slam thing. And how I felt about Kenny, especially after my arrest. Art said he didn't want to color my feelings.

How do you color over black?

I don't know exactly when Brad found out about Kenny, if Art McLaughlin told him during one of their interviews, or if maybe Detective Marketta told him just to kind of rub things in, you know. I guess it doesn't matter. Anyway, since Brad and I will be doing our time here on the island, we'll get to talk, I'm sure. Through the fence that I hear separates the men's exercise yard from the women's.

The two of us were sentenced yesterday. Sixteen years each. I guess it could have been a lot worse. I could be like Arielle. It was only at that sentencing hearing when I found out that Brad knew about Kenny. How he died, I mean. Brad and me were chatting at the defendants' table during a short court recess. Brad's eyes were focused somewhere beyond the far wall.

"What're you thinking?" I asked.

"Huhm?" Brad said, focusing on me instead. "Oh, just thinking."

"About?"

"Kenny. I guess he kind of got what he deserved." His eyes narrowed. "He always bragged about becoming famous. You know, like his big ancestor, Alexander. Guess he was more like old Al than he knew."

I didn't get it.

"Have to explain that one, Brad."

Brad chuckled, "Well, it was kind of Alexander's pride and bluster that got him killed, wasn't it," he said, but it wasn't really a question.

"I'm still not following you."

"Traci," Brad said with amazement in his eyes, "it was one of the most famous events in American history."

"I never was much into that history stuff," I confessed.

"You don't know about this?" Brad asked, his amazement turning into disbelief. "Alexander was always shooting off his mouth about people he didn't like—one of whom happened to be the Vice-President, Aaron Burr. Old Al kept pushing his stuff and they ended up in a duel. Burr shot him. Hamilton died the next day."

I know my blank look didn't surprise Brad. My reaction did, though.

"Brad, what are you talking about? Kenny didn't die in a duel."

There was Brad's little chuckle again.

"Are you sure?" he said.

But about then, the judge rapped his gavel and we were back in session.

Broadman got sentenced about an hour after us. He's getting forty-five years, for killing that tour guide at Pedro Saint James—and everything else. Well, couldn't happen to a nicer jerk. I don't think the prosecutor up in Philly much cares what happens to Broadman. They haven't even taken him up there yet for plea agreement talks. I'm guessing he'll rot down here inside a Cayman prison. He'll be either eighty or dead when his sentence runs out.

Some of our Grand Slam crew are still waiting to get sentenced. Most so far have gotten ten to twelve years. Except Mark Gillman, the moron who killed that policeman and fireman at Pedro Saint James. They put him away for sixty-five years. Maybe he and Broadman can share a cell.

Broadman would probably kill him the first week.

Brad and me both dodged a really big bullet back home in Philadelphia. We were both facing life sentences up there for the armored car heist and the deaths of those two guards. But the Pennsylvania prosecutors—with a little prodding from Marketta and his chief—let us plead guilty to a lesser charge of reckless homicide, with a promise that we'd get just twenty years each. The best part is, those sentences will run concurrently with our sixteen down here on the island. I guess the folks in Philly were more than happy to let the citizens of Cayman clothe and feed us for the next sixteen years.

The bad part, of course, is that Brad and I will both get shipped back to Pennsylvania someday, once our sentences run out down here. We'll have to do the last four years of the Pennsylvania sentence in a state prison up there. Unless maybe our attorneys can finagle something, like some "time off for good behavior."

Good behavior. In prison. That's funny.

But you never know, do you?

Poor Brad. He's been so faithful to me—through all this. I never saw that in him, that loyalty. And I was totally in the dark about how much he really cared about me. Stupid me.

I wonder what he'll think after sixteen years of staring at me through a chain-link fence.

I just caught Brad's eye as they led us off in separate directions after our sentencing yesterday. I don't know how to describe his expression, and I don't know what mine was like, either. But I called after him. I don't know if it was hope, or desperation.

"I guess we just have to wait, now, huh?" I said in a

really loud whisper. "You and me?"

The guard leading Brad had ahold of his arm but Brad tugged him to a stop and gave me a smile that was a promise.

"I've waited this long, haven't I?" he said loudly as the guard pulled him out the door.

Some moments are just bittersweet, yet I felt a flicker of hope. They say love outlasts everything else.

I hope so.

I used to think I was pretty sharp about life—that I understood a lot more than I guess I do. I don't really even understand my own feelings, much. Even with my misgivings, I thought Kenny actually cared for me. But then Brad was always there, in the back of the picture. Life is so crazy at times, so unpredictable, full of choices that seem impossible to make. And I made so many bad ones.

I thought I loved Kenny. Still, I can't deny that when Art told me how he died—blown out the hole in that plane into oblivion—I felt a kind of secret joy. How strange.

But then, so is life.

Acknowledgements

I want to express my gratitude to Julia Skwierawski, my niece and an avid lover of books, for challenging me to create a story in this new—for me—format in which multiple characters narrate the story from various points of view. It has indeed been a challenge. I thank her also for the suggestions and thoughtful criticism she offered along the way.

I thank my wife Candy, as always, for her support, literary and literal. Her encouragement through twenty-nine years (and counting) of marriage has enabled me to pursue writing as more than a hobby. I'm grateful that she's willing to give me up for the many long hours needed to complete each work.

And not least, I thank my many readers who keep asking for more.

About The Author

John R. Spencer grew up in Kansas and Colorado and holds a degree in English Literature from the University of Northern Colorado, where he wrote a weekly column for the campus newspaper and was, for two years, Editor-in-chief of the student literary magazine, *NOVA*. He also holds a Master of Divinity degree from Nashotah House.

In addition to writing, he has enjoyed a diverse career as a police detective, coroner's investigator, EMT, social worker, community corrections supervisor, and parish priest. He has been dramatic director for several community and children's theaters in Colorado, Wisconsin, and Illinois, as well as performing in numerous stage productions.

He is the father of three grown children and lives with his wife, Candice, in Eastern Iowa.

Also by John R. Spencer

Solarium-3, Haeven, ReGeneration
(THE SOLARIUM-3 TRILOGY)

www.solarium-3.com

CPSIA information can be obtained
at www.ICGtesting.com
Printed in the USA
LVHW09s1324170918
590413LV00001B/16/P